FEELS LIKE FAMILY

JO COX

1

Staring at a wardrobe full of the same damn dress on repeat, V sucked her teeth. Picking the blue or green version shouldn't be hard, and yet... Slamming it shut with a flourish, she fell forward onto the bed and buried her face in the duvet. Years of work to get here, to her first real proper teaching job, and all she could think about was what to wear. Had she finally lost her mind? Had pages of student attainment statistics and lesson plans tipped her over the edge? Or was it the drone of "muuuum" from the hallway?

"What's up, sweetheart?" she mumbled, barely lifting her face as she swept a chunk of glossy red hair from her eyes. Sight was imperative if Grace were about to launch an attack, but she'd also freshly washed it as a confidence boost for her first day and wanted to save her efforts from sticky little fingers.

The hinges creaked as Grace inched open the door. "I can't sleep." She threw it wide now and bunny hopped across the floor. Then there was a little squeal as she flung herself at the bed. "I'm too excited."

Turning her head so they were facing, V couldn't resist a

smile at the comical little pout. Grace's freckled nose wrinkled a few inches away from her own, and she gave it a quick peck. "What about?"

"School."

"I'm afraid you'll have to cope with two more days of fun, sorry." She didn't go back until Wednesday. V was the only one being subjected to a Monday morning, and it was a royal pain in the butt. Why the primary and secondary schools started on different days was a mystery whose answer was known only by some officious bureaucrat who had clearly never needed to find childcare. Add a training day into the mix and it'd meant begging for help. Again. "What are you doing with Auntie Jess tomorrow?"

"I don't know, she won't tell me. Maybe she hasn't decided yet."

"I'd say that's highly unlikely." Jess would've planned their time together meticulously, and Grace was about to be spoiled rotten. How she was more excited about starting her second year of school was baffling. She should know by now that she had the rapturous attention of all three adults in the house.

There was a jingling noise and V twisted, propping herself on an elbow. "Have you had that dog in your bed again?"

"No."

"*Grace?*" She tried to make eye contact with her suddenly subdued daughter as he trotted in and put his paws on the edge of the bed, his long pink tongue lolling to one side.

"He sleeps on the *end* of the bed, Mummy." Finding her confidence again, Grace sat up and patted his head. "I don't let him under the covers anymore, like you said."

"Are you arguing this on a technicality?"

"A what?"

"A tech—" V waved a hand to end this pointless conversation. "You know what, never mind. You should be asleep, and I need to finish unpacking from holiday so I can get sorted for work in the morning. No arguments tonight, come on." She ushered Grace off the bed, then shooed her —and Hal the spaniel—onto the landing. When he went to follow them into Grace's room, she shut the door in his face. "Sorry, my friend. You are not coming in."

"But Muuuum." The pout returned as Grace stomped her foot on the carpet, but this time it was neither cute nor little. She wasn't getting away with it, though. He was covered in sand from the beach and having the same argument every night was getting old.

"Don't *but Muuuum* me. You know tomorrow is important. Can you just do as you're asked this once? I'm begging you."

"Fine." Grace expelled the word with an exaggerated breath, as if it were the hardest thing in the world. Then she scraped her feet across the floor, her arms floppy and her back bent over, and fell forward onto the bed. For a five-year-old, she already had some impressive attitude. At some point, she might need her own place and a robot carer who had no emotions, because she was going to be a nightmare with the addition of hormones.

"Thank you, sweetheart." V stood with her hands on her hips and watched Grace climb under the covers, having long ago ceased worrying about the amount of sarcasm she employed while parenting. "I can see that was an effort, so I appreciate it."

"Will someone come and read to me if I can't have Hal?"

Were they bartering now? Perhaps if it settled her, though, a book wasn't such a bad idea. She was probably still hyped up from all the ice cream and a week out of routine. "Okay, what do you want?" Running a finger along the books on the shelf, V pulled out Grace's favourite and held it up. "This one?"

"No, I don't want *you* to read to me."

She said it as if the idea were utterly ridiculous and V tried not to convey how much it stung, even if it wasn't a surprise. "Of course you don't," she muttered, returning the book to its place. "Fine, I'll go and ask."

When she opened the door, Hal was still on the other side. He followed her downstairs and trotted into the kitchen, then curled up in his bed, peering up through a pair of big brown eyes. He was out of luck if he thought he was getting a reprieve.

It would be Melissa who Grace wanted, and she stood next to the work surface with a mug of tea and a half-empty packet of chocolate Hobnobs. As V entered, she dunked one in and waited as long as possible before risking that it might break off and disintegrate. "Hang on." She held up a finger, concentrating intently. Then she whipped the biscuit into her mouth and caught some dribbles with her other hand. "Sorry, that was intense."

"I gathered. Would you be up for reading Lady Muck a bedtime story? It seems I'm completely redundant these days." She had Auntie Jess for days out, Auntie Melissa for story time, and V often felt she was only good for doing Grace's washing. It wasn't strictly true that her housemates got to experience all the fun bits, but it wasn't far off.

"Sure thing." After bashing her hands together, Melissa wound the top of the packet, tucking it back into a cupboard. "It gets me out of unpacking."

"Unpacking?" Why on earth was she doing that? When you were lucky enough to have a partner who would walk on hot coals if it made your life easier, it was a terrible waste. "You really aren't exploiting this pregnancy to your full advantage if you haven't already got Jess carrying out these menial tasks. We'll discuss that later."

"*More* exploitation?" Melissa nodded as she took a quick slurp of tea and then dumped her mug into the sink. "Noted. I'll see what I can do." She paused to tie back a mass of unruly blonde hair with the band from her wrist, then adjusted the ring through her nose. "Now, shall we go so I can be exploited by a five-year-old?"

They circled through the living room. The entrance hallway had two doors: one to the kitchen and the other to the lounge, but the rooms were in an L-shape and joined by an archway so it felt almost open-plan. When they reached the top of the stairs, Hal had taken the other route and was patiently waiting for them. That dog didn't miss a trick.

"Not you again," V muttered, bending to ruffle his ears.

Melissa stepped past and sat on the edge of the bed, where Grace was propped up on some pillows with two books held to her chest. "What have we got this evening, Monster?"

"Have you been eating biscuits?" The dog wasn't the only one you couldn't get a single thing past, and Grace was carefully eying the flecks of oat stuck to Melissa's T-shirt.

"No." She brushed away the crumbs and shuffled up the bed, laying on her back and crossing her legs. "As if I'd be eating biscuits without you. We had a pact." Grace was still regarding Melissa with suspicion but handed her the books all the same and cuddled in alongside. Hal took this as his cue to jump on the end of the bed, crawling up Melissa's legs and resting his head on her lap so his nose nudged the underside of her belly. "Would you mind just grabbing my glasses? I left them on the bedside table earlier."

Taking at least her nineteenth deep, calming breath of the evening, V found a bit more sarcasm. "Of course. And for your companion? An ear scratch maybe?"

Peering down her nose, Melissa laughed. "No, that will be all, Jeeves. Thank you."

When she stepped onto the landing, V bumped into Jess coming out of her bedroom with a pair of glasses in hand, clearly having heard. "Are you alright? You seem a little highly strung this evening."

Once the glasses had been flung at Melissa, V followed Jess downstairs. "Oh, you know. No big deal, I'm only absolutely shitting myself."

"I see." She opened the cupboard under the stairs and pulled out a bumper pack of nappies. They'd been buying in bulk to save money and there were boxes piled three or four high of everything the overly cautious first-time parent could wish for. At some point, V was expecting Mary Poppins herself to spring forth. "Any help?"

She narrowed her eyes, trying to halt the smile beginning to twitch across her lips. "I suppose you think that's funny."

"I did think it might lighten the mood, yes." Jess returned the box and continued to the kitchen where she flicked on the kettle and pulled out a couple of mugs. Tea was her catch-all solution to any sort of problem.

"As much as I appreciate it, could you not? The only thing I need right now is an early night. Have you seen my phone anywhere?"

Leaning back against the work surface, Jess wriggled and reached into the pocket of her jeans. "This phone?" She held it up to show the new photo of Grace's tongue, which now adorned the lock screen. "She was using it to FaceTime her dad earlier."

"Little bugger. She's too clever for her own good."

"Takes after her mum." As she stepped alongside, Jess nudged V's shoulder and grabbed the packet of Hobnobs from the cupboard. She pushed one forward with her thumb so it poked out and waved it in the space between them. "Go on, before my fiancée eats them all."

V grumbled but took one, wedging the entire thing in her mouth. When she'd finished chewing, she gestured for another. "Keep them coming. I'm stress eating." She nibbled the next, sighing and almost choking on a crumb so that Jess had to slap her back. "Thanks," she spluttered. "Seems I can't even rely on biscuits tonight. What has the world come to?"

It merged into a laugh when Jess wedged her in a tight hug which lifted her off the floor. There was something comforting about the act. She was several inches shorter and had always liked a strong pair of heavily tattooed arms. It would be nice if they didn't always belong to her best friend, but she'd take what she could get right now.

"What are you worried about?" After Jess dropped V to the ground, she playfully shoved her shoulder again. "You'll be great. Just relax, get some sleep, and then knock 'em dead. I have total faith in you."

She had total faith in herself too. Sort of. Probably. She'd definitely had it back in March when she was offered the job, but six months had passed since then. Taking one last Hobnob, she tried to snap out of this uncharacteristic panic. Teaching was what she wanted. What she'd worked for. Come to think of it, what everyone else around her had worked for too. She was a capable, confident, twenty-eight-year-old woman. Now she needed to prove it.

2

The following morning, while wriggling on an uncomfortable plastic school chair, that capable, confident, twenty-eight-year-old woman was already wavering. "Five more minutes. Get through five more minutes," V muttered, crossing her legs and clenching. She'd only just made the morning briefing and leaving early to use the toilet would not make a good first impression. Of all the things she'd expected to derail her, needing a wee wasn't one of them.

She shuffled sideways, trying to concentrate on whatever the head teacher was waffling about, and tugged her new lanyard. It was only a training day, though. How important could it be? She snuck off the seat and tiptoed across the back row, bent over as if it made her less conspicuous, but was so focussed on her task that she ended up head-butting a figure in the corridor as she rounded the door.

"Shit, bugger, fuck," she blurted, covering her mouth and pulling away the strands of hair which clung to her lips. "I'm sorry."

The woman slid both hands into the pockets of her

loose-fitting but perfectly tailored navy trousers. "I think you're one of mine."

"Excuse me?"

"Maths? I'm told I've got two newly qualified teachers to guide and shape this year. Budget cuts."

V straightened and pressed her legs together. "Then I'm sorry for that, too. Would you mind if I just...?" She gestured towards the bathroom. "I'm desperate."

Navy Trousers stepped aside. "Go ahead."

"Thanks." As V jogged off, she turned back to whisper, "Nice to meet you, by the way."

She threw open the door and landed in a cubicle, hoisting up her dress and letting out a grumble of frustration that her first interaction with one of her colleagues was asking to use the sodding toilet. They could pull this back, though. She knew she was a good teacher. Eighteen months of tutoring had ended up being useful practise, and she was streets ahead of most of the people she'd trained with last year. Jess was right; she just needed to relax and remember that.

When she emerged, the rest of the staff were filtering from the briefing, chattering and laughing. She ducked through the door and grabbed her bag, then tacked herself on the end in the hope they'd lead her to wherever the next activity was taking place. As she reached the door again, Navy Trousers leant against the wall with her hands still in her pockets.

"We're heading in this direction." She nodded towards a different corridor illuminated by a flickering strobe light, and V had the ominous sense that they were about to leave the nice shiny new part of the school and head into the maze of run-down old buildings. Lost to time and avoided by anyone in maintenance, the maths department was not a glamorous place.

She followed, fiddling with the lanyard around her neck again, and nodded appreciation as a set of double doors were held open for her. "So, when you said I'm one of yours, what exactly did you mean?"

"I am the head of department."

"How come you weren't in the interviews, then?" She'd certainly have stood out. The accent alone, which was some drawling Southern European configuration, was distinctive enough. The woman V had been introduced to as head of department was entirely unremarkable, if you discounted bad breath and a penchant for hideous parrot themed cardigans.

"I wasn't head of department at the time. It was what you might call an emergency appointment, I'm covering for long-term sick leave."

"I was going to say, I thought the woman I met was older and less—" It was imperative to find the right words. Saying she was a bit rough looking, while technically a comparative compliment, probably wasn't a good idea. "Well, just older."

"She is, and she's been in a motorcycle accident. A broken pelvis, punctured lung, fractured wrist... a mess. It's possible she'll take early retirement."

"A motorcycle accident?" V's eyes widened. She could well have imagined injury by errant knitting needle putting her out for a while, but not a motorcycle accident.

They reached the end of the corridor where a low hum of conversation emanated from a classroom. Inside was a face V recognised. One of the girls she'd trained with, a twenty-two-year-old with mousy hair and a shrill voice, was perched on the edge of her chair saying characteristically little. Those year nine shits were going to eat her alive. The other two V had never seen before—a large bubbly blonde who must have been in her mid-fifties and hadn't shut up since they walked into the room, and a balding guy who looked decidedly bored. Not just with her, but with life.

"Hello everyone. I hope you're ready for this because I'm not." Navy Trousers leant against the desk at the front, oozing a lot more confidence than her words implied. "For those of you who don't know me, my name is Sofia Pisano. I'm filling in as head of maths temporarily and it's been a rush so if I'm not up to speed, that's too bad. We're all going to have to muddle through together this term."

The mousy girl raised her hand and waited for Sofia to look in her direction. "Does that mean you'll be my mentor?" A sideways squint made it clear why she felt compelled to ask, because Sofia seemed like the only safe choice if you didn't want to be either bored or talked to death. "I had the old department head."

"I will mentor one of you, yes, and Bob will take the other. Rest assured you will be in quite capable hands, he's a very... *experienced* teacher." She hadn't been able to maintain eye contact through that last bit, her mouth curling into a slight smile as she glanced at V and saw her smirk.

V's good humour didn't last for long, though, when it turned out Sofia had awarded herself to the other girl. It was the first of a string of disappointments she would face that day. Not only had she missed out on being mentored by the cool Italian—as she quickly learned—in favour of bored Bob, but she also discovered the canteen wasn't open on training days and she had nothing to eat. As they all broke for lunch and everyone else pulled out a box of salad or pasta, she twirled her thumbs and tried to stop her stomach from growling, until Bob held out a manky looking banana.

"Would you like it?" he offered, nudging his hand forward. "I'm not big on over ripe fruit."

No, me either.

V took it with a gracious smile. Right now, beggars couldn't be choosers. Perhaps she'd judged him too harshly, and the whole responsible grown-up teacher thing could start tomorrow with packing a proper lunch. "Thank you. It was a bit of a rush this morning and I came out without anything to eat. My daughter turned off the alarm when she was playing with my phone."

Sofia peered over her dish of pasta, still sitting on the edge of her desk. "You have a daughter? How old is she?"

"Almost six."

"They're quite cute at that age," Bob cut back in as he tore the lid off a full box of sandwiches. "Just you wait. I've got a couple of teenagers and they're a bloody nightmare. I leave them for my wife to deal with."

"I'm already at that stage. Grace goes to her dad's every other weekend but the rest of the time she's mine to deal with—nightmare or otherwise."

"You love her, though. I can tell." Sofia wore a warm smile, setting her pasta down with the fork poking out of the box. "For a start, your face lights up when you speak about her. Bob's never does that."

V laughed. "Are you suggesting Bob doesn't love his kids?"

"Bob, do you love your kids?"

He shook his head. "Can't stand them."

"There you go." Sofia raised her hands and then her palms slapped down on her legs. She stood with a brief sigh and the mass of rings on her fingers glinted as she ran them through waves of mahogany coloured hair which were blunt cut just past her shoulders. Stepping in front of the interactive whiteboard again, she began tapping through to their next activity. "I suppose we should resume if we ever want to get home to the children we despise." She turned and pointed at V. "Or love."

The afternoon proceeded as the morning had, only with a lot more hunger. One banana really wasn't cutting it and by four o'clock V was yawning, her eyes nodding as she watched Sofia gesture at the board. She was both enthusiastic and completely cool, but it wasn't being matched by anyone in the audience. When a hand raked through Sofia's hair again, though, V found there was finally something worth paying attention to. She inclined her head as she caught sight of the start of a tattoo and tried to follow it, now very definitely awake.

"That is all for today." As Sofia sat on the edge of the desk in front of V this time, her knee hitched up and a hand splayed.

It wasn't a body part she usually paid all that much attention to, but Sofia's hands were tanned and perfectly smooth, and V admired them. All those rings would need to come off because they could do some real damage, but that was workable. Short, clean nails were also a good sign in this imaginary world she was rapidly concocting where they were going to have sex in a store cupboard. Her eyes travelled over the turned-up cuffs of a sky-blue shirt, her head drawn forward by the hint of spice in Sofia's perfume, which may on reflection have been a cologne.

She was not your typical maths teacher. Art, maybe. Something with a bit of sex appeal. Maths was a Bob subject —middle-aged male teachers who looked a bit pissed off with life and had never experienced what it felt like to have women interested in them. Sofia would definitely have women interested in her, regardless of her sexuality, although all the signs were present. There was something about the way she carried herself which implied she knew how to hold a woman, and V was still imagining the thrill of that a good ten minutes later.

When she realised Sofia was staring at her, expecting her to speak, she shook her head. Everyone else was already filtering out of the room, but she was too engrossed to notice. Indulging in a fantasy was a helpful diversion from the stress of an impending real first day, when she'd need to get up in front of a class of actual children, but now she needed to think of something appropriate to say. "Thank you for today."

"You're welcome. How are you feeling about tomorrow? Is there anything else you need? I know you have Bob, but my door is also always open."

As V went to stand and leave, she reconsidered and relaxed back into the seat. "Actually, there is something." It might be a regrettable request but, contrary to where her brain had diverted, she was here with a very set agenda. It involved progressing her career as quickly as possible. "I was wondering what there was to get involved with. Hockey club, stuff like that." All advice had pointed towards volunteering for extracurricular positions if you wanted to make a good impression. "I play occasionally when I have time—so rarely these days—but I could still be useful. Who would I need to speak with?"

Sofia nodded slowly; her gaze fixed on the ceiling as she considered. "You could ask the PE department, but they are a little protective of sports clubs. Any other talents or interests?" When her eyes dropped to meet V's there was a devilish glint in them and the hint of another smile.

The only answers popping into V's head were not school appropriate, so she shrugged and kept them to herself. She was probably reading more into Sofia's subtly suggestive question than she ought, based on wishful thinking. "No, but thanks. I expect I'm getting ahead of myself, anyway." And in more ways than one. She needed to get a grip on herself before tomorrow, or it would be difficult to tell who the hormonal teenagers were and who was teaching them.

"Not at all. If you're serious, we are now a teacher down on the half term orienteering trip. It doesn't hold any of the glamour of hockey club, admittedly, but we have fun. Sleeping in log cabins, long hikes in the woods, trying not to lose too many kids... I enjoy it, anyway."

Sofia was right, that didn't hold the same appeal. She could dress it up however she liked, but sleeping in a Scout camp for a few nights with a bunch of spotty pre-teens was unlikely to be enjoyable. On the other hand, it fit the bill in providing a highlight for future CV's. That was the important thing right now, over short-term inconvenience. "Who would I need to speak with if I'm interested?"

"That's the beauty part, I'd already signed you up thirty seconds ago." As Sofia slipped off the desk, she shoved both hands back in her pockets. "Just make sure you don't take on too much this term. The first is always the toughest. I know it's tempting at the start of September, but you need to keep enough in the tank to get past Christmas. Okay?"

"Okay." V pushed back her chair, knowing she had no intention of taking that advice. It was alright for the mousy twenty-two-year-old who'd gone straight from school to university to a teacher training course, but she couldn't help feeling like she was playing catch-up. "I do just need to check I can get childcare before I commit to half term. My housemate will be on maternity leave so I'm sure she'll do it, but can you hold that thought?"

"Of course." Halfway towards the door, Sofia turned to

walk backwards. "Don't take too long, though. I'll have people queueing up to spend three days in the woods with me." She grabbed a satchel from a peg on the way out, then waved through the glass as she wandered down the corridor.

"I bet," V murmured, waving back. It sounded more enticing by the minute.

3

Pushing through the front door half an hour later, V let everything drop where she stood—coat, bag, lanyard, shoes. The smell of roast chicken wafted down the hallway and she sighed, closing her eyes and slumping forward. There were many compensations to living with someone who seemed happy to play the role of perpetual carer. "God bless you!" She took another deep breath as she stepped into the kitchen. "I'm starving."

Jess looked up from the hob as she stirred, reaching to switch off the oven. "That's fortuitous because I made you a special first day meal."

"Tell me why I'm not marrying you myself. C'mon." V playfully nudged Jess's shoulder. "We don't have to sleep together—you can still make Melissa scream every night—I just want to know you'll cook for the rest of my life."

Somewhere in that comment, Jess had got lost, and there were no prizes for guessing where. She stared absently into space and then grinned, finally snapping out of it as she stirred her gravy pan again. "How about I cook, but we don't get married?"

"Deal. Where is Melissa, anyway? And my daughter, come to think of it." The house was suspiciously quiet, which usually meant there was mischief afoot.

"Walking the dog." Dropping the spoon, Jess grabbed an oven glove from a hook and batted V out of the way. "Together, obviously. I didn't send Grace out on her own."

"Thank you for watching her today. I owe you a million return favours." And she knew exactly how she'd end up giving them. It'd be tit for tat, except Jess and Melissa were having twins and that meant they would be getting back two-fold what they put in. It didn't even bear thinking about right now, trying to babysit two wriggling babies. Especially ones with *those* troublemaking genes.

"No bother, I just extended my annual leave by a few days. We went to the zoo, and tomorrow I said we'd go swimming."

"Oh, I see." V laughed, stealing a piece of chicken breast from under some foil on the counter. Her stomach was making a disturbing variety of growling noises and the monster in there needed feeding. "You're having children so you can go to the zoo without looking like a weirdo. Excellent."

"You got me. We've been through all this expensive fertility treatment so I can go to the zoo." The goofy smile Jess wore showed it was worthwhile, and she was now busy staring at all the photos on the wall in front of her, charting the entire journey with scans and week by week progress updates. She'd already added the pictures from last week's holiday to Wales, which had become an annual pilgrimage for the entire household given everyone was chronically skint. Melissa's grandparents lived near Cardiff, so they all got free accommodation.

"I had a pretty great day too. The new head of department is this swarthy Italian and work suddenly became a lot more enticing."

As she turned, Jess raised an eyebrow. "Man, woman, other?"

"Woman. Sofia," V drawled, trying to get across the accent but ending up sounding like an extra from 'Allo 'Allo. "Contrary to what I just suggested, maths has never sounded so sexy. I know you're only into heavily pregnant blondes, but even you'd look twice, she's gorgeous."

"Yeah?" The eyebrow raised about another inch, although she wasn't Jess's type at all. This was only an excuse to talk about Sofia. "Do you reckon she's into women?"

V shrugged. "Who knows, but it doesn't hurt to look. Right?"

"Don't ask me, I've never slept with my boss."

Slapping down a hand on each of Jess's shoulders, V laughed. "Oh no, but I seem to recall Melissa technically did. Don't think I didn't find out about that incident in your office."

Jess turned sharply this time, her mouth dropping open and her face flushing from a lot more than just the steam off the gravy. "Who told you about that?"

"I have my sources but don't worry, I was proud. Didn't know you had it in you." She was depressingly well behaved, but learning she'd had sex over a desk when Melissa was working for her had raised some hope that she wasn't completely lacking in imagination.

"It only happened once."

"Alright, don't ruin it." V laughed again as she shook Jess's shoulders. "It's the most interesting thing you've done in the past five years, so I'd milk it for all it's worth."

"Rude."

"True." Not that it was a bad thing. Jess was steady, reliable, and just about the best friend you could ask for. If it weren't for her, Grace would've spent the last few years living with her grandparents in a cramped back bedroom under the glare of disappointment and thinly veiled disapproval. Apparently even in this day and age, accidental pregnancies when you were getting a degree weren't exactly celebrated, even if they loved her dearly.

"Yeah, well. I enjoy being boring," Jess continued with a defiant nod. "You can keep your casual sex."

"Thanks. I will." Although she was lucky if there was room even for that, between study, work, and caring for Grace. It'd been months, and she was having to get by with the help of her strategically hidden little friends. On the other hand, at least they didn't pout if you skipped out on a date to deal with a childcare crisis.

Fifteen minutes later V and Jess were still sparring, and Jess was eying the clock on the wall, fretting over her roast dinner. It was all ready, and she wanted to serve, but Grace and Melissa were nowhere in sight. They'd have stopped to talk to another dog walker, or Melissa would've sneaked Grace some sweets from the shop and held them up while hiding the evidence, but Jess wanted to call her.

"Just let her be," V pleaded, pulling out a chair and sitting to set out the cutlery. "She would've phoned if there was a problem."

"I know, but she keeps insisting on going to the woods and I don't like it up there, especially when it gets dark. The place is swarming with doggers and kids smoking weed."

"Neither of which will pay the slightest mind to a pregnant woman walking her dog with a five-year-old in tow. Honestly, you need to relax. If you're this strung already, you'll be a basket case by the time those kids are three months old." Melissa was a bit naïve sometimes, but she wasn't an idiot and wouldn't have taken Grace anywhere they weren't safe. Not that it would stop Jess from worrying.

She held up her hands, hopefully in defeat. "Okay, you're right. Sorry, I'm just stressed out right now."

"No shit. Tell me what's going on." A loud sigh followed, and V hoped she was finally going to talk. Her anxiety was increasing week on week and she needed to stop bottling it up.

Jess stuck her hands in the pockets of her jeans and shuffled on the tile. "I don't want anything to go wrong, that's all. I know I'm being overprotective, but I can't make myself stop. After everything we've been through the past two years..." She trailed off; her gaze firmly fixed on her Sesame Street socks. "I feel so powerless."

That was relatable, at least. "Welcome to parenthood."

"Gee, thanks for the reassurance."

V shrugged and hooked her arm over the back of the chair. "I didn't mean to sound dismissive; I'm just saying we're all in the same boat. I've been at it for almost six years and I still don't have a clue what I'm doing. You have to submit to that and realise some things are simply out of your control." Although the irony of who was delivering these words hadn't been lost on her. She was quite aware she spent as much time worrying, only perhaps not so openly. In any case, it didn't seem to help, and V tried to work out what else to say. Usually, she was good at giving Jess pep talks—they'd been doing it for each other since they were teenagers—but perhaps she was losing her knack. "Hey, come on. You're going to be a great mum."

"Really?" As she pulled the phone from her pocket, Jess drew a deep breath and then tapped it in a slow rhythm on her palm. She was still considering calling when the front door rattled open.

"Something smells good," Melissa yelled from the hallway. She wandered in with Hal by her feet, her cheeks rosy from the fresh air—or perhaps the weed. "Hello sexy."

Instinctively puckering up, V leant forward as Melissa pretended to go in for a kiss, and Jess shook her head, finally cracking a smile. "You two need to come up with some new material."

"How do you know it's just a joke?" they both challenged at almost the same time, proving the material probably was getting a little worn.

Jess gripped Melissa's cheeks in both hands and leant in to kiss her, smiling at her mumbles of pleasure as she closed her eyes and sunk into it. Then she pulled back and shrugged. "That's how I know. Four and a half years and I still make you weak at the knees, admit it."

"I'll admit nothing," Melissa protested, trailing Jess across the kitchen and stroking both hands under the bottom of her T-shirt while she tried to serve the food. "But for the sake of argument, what are you doing later?"

"Watching you drool, I expect. I've got a fiver that says you're asleep in my lap by eight."

They'd all be asleep in a pool of drool by eight, so long as Grace would settle tonight.

Right on cue there was a thumping noise on the stairs and down the landing, then the sound of running water. It played out in reverse and Grace whizzed across the floor, sliding on her socks and almost crashing into the kitchen unit.

"Can I feed Hal?" She was already reaching into the cupboard for his food, completely ignoring her own mother. If Jess wanted to know what parenthood looked like, it was this: being usurped by a dog. "Good boy. Sit." Grace waited for him to do as instructed before filling the bowl and crouching next to him. "Okay, eat."

It always seemed to fascinate her that he did what he was told, and she watched intently as he ate his dinner, her head resting on her knee. There was no point trying to talk with her until she'd finished, so V turned her attention back to Jess, who was busy plating up their roast and muttering about it going dry. "Do you need a hand?"

"Don't worry, I've got it." Melissa reached for the oven glove and swatted Jess across the top of the legs with it. "Sit down. I'll have you as my slave soon enough."

As Jess went to protest, V caught her eye and mouthed "she's not ill" so she stopped. Instead, she sat and bumped their shoulders together, finally looking something close to relaxed—long may it last.

* * *

It'd taken until nearly nine to get Grace into bed because she wouldn't rest until she'd laid out every item required for school on Wednesday and video called her dad to tell him how excited she was. Again. Even as she lay with the duvet tucked up to her chin, she was still smiling maniacally, although really it should have been a relief. Lots of kids struggled, but she'd always been confident and outgoing. It was serving her well.

"Goodnight." V kissed Grace's head and grunted as she hauled herself off the floor, but as she made her way to the door, there was a long "muuuum" which halted her escape. She scrunched her face, berating herself for naively assuming she'd gotten away with it tonight, and slowly turned. "Yes, sweetheart."

"When the babies come, can they sleep in my room?"

Shit.

This was not the time to explain they wouldn't still be living here. Everyone had always agreed as soon as this first teaching post was underway, they would find their own place. Years of planning and work had gone into getting to that point, but Grace was unlikely to see it that way.

"No, the babies will sleep with Jess and Melissa, and then they'll have their own room."

"Why?"

Slowly tracking back, V perched on the edge of the bed. "They'd wake you up. Babies cry a lot." It was even more reason to find a place before they arrived. One ride on that merry-go-round was more than enough, and V bit the bullet. "We might have our own house by then, too. What do you think of that?"

"Don't we already have a house?"

"This is Auntie Jess's house. She lets us live here, but one day soon I'd like to have our own. Just you and me."

Grace considered for a second. "Can I stay here?"

It was hard not to take that personally, and V rolled her eyes although they were welling with tears. "No, sweetheart. You have to come with me. Sorry."

"Can Hal come, then?"

"No, he's Melissa and Jess's dog. You can still walk him, though."

"But he's my dog too. Can't we share him, like you do with Daddy? He could come every other weekend."

V laughed at the notion. Was Grace really comparing herself to a spaniel? "I promise you'll still see lots of him."

"Do you really promise? This can't be like when you promised me a pink bike and got me a purple one."

"I know. I extra promise this time. Hal, Jess, and Melissa love you, wherever you're living. Okay?"

She nodded but didn't look sure, pulling the duvet tighter under her chin. "I guess."

"It'll be fine, sweetheart. Try to sleep now, you're going swimming in the morning." V kissed her head, tucked her favourite teddy in next to her, and questioned who she was trying to convince. It had been a long time for them both, not just Grace.

She wandered down the stairs and leant against the living room door frame, watching Jess rub Melissa's calves on the sofa while she read a book. There'd be no one to talk to past eight o'clock when they lived on their own. No one to cook roast dinners and make sure they were both okay. The thought was wholly depressing.

Hal got up from his bed and trotted across, rubbing his face against V's leg. "Daft mut," she whispered, bending to stroke his ears.

They were soft and curly, and Grace would sit for hours playing with them. Perhaps she could have her own dog, except there'd be no one to walk it during the day. Hal went to Jess's dad's house when everyone was at work because he'd retired, but V didn't have that luxury. A hamster was more viable, but you couldn't really walk one of those because something would eat it.

"I'm heading to bed; Grace has worn me out." Jess stretched and yawned, lifting Melissa's legs from her lap and then leaning over to kiss her.

She didn't look up from her book, a page between her thumb and forefinger. "Okay, be there once I've finished this chapter. Don't bother putting on pyjamas if you know what's good for you."

When V laughed, they both turned around wearing

guilty expressions. "I'm glad to see the romance isn't entirely dead," she teased. "Will you be leaving your socks on?"

"No but remind me what options we have besides the missionary position because that's a little tricky these days." Jess's voice was dripping with sarcasm as she raised both her middle fingers.

Melissa smirked up at her, the book resting on her bump. "Don't worry, you'll get there with this sex thing." She let out an exaggerated sigh, and it almost fell off. "I'll have an orgasm, eventually. Just keep trying."

With a quick roll of her eyes, Jess left via the kitchen, pouring herself a glass of water before heading upstairs. V waited until she heard the bathroom door shut and perched on the edge of the other sofa, sniffing into her sleeve. She wasn't much of a crier, but now that she was going to be alone with only the television for company the tears were pressing hard.

Closing the book and setting it on the floor, Melissa grunted as she swung her legs around. "Are you alright?"

"I had to introduce the idea of us moving and it caught me a bit off-guard."

"Ah. You know there's no rush? We're happy to have you here for as long as you need."

"I appreciate that, but you'll change your mind. Believe me. When those babies come, you'll want to be a family. Alone."

Melissa shrugged. "We've always been a little unconventional family." She clasped both hands over her bump and then reached up to stretch her back. "We're just adding to it."

"Yeah, I know, but it needs to happen at some point and it's probably easier before the babies arrive." It would be hard enough tearing Grace away from Jess and Melissa, although that relationship would change when they had their own daughters to dote on. "It'll be fine," V assured herself out loud. She seemed to do a lot of that recently. "We've got months to transition. Everyone needs to reinforce that she's loved, and safe, and not losing people from her life because of this."

"Hate to burst your bubble but I'm twenty-eight weeks today, you've not got *that* many months. You should do what's right for you, though, so we'll fall in line. Will you just let me talk to Jess first? This is going to be tough on her too."

V nodded. "Is she doing okay?"

"You know what she's like. Gets all practical and won't admit she's terrified. It's taken us both a long time to believe this is happening and we're bringing home two babies."

"Be worth all the effort and heartache in the end."

Melissa's smirk returned. "Jess or the kids?"

4

A fortnight later the deed was done, and Jess knew about the plan to move. She'd reacted exactly as everyone should've expected—insisting on booking in a tonne of appointments and showing every property she had in budget until V found the right one. Or until Jess found the right one, it was hard to tell. Having a live-in letting agent was great, but she was taking the assignment very seriously.

By Friday they were on potential home number four and V was praying it was better than the last three which had all been quickly vetoed. There *were* genuine issues, but she also knew at the back of her mind that she was being a bit nit-picky because she still hadn't got her head around the idea. It all seemed to have happened so suddenly, even though in reality it hadn't, and she felt like she was hurtling off a cliff at speed.

She gathered up her things from the desk, way past the end of the school day, and checked the time. Cursing that she'd become distracted by lesson plans and wouldn't make it to the childminder to say goodbye to Grace before her dad collected her for the weekend, she slumped back into her seat. It was the first time she'd leave without a hug, and a gasp of air as the headrest deflated mirrored her mood.

Minutes later she was still sitting there until a noise made her jump and she swivelled to find Sofia stood in the doorway. She rubbed her face and tried to look awake, which was a challenge given she almost wasn't. "Sorry, I was just leaving. I hadn't realised how late it was."

"Now do you believe me that this will be a difficult term?" Sofia's tone was sympathetic rather than heavy with judgement. "We're all heading to the pub. Will you join us?"

"I'd love to—believe me—but I'm about to view a flat." She closed her eyes again and let her head once more loll against the back of the seat, imagining sipping a cool glass of wine instead. After a double period of trigonometry there was nothing she wanted more, and it was the third week in a row that they'd invited her. At some point she should socialise, not least because she was forgetting how.

"Well, I expect we'll be there for some time. I like to play a game where I see how long Bob can hold out while his wife calls him, wanting to know when he'll be home and checking he isn't too drunk."

V laughed and unhooked her leather jacket from the headrest, slipping it on as she stood. "Yeah, he's a... character. I had my first one-to-one with him earlier in the week." She stopped in her tracks, remembering another task she hadn't yet completed. "That reminds me. I need to book in to observe one of your lessons."

Taking a step back to hold the door wider, Sofia nodded. "Okay. Come and see me next week. For now, though, get out of here and don't think about work for at least the next hour."

As V went to move past, she couldn't resist lingering in the doorway. She hadn't yet had her fix of Sofia, which was unusual because they'd spoken most days. One or the other was always popping their head around a door at lunchtime or during a free period. "What are you up to this weekend? Anything exciting?"

"Oh yes, very." Sofia's face became serious, and she nodded slowly this time. "I have a stack of books to mark, and a risk assessment to go over for the orienteering trip. I've added you now, so there's no turning back." She leant forward as she said the last bit, then shrugged as her smile returned. "I may also meet up with a friend tomorrow evening, so I'll have a little fun."

Fun, or *fun*? Sofia was easy going and always happy to chat, but she revealed very little about her personal life. When Bob was complaining about his wife and kids, or anyone else was discussing their weekend, she kept quiet. Saying she had nondescript plans with a friend was the most information she'd divulged over the past few weeks, and V couldn't resist trying to bait her for more.

"My little fun will be bashing the hell out of a hockey ball tomorrow morning. It's a great way to relax, I highly recommend it if you haven't tried. Not that it looks like you're carrying any tension, you're always annoyingly calm and collected. One day I'm going to learn your secret."

With her hands safely in her pockets as they walked down the corridor together, Sofia laughed. "You'll have to work for that, I don't give away my secrets easily."

No, I don't think you do.

V watched Sofia bend to pick up a duster, handing it back to a cleaner with a warm smile. She was so unlike anyone who'd piqued V's interest before. Jess liked to describe her type as edgy, but in truth she'd just gone for some arrogant tossers since splitting from Grace's dad. Sofia had a real ease with herself which implied the confidence was genuine, rather than a mask to hide a host of insecurities.

When they reached the car park, V continued towards the gate, but Sofia stopped, hitting the remote on her car key. "Where are you heading?"

V turned to walk backwards but didn't slow down because she was running late. "Town. My housemate is also the letting agent and we're meeting at her office."

"Then jump in, I'll give you a lift."

She paused and considered for a second, but it didn't take long to decide that she wanted to spend more time in Sofia's company, even if it was only a three-minute drive to the High Street. She tracked back and popped open the passenger door on a black Mini. The lights revealed a pristine interior, and it almost changed V's mind. "Are you sure I should be in here? I might sweat on it or something."

As Sofia slid in on the driver side, she let out a little grunt. "Yes. Don't worry, I'll disinfect it all the minute you get out."

"It's just so... clean. I can tell you don't have a five-year-old."

She'd never sat so straight in a seat, trying not to let any part of her body touch the fabric unnecessarily. The only person V knew who came close to the same level of cleanliness and order was Melissa, but even she left the odd biscuit crumb on the seats—it was inevitable when you ate so many of them. This looked like she kept it in a sterile container and meticulously returned it to factory condition every evening. It even had that new car smell, although it was rapidly overtaken by the spicy notes in Sofia's perfume and V's chest contracted as it overwhelmed her too.

"I am a little particular about how I treat things." Sofia revved the engine, quickly nudging off the stereo and hooking her arm over the back of the seat as they reversed out of the bay. "And no, I definitely don't have a five-year-old. No children at all, actually, unless you count my sister who's always calling me up and asking for money."

As they slowed over the speed bump at the school gate, V smiled. Each new bit of information or insight felt like Sofia handing her fragments of trust, and she liked it. She wanted to know more and piece her together. "At least you can say no, although I've had to do that through necessity with Grace. When I get my first proper pay packet this month, I'm taking her for a burger and letting her order anything she wants. I know that sounds ridiculous, but I've never been able to do it."

"It doesn't sound ridiculous at all. Money is a funny thing. I have never believed it makes you happy, but an absence of it can make life very hard." Sofia turned briefly, flashing another of those thousand-watt smiles.

"I'm relatively lucky, there have been lots of people who've helped me out. My friend Jess has let us stay in her house almost rent free."

"Wow." As Sofia turned again, her eyes widened.

"I know. It's a bit of an odd setup. Jess is technically my ex-girlfriend, and then not long after we moved in, she got together with her current partner—Melissa—so there's the three of us. Plus Grace. And Hal the dog." V waited to see how that landed. A lot of people didn't get it, including her parents, who had never fully understood why it was a better option than their spare bedroom.

"I hope you don't mind me asking, but does it never become awkward?"

It became awkward plenty of times, when there were four people trying to use the same bathroom. Either that or Grace wanted to know why Jess and Melissa had locked their bedroom door and it sounded like they were herding livestock in there. Not in any of the ways V was sure Sofia meant, though. "Nope. We bicker a bit sometimes, but everyone muddles along, and Grace loves it. She's got a squad of adults on hand at all times of the day. It's a five-year-old's dream."

Sofia laughed and nodded. "I can imagine, and I'm wondering why you'd ever move out."

"Me too," V mumbled as they pulled into the car park behind the supermarket. She waited until they'd stopped and unclipped her seat belt, but then held it in place. She wasn't quite ready to get out yet. "Thanks for the lift." Realising Sofia was staring at her with a confused smile, she let go and grabbed the handle. "Maybe we can chat again." *Chat again?* Of course they would chat again, they saw each other almost every day. "Later, I mean." She shook her head and popped open the door, her cheeks flushing with embarrassment, then slung her bag over her shoulder.

As they walked through the alley to the High Street, Sofia pointed to the chain pub a few doors down. It was the grimy one with ripped posters advertising two-for-one drink deals and didn't seem her sort of place. V had pictured a wine bar or something more stylish, but then perhaps it wasn't Sofia's call. "This is where we'll be if you make it back." Her lip curled up as she tried to suppress another smile. "I'd love to *chat again*."

V's eyes rolled, at herself rather than Sofia. She waved and pushed open the door to Jess's office block, leaning back against it and slapping her palm to her forehead. "Get a grip," she muttered. "You're acting like a teenager with a ridiculous crush. It hasn't been *that* long."

She pulled herself together and climbed the stairs, meeting Jess halfway with her phone and a set of keys in hand. "Oh. I was just about to text you and say I'd swing by the school."

"No need, I got a lift."

"That's good." Jess stopped in the entrance hall to check the post. "Sounds like you're making friends already. Who gave you the ride?"

Her cheeks warming again, V stuttered. "Do you remember the Italian I told you about?" She cringed, hoping Jess wasn't about to tease her. She was feeling self-conscious enough about her spiralling feelings for Sofia. "They all head to the pub on a Friday so she was coming, regardless."

"That was nice of her." As Jess turned, she had a daft grin plastered across her face, and V rolled her eyes again. So much for that wish. "Are you going?"

"Maybe, if there's time, but I've got a lot to do and we're going to be late. Come on." V held open the door and tried to shoo Jess onto the street, but she wasn't budging.

"You've gone all red."

"Yeah, yeah." She knew she had. "Hurry up."

* * *

Five minutes later they'd left the town centre and pulled onto a housing estate. It was all dark wooden window frames and chipped fascia boards, but they'd made a more promising start than with any of the other properties. Jess drove down a long winding cul-de-sac, which stopped at a large block of flats. In the centre was a car park with a sandstone building wrapped around it.

"What do you think so far? Better?" She looked hopeful, and V nodded.

She could see herself living here. For a start, the neighbours all had decent cars. It shouldn't be the first thing she looked at, but after the last place where there were burnt-out vehicles along the verge and people hanging out of balconies to smoke cigarettes, she'd become a bit of a snob.

The flat was on the ground floor, which was also a bonus because it meant no stairs to trudge up with shopping, but the positives stopped there. It was tiny, and although that was manageable because there were still two bedrooms, the kitchen and carpets really needed gutting. As she followed Jess in and ran her hand over the gouged work surface, her heart dropped into her stomach.

Jess was eying a hole in the door with a grimace. "They only gave notice yesterday, and this is the first viewing. No wonder they wanted to be out for it and told me I could let myself in…"

She was muttering more to herself than anyone else, and V cut her off. "Sorry, I know you've put in a lot of effort and I appreciate it, but I don't think this place is for me. What else do you have?" She made a move towards the entrance hall. There was an indistinguishable foul smell emanating from somewhere and she didn't feel any compulsion to stay. Jess followed and locked the front door behind them, and when she didn't answer the question, V playfully slapped her shoulder. "Earth to Jess. Come on, the next one can't be any worse than this."

Jess bit her lip and then sucked it loudly. "It's not… but there is a slight catch and Melissa is going to kill me."

"I'm listening…" But she had to wait until Jess had led her outside and they were back in the car to find out more.

Shuffling on the seat and twisting so they were facing, Jess let out a brief sigh. "Okay, so you remember the house we were living in before I bought the current one?" When V nodded, she continued. "Well, the tenants are buying some-where and have already told me they won't want to renew their contract. I immediately thought of you because that place would be ideal."

Too right it would be. There were two double bedrooms, Grace would love the garden, and it was in a great area. The whole idea made perfect sense apart from one bit, and that was why Melissa wouldn't be happy. Her mum—Rachel— was the landlady, and they didn't always get along, but who she chose as a tenant shouldn't cause any friction. "I don't understand what any of the catches are, I think being able to take Rachel's house would make this so much easier."

"They're sort of interlinked. Melissa made me swear that I wouldn't try to convince you to stay, and the current tenancy doesn't run out until February. It would mean you staying with us for another few months, but before you say no, think about it." She held out a hand to halt a torrent of objections which weren't even coming, but the fact she was doing so gave V pause for thought. "It'd give you some extra time to save for furniture and whatever, a little longer for Grace to get used to the idea, and we could have one last Christmas together. Besides the fact you get a properly nice place to live, and I'm pretty sure you wouldn't have to pay market rate."

On the surface, it was an easy decision. Something stopped V from agreeing straightaway, though. Perhaps it was the look of pleading on Jess's face, as if it were a bad idea that she needed to make a strong case for. It may also have been lingering doubts about whether Melissa really wanted them there. She said she didn't mind, but Jess had never given her much choice because the live-in best friend and toddler had been part of the package from the start. At some point Jess's priorities needed to change, for her own sake, and if there was one thing V wanted less than living in a grotty flat, it was to compromise her best friend's happiness after she'd done so much.

It was too big of a decision to make on the spot, and V stalled. "I'm interested, but can I think about it?"

"Of course. No hurry, I could just do to know over the next month."

"Thanks. And Jess?" She'd gone to turn on the ignition but stopped and looked over. "Would you mind dropping me back in town? I'm going to get out of your hair this evening so you can spoil your fiancée, okay? Make sure you pick up her favourite takeaway."

Jess laughed. "You mean so you can drool over that woman again."

V smiled and whispered, "You got me."

5

She pushed through the pub doors and surveyed the scene. Having never had colleagues, this was unfamiliar territory, and she needed to tread carefully. She was one of them, or at least would like to be. Sort of. Perhaps not Bob, because she never wanted to become that jaded. Maybe more like Sofia. She was the sort of teacher V aspired to become—respected by the students rather than feared and simultaneously liked by everyone else. On that basis, doing her usual trick of getting blind drunk and dancing on tables at the first sniff of a night out probably wouldn't make the right impression.

After elbowing through the crush and waiting a good ten minutes for a glass of white, V wandered down the long, narrow building until she found the group of teachers around a large circular table near the back doors. Several were on the patio smoking, and the rest were eating dubious looking burgers and working their way through the drink menu. Perhaps she didn't need to worry after all.

There was no sign of Sofia, though, and V's shoulders slumped forward with disappointment. She'd obviously given up on Bob this week, and when he patted the seat next to him, disappointment turned to regret. "Come and tell me how your viewing went."

"How did you know about that?"

"Ah, you'll soon learn nothing stays secret around here for long."

"Is that right? I'd better be careful, then." V set down her glass and then wriggled out of her jacket, hooking it over the back of the chair. "The flat was a dud so I'm here drowning my sorrows." She inclined her head as she considered the other house. "Well, that's not quite true, but it's complicated."

She was about to clarify, deciding having Bob to talk to was better than nothing, when a hand landed on her shoulder.

"A complicated flat? Do they often have emotional issues?"

It was an effort for V not to give herself away with a smile or blush when she looked around to find Sofia stood behind her. She cleared her throat and took a sip of wine, determined not to devolve into a bumbling wreck this time. "The ones I view seem to, yes, although it isn't the flat that I just looked at which is on my mind. I've got the opportunity to take a great house, and we even know the landlady, so I'll probably get cheaper rent."

"Ah, a house it might be worth moving out for, that's exciting. Are you worried it's too good to be true?"

"Something like that, but it's not important."

"Sounds as though it is. Please tell me." Sofia pulled out a chair from another table and swung it around so she could sit. "Perhaps I can help, or at least it will entertain me for five minutes."

Things were slow if this constituted entertainment, but

V nodded all the same. She'd happily sit and talk about anything if it meant more time with Sofia. "Okay, well the main issue is that it means staying with Jess and Melissa until February. I know that *sounds* like a good thing but they're about to have a baby—two actually—and I'm worried we'll be in the way. It's making me wonder if I should find something sooner, even if it's not ideal, to give them some space."

Sofia considered for a second, hitching up her knee and resting her chin on top. She was giving the matter her focussed attention and for a moment it felt as though the rest of the crowd had dissolved into the walls, which they might as well have done for all V now knew or cared. "Have you asked them about this? Do they mind you staying?"

"They say they don't, no, but I'm not sure I believe them. Not so much Jess, she'd let us stay forever if we wanted to, but it's different for Melissa. I can't help feeling like having her fiancée still so caught up with us is a bit..." Trailing off, V sucked her teeth and tried to find the word. "Unfair? If I don't give Jess a bit of a shove to put her own family first, it might all blow up at some point."

With the greatest respect to her, Jess didn't have a clue what it felt like to be pregnant and vulnerable. V did, even if she recognised that Melissa's situation was different. It was a planned pregnancy, they were engaged, and to all intent and purpose their relationship was secure. She still deserved to be the focus of Jess's attention, though.

"Perhaps." Sofia shrugged. "Or maybe Jess *is* considering her new family. The prospect of twins will be very daunting, and they will both appreciate your support. She probably knows that and realises having you around could make life easier."

"I guess," V conceded. She knew they were both

bricking it, and perhaps that was part of what Jess's pleading look came down to when they were in the car.

"It seems you have a very strong friendship and you are worrying—"

"For nothing," V finished. "Yeah, I get it."

"No." Sofia shook her head, then leant forward again as she whispered, "Because you love them." She sat back and her foot dropped to the ground. "And they clearly love you too. My opinion, for what it's worth, is that you should double check but then accept what they tell you. Don't let this be the reason you miss out on an excellent opportunity."

It wasn't the only reason she might want to pass on this excellent opportunity—her own fear still played a gigantic role—but at least she'd broken down one barrier. She'd talk this through properly with Jess and Melissa, but the rest could wait because Sofia had already provided her enough counsel for one night. "Thanks. That was actually really helpful, so I appreciate it."

Sofia squinted and let out a shot of laughter, her brown eyes glistening in the warm light from the wall lamps. "Did you just insult me?"

"Of course I didn't, that would be no good for my career." With a quick shrug, V took a sip of wine.

"Oh, I see. You only want to *chat again* so you can kiss up to me, you didn't need advice at all."

Resisting the urge to say anything about kissing her, V looked Sofia dead in the eye, her eyebrow lifting a touch over the glass still raised to her lips. "Absolutely."

Sofia met her gaze for a second and then pointed to the dregs of Bob's pint. "Sorry, Bob. I interrupted. Can I get you another while I'm at the bar?"

"Suppose you could persuade me." He pulled the phone

from his pocket and chucked it at the table. It skidded over the surface, the screen flashing up a photo of a middle-aged woman next to two tall teenage boys. When V made eye contact with Sofia again, they both grinned.

"I'll be back, don't go anywhere." Sofia's hand glanced across V's shoulder more delicately this time as she stood and moved towards the bar.

The gesture caused her stomach to flip and, when Sofia turned back momentarily, she knew the desire was written all over her face. The only thing she could do was own it and return the smile. She continued to watch as Sofia ordered, half listening to whatever Bob was saying. When he stopped, she shook her head and tried to catch up. She'd heard something about university fees but not a lot more besides.

"I was thinking perhaps dinner after this?" Sofia set down Bob's drink and then another Coke for herself, getting V off the hook. She didn't sit right away, though, leaning with a hand on the back of each of their chairs. "I haven't eaten yet, but I cannot face anything they serve here."

Bob folded his arms and let out a short sharp huff. "Count me out, I'm afraid. Won't get away with that."

"V?" Sofia's index finger drummed a gentle beat on the top of V's arm as she waited for a response. "Can I tempt you?"

Sofia could tempt her into pretty much anything, and food was the least of it. With half a glass of wine hitting her empty system, V was already lightheaded and game for whatever came her way tonight. It's not like she could go straight home, anyway, after she'd offered to give Jess and Melissa some space for the evening. Even if that hadn't been the case, she'd earned some fun. "Sounds good to me."

"Excellent, and what sort of food would you like?"

V shrugged. "I don't know. Quite fancy Italian." She raised the glass to her lips and waited, wishing she could see how that'd landed.

"Yes, I'm sure we could find you an Italian if that is what you desire." Sofia sat and rescued Bob's phone from a pool of spilt beer, leaning across to pass it over. She placed a hand on V's knee to steady herself, but it lingered a beat longer than needed.

It was still mild enough that V wasn't bothering with tights under her dress and the contact with her bare leg created a tingle of goosebumps. She crossed them in Sofia's direction, glancing down at her ankle boots to hide the look of satisfaction on her face.

"Yep, I definitely desire Italian." She took another sip of wine hoping once she'd finished their drinks, they could leave. No longer was she remotely interested in hanging around to chat and fit in with the rest of her colleagues. There was an entire term in which to do that, but a chance for dinner with Sofia might not come around again.

Twenty minutes later when Bob finally submitted to returning to the loving bosom of his family, V and Sofia followed him out. He trudged off down the High Street like a kid sulking about needing to get home before curfew, and V pointed to the independent Italian a few doors down from the bookshop where Melissa worked.

"Shall we go there?" Given there wasn't anywhere else besides a ropey chain restaurant, it seemed like there wasn't much of a choice and she walked in that direction. Sofia, however, hadn't moved, and when V glanced back over her shoulder she stopped. "What's up? Have you changed your mind?" The idea caused her stomach to sink.

"No, I was just thinking." Sofia pulled out her car keys

and pointed towards the archway leading to the car park. "My cooking is far superior to anything they will serve us."

"Oh naturally." V took a few steps back towards Sofia, her mood buoyed.

"I would also like a drink, but I can't because I'm driving..."

"Mhm."

"So perhaps you could come to my house and I will order you a taxi home later? It is only a ten-minute drive away; I live near the canal." When there was no immediate response because V was too busy trying to halt a ridiculously disproportionate smile, Sofia seemed to think she needed to make a stronger argument. "I can prepare anything you like, just name it. There may even be the remains of a homemade tiramisu in the fridge."

The way the word tiramisu rolled off her tongue sent a shiver down V's spine, but watching Sofia plead was far too enjoyable and she dragged it out a little longer. "I don't know, you're practically a stranger." She stepped closer and tugged on the bottom of Sofia's jacket. "What if you take advantage of me?"

A delighted grin spread across Sofia's face. "I think it's more likely to be the other way around, but I'll take the risk if you will."

6

The Mini stopped alongside a high stone building butted against the edge of the canal, and V stared up in awe. It was just enough surprise to halt the excitement that'd been swirling since they'd left town. "Holy. Holy. Fuck."

"What?" Sofia had her hand on the door handle but paused and turned, her face written with an unusual amount of worry.

"Your house." It looked like something out of a picture postcard. They were only a few minutes out of town on the outskirts of one of the satellite villages, but it could've been a whole world away. No wonder Sofia looked so relaxed all the time, if this is what she came home to every night. "Is the whole thing yours?"

Sofia laughed, her shoulders dropping as she popped open the door. "No, of course not. You know what teachers earn. Mine is a tall, thin sliver, and I have only two bedrooms." She jingled the keys as she sought the one for the front door, carrying her satchel in the other hand. "Don't set your expectations too high, okay?" She stuck the key in the lock but then paused again. "I won't have you disappointed."

"Given I live in my friend's spare bedroom in an ex-council house I don't think there's much risk of that, do you? It'll be a novelty not to tread on Lego every five minutes or find a spaniel has snuck in and left hair all over the bed."

The smell of sandalwood mixed with earthy real oak flooring was also a welcome change from dog related odours, which even Melissa's many vanilla candles and diffusers couldn't combat. When they stopped in the entrance hall to take off their shoes, V tracked the scent to a fancy incense burner on a low table just inside the kitchen beyond. That was Melissa's Christmas present sorted, at least.

"Don't worry, you'll find no dog hair in my bed." The comment was made absently, and probably innocently enough, but a little colour rose on Sofia's cheeks and she cleared her throat. "Anyway, tell me what you would like to eat."

"What are my options?"

V tiptoed barefoot across the floor and into the kitchen. It was a square room with a tall window looking out over the canal. On the far wall were solid oak base units, and they extended in an L-shape to divide the room in two. It was warm and inviting, but of course perfectly neat and clean. Even the little round dining table was clear from clutter, which was unheard of at Jess's. There was always something —Melissa's books, Jess's laptop or video games, Grace's homework.

Sofia crouched and opened the fridge. "The tiramisu is still here. If you would like a main first, I could whip us up a quick bowl of spaghetti. There is sauce already prepared."

"Prepared? You mean it doesn't come in a jar?" V knelt

beside her and pulled out a tub. "This is very impressive, you know. Is there any end to your talents?"

"Absolutely none." As Sofia took the sauce, she spotted something else on the bottom shelf. "Oh, and I have some ravioli here. Left over from last night but it should be fine still, perhaps just a little soggy."

The tray she pulled out was dotted with perfect parcels of pasta, and V prodded one with her index finger. "Are you a walking advert for Italy? I love fish and chips or shepherd's pie, but I don't make them from scratch every day." Or any day, come to that.

"What can I say? I love to cook." The sauce and the tray were raised alternately. "Which will it be?"

V held out both hands and then clapped them together. There was nothing in Sofia's fridge that she didn't want to eat. "I will take the ravioli, with sauce, followed by tiramisu please." She'd tried to imitate Sofia's accent again, but it was nowhere near as seductive and she only ended up laughing, grabbing hold of the work surface to haul herself back up.

"As you wish. Will you find us a bottle of wine from the rack in the corner while I get started on this?" Sofia set down their food choices and opened a cupboard, pulling out a large metal pan and filling it with water. Then she set it on the gas ring and lit the burner.

"Which one?" There were a lot to choose from, and all red.

"Any will be fine."

"Let me guess, you have excellent taste in wine, too?"

Sofia shrugged and grabbed a corkscrew from the drawer, turning to take the random bottle as V handed it over. "I'm not a connoisseur, I've just learned what I like and buy it in bulk."

"Yes, we're the same with biscuits in our house." The

favourite was Hobnobs, and there were at least two packets on every weekly shopping order. If they ever ran out, there was widespread panic and someone ended up at the local shop.

Sofia didn't know how to take that, and she stared blankly for a moment. "Biscuits?"

"Yes, and ice cream. I do have to get strict or it's all anyone would eat."

"Oh, I see." This seemed to pique Sofia's interest, and she raised an eyebrow as she popped out the cork. She dropped it into a wide glass bowl on the windowsill, on top of dozens more. "How strict?"

"Very strict indeed." V stepped forward and lowered her voice, spurred on by the lascivious smile it'd elicited. She was at least three inches shorter than Sofia with her boots off and peered up as she took back the bottle and set it on the counter. Her heart was thudding, and she prayed she wasn't reading this wrong.

"Will you be strict with me?" Sofia whispered.

"It depends, what have you done?"

Sofia backed against the unit, her arms bent behind and her palms flat on the work surface. "Well, lately I've been having lots of inappropriate thoughts. Do they count?"

"I don't know yet, tell me more."

"It involves another teacher."

"If it's Bob, then you're in for a real talking to." This probably wasn't the time for jokes, but it was a useful way for V to ease her own nerves. She had a feeling Sofia's sense of humour could take it, and she was right. Her laugh was deep and throaty this time, like a growl which caused V's clit to twitch. She ran a hand down the lapel of Sofia's shirt, inhaling the spicy scent and finding the same thing happened.

"Bob isn't my type," Sofia clarified. She paused for a beat and then whispered, "But there is someone in the department who I can't keep away from, however hard I try. I wonder if she has noticed me calling by her classroom and finding any excuse to see her."

Leaning closer, V whispered back, "You don't need an excuse."

"I don't?"

As she shook her head, V casually flicked open the top button of Sofia's shirt. At least, she hoped it looked casual because her fingers were trembling. Then she stroked the fabric away from Sofia's shoulder, in search of the tattoo. There were geometric shapes which morphed into an eagle, and V was gradually opening more buttons to trace it all until Sofia had to take her arm out of the sleeve, revealing the bird spread right across her back.

Standing with her shirt awkwardly half hanging off, Sofia slipped out of the other sleeve and threw it aside, resting her palms on the work surface again. "Are you happy now you have seen that?"

V ran her eyes over Sofia's torso, her slightly soft stomach, and her muscular arms. "Yes, thank you." She tilted her head and let out a gentle laugh. "I have been easily distracted from the tattoo." Then, meeting Sofia's gaze, she became more earnest. "You're gorgeous."

Saying it out loud, even with the aid of wine, still made her cheeks colour. It had the same effect on Sofia, and she diverted her eyes to the floor. Peering up again with a shy smile, she wrapped her right arm around V's waist to pull them closer.

Lightly trailing her fingers over Sofia's throat, V felt the pulse quicken under her touch as she kissed Sofia's chest. Her skin was as smooth and soft as V had imagined, and she closed her eyes as she stroked a thumb along Sofia's jaw and then curled it over her cheek. Glancing up to find Sofia's eyes were heavy, her tongue running over her bottom lip, V became bolder.

Tilting down Sofia's chin, she kissed the corner of her mouth, lingering and then nipping across her lips as they parted. She almost let out a moan when Sofia's hands pressed firmly down her back and over the curve of her arse, pulling them flush together this time. It was exactly the reaction she'd hoped for, but it still took her by surprise.

As their lips connected fully and Sofia's tongue slipped into her mouth, it knocked all the air from her lungs so that she gasped. She hadn't been lost to someone like this for a long time, the hands working over her back and hips causing everywhere to pulse with arousal. Running her fingers through the waves of mahogany hair as the kiss deepened, she pressed Sofia harder into the kitchen unit, an urgency building.

Her core pounding with the rush of blood, V diverted to Sofia's ear and whispered only two words: "Fuck me".

Suddenly lifted, cold marble hit the back of her legs and she wrapped them tight around Sofia's back, her hands roaming across the defined muscles of Sofia's shoulders. Then she raised herself to allow Sofia to remove her underwear and it was flung across the kitchen.

When Sofia's hand grazed the inside of her thigh, she spread her legs wider and let out a breathy moan, wriggling to the edge of the counter and then tilting her hips. She was so wet already that she could feel it seeping into her dress, but Sofia made her wait while she desperately pulled off her rings and threw them at the floor. They clattered on the wood and then Sofia's first two fingers parted her lips, gently trailing the length of her desire and causing her to shiver.

She circled and played while they kissed again, every touch sending out waves of heat which flushed up V's throat. She was desperate to feel Sofia inside her, an anticipatory throb of her walls quickly repeated when a finger circled her entrance. It was slow at first, then faster, until Sofia pulled back her head and their eyes locked. She swallowed hard as she pushed inside, little by little, then when she curled her fingers and V let out a long low guttural sound her eyelids fluttered.

V palmed Sofia's breasts through the fabric of her bra and rubbed firmly over her hardened nipples, then reached around to unhook it and took the weight of a breast in her hand. Flicking her thumb so that Sofia moaned with her, she pulled them tighter again and her lips fell to Sofia's neck, sucking hard.

Sofia's arm wrapped low around V's waist to draw her into each thrust now and she was being pounded, each breath escaping with a short sharp cry of pleasure. She dug her fingers into Sofia's back and rocked into her hand, completely lost in the moment, and as the pitch of her cries climbed, Sofia's thumb against her clit sent her higher.

A jumble of words strangled in her throat, rising slowly with the heat that had started from her feet and was creeping through her entire body. She pressed their mouths together again, feeling herself tighten around Sofia's fingers as they continued to drive in and out, her toes curling as her thighs clenched against Sofia's sides.

"Fuuuuck," echoed around the room as she climaxed, but it didn't seem to want to stop and Sofia kept going, sweat dripping down her back and her face red with exertion. She continued to stroke and twist, eking out every sensation until finally V could take no more and grabbed her wrist, forcing her to pull out. "Enough."

She was still grasping the wrist as Sofia kissed her again. It was more tender this time, V's swollen lips throbbing along with the rest of her body. She cupped Sofia's cheeks and gently stroked along her jaw with both thumbs until the banging of the pan lid where the water was boiling disturbed them and Sofia jumped away to turn down the heat.

"Sorry," she whispered, wrapping her arms around V's waist to help her down. "I haven't forgotten about dinner."

V adjusted her dress, the tops of her thighs still slick and slipping together. "Oh good, that was my worry." She laughed a little and stepped behind, reaching her arms around Sofia's torso and massaging her breasts. Her skin still buzzed wherever they touched, and she laid kisses over the tattoo again. "You do that, while I do this." Sofia's breath hitched as her trousers were deftly unfastened and a hand slid into a pair of tight black boxers. She was soaking, her clit pulsing against V's fingers. "You're a little excited."

A mumble of something in Italian, and then Sofia moaned again. She braced her hands on the work surface, her hips rolling into V's touch as kisses peppered her back. "You must know how much I want you."

"I'm getting an idea," V whispered. She was desperate to feel Sofia's skin against her own but got the sense there wouldn't be time to take off any more clothes. Sofia threw back her head, her face flushed with excitement, clearly already close. "Did fucking me turn you on?"

"Uhuh," she whimpered, her hips surging forward as her nipple was rolled between V's thumb and forefinger. She clasped her hand over V's, with only the cotton of the boxers separating them, her breathing still heavy, and closed her eyes as she was held. After a few seconds, she turned to wrap her arms around V's waist, kissing her neck and pushing her back.

"Don't you want to finish dinner?" The pan was still boiling on the stove, and V pointed at it as she hooked her hands around Sofia's shoulders.

Sofia shook her head, her eyes glistening as she smiled and pulled V's hips tight against her own. "It can wait."

* * *

An hour and a half later they were on the sofa in the first-floor lounge. The room was the same size and shape as the kitchen but with a balcony over the water, although it was too dark and cold to use it. Instead, they were sitting in the shorts and T-shirts Sofia had grabbed from her bedroom, both cross legged and facing each other with a dish of tiramisu in the space between them.

"This is spectacular." V licked the back of her spoon and then went in for another scoop, velvety soft cream lingering on her tongue. It was about the weirdest thing she'd done after sex. Few times had anyone offered her a tray of dessert and some comfy pyjamas, but then perhaps that just went to prove she'd been doing it with the wrong people. Grown-up teacher V was also raising her standards in this department. "I'm going to be disappointed when we run out."

Sofia shrugged. "I will make you more."

"That would be great. If you could send me home with a couple, I'd really appreciate it. Some of that ravioli, too. It was excellent."

With a waggle of her spoon, Sofia laughed. "Ah, but if I do that, how will I ever convince you to come back?"

"Come back, huh?" V nodded and scraped up the last blob of cocoa dusted sponge. She hadn't even considered yet whether she'd be staying the night, let alone coming back. It was only nine, she could easily still get a taxi, and her stomach knotted. They probably should've discussed what would happen next *before* having sex, given they still had to work together, but she'd got a little carried away.

Another shrug, and Sofia dropped her spoon with a clang. "Yes. Of course I want you to come back."

"Is that a good idea?" V's finger trailed slowly around the left-over streaks of dessert. "Wouldn't it become difficult at school if we were... you know, sleeping together?" She sucked away the cream and then set the empty dish on the coffee table, wriggling forward and taking Sofia's hands in her lap. "I'm having a great time but I'm a bit worried it'd get all awkward."

"What we do in our own time is our own business, but if what you mean is that you don't want to see me again, just come out and say it." With a quick laugh, Sofia scrunched her face and leant in for a kiss. "I am a big girl, and I promise I won't sulk."

"This isn't about not wanting to see you. I can't begin to tell you how much I'd love to continue having rampant sex over the first two floors of your house, but I'm not sure it's practical." Had she really used the word 'practical' in relation to sex? Yes, she had. Jess would be proud. "I don't want a reputation. My job means a lot to me."

Sofia tucked away a wedge of red hair. "As does mine, so I understand. If you feel uncomfortable with this, we won't do it again, but I would never tell anyone. I would never betray your trust."

She believed that, oddly, even though they didn't know each other all that well. The knot in V's stomach dissolved, and she relaxed again. "I know you wouldn't." She hooked her hands behind Sofia's neck. "My life is complicated, and full on, and I don't want to tell you we can do this again when I have absolutely no idea whether I'm coming or going right now. Can we leave it as something we might do again if the mood takes us...?"

Sofia laughed and then whispered, "Of course." She gently took V's face in her palms and kissed her, their mouths lingering together as she smiled. "Do you have some more time now, though? I will drive you home soon, I haven't had much to drink, but can you stay a while?"

"Oh yeah," she whispered back, pressing her lips against Sofia's again and feeling a familiar heat. There was no harm in enjoying it a little longer. "I think I can manage that."

7

True to her word, Sofia remained as friendly and professional as ever, continuing to check in whenever she had the chance and casually breezing through life in her usual carefree manner. If only V could manage the same. She was now five weeks into the term and understanding what Sofia had meant about the first being the most difficult. The nights were drawing in, and Grace had been suffering with a cold which had delayed her most recent visit to her dad, putting their entire schedule out of whack.

In any pockets of free time, she was trying to think through the house properly and do some budgeting. Talking it over with Jess and Melissa had helped, and she was swaying towards saying yes, but the idea of moving anywhere was still overwhelming. Even her trusty spreadsheets weren't helping. Every time she opened them up and went over the figures, she got lost in imagining how empty the place was going to be again and almost burst into full floods of tears.

Trudging into Sofia's classroom on Wednesday lunchtime with two black eyes owing to lack of sleep, she tried to stifle a yawn and show some enthusiasm. She'd actually been looking forward to observing Sofia's lesson, hoping it'd be an antidote to Bob's, which had made her want to quit. Not just teaching, but possibly everything.

She dropped her bag by a seat which was left for her at the back of the classroom. "Sorry, I'm a bit early."

"Never apologise for being eager. Are you ready for your masterclass?" Sofia's eyes remained fixed on her interactive whiteboard as she tapped through her apps.

"Eager?" There was a flourish of demented laughter as V slumped into the chair. "Eager went out the window weeks ago but I'm here, sort of willing, and kind of able."

As Sofia turned, her expression was written with sympathy and perhaps a touch of concern. "Are you alright?" She weaved through the sea of tables and pulled up another chair, inclining her head and smiling.

V waved a hand as if it might waft away her troubles, then her arms hung limp by her sides while she slouched and closed her eyes. "Oh, yeah. Just feel a bit like I'm sinking. Too much to do, Grace has been ill, and I still haven't decided whether to take this house. It's all good, though. I'm having a quick nap here before you start." She smiled and sighed.

"Is there a rush? Give yourself a break. Not everything must be accomplished in one go."

Trust Sofia to be so nonchalant. "I know, but some of these things have time pressures. The house is a great offer, and I should take it but I'm just..." V peered through one eye and smiled again, hoping to have conveyed the gist without needing to admit out loud something which made her feel like a right wally.

"Scared?"

She laughed at how ridiculous that sounded. "Bingo. I'm

almost thirty and I'm responsible for keeping a whole other person alive. I can hold down a full-time job—pretty much —but I'm worried about living on my own."

"Perfectly natural." The chair creaked as Sofia relaxed into it. "I remember when I first lived alone, making any excuse to stay at work so I didn't have to go back to an empty house. It gets easier, though, and you have Grace."

That was part of the problem, V was realising. It had never been only the two of them. What if she couldn't do it on her own? The thought was too scary to vocalise, so she only nodded and opened her eyes fully, sitting straight in the chair. "I know. Thanks for letting me vent. Everything will work out; I think I just have to take the plunge."

"You are welcome, any time, but don't be alarmed when you get my bill at the end of term." Sofia looked down at her watch and sucked her teeth, then laughed when V shoved her knee. "Are you at least finding your feet here? Has everyone been friendly?"

As V tried to halt any number of ridiculously inappropriate comments, her eyebrows shot up. "Spectacularly so." She shoved Sofia's leg again. "That Bob is *extremely* friendly. What a rock."

"Oh, I know. A real treasure, which is of course why I selected him as your mentor."

"And then there's you, also around whenever I have a problem. Is that because you have a wealth of experience to share and take your job so very seriously?"

With her gaze now fixed on the ceiling, Sofia pursed her lips and then laughed. "Well… I probably can't pretend it's all professional obligation." She grinned and shrugged. "But I also want to help because I know what it's like. I was worried I wouldn't fit in *at all* when I first started. I was sure everyone would look at me and wonder why on earth they hired me."

"Pfft, yeah…"

"It's true!" Her eyes widened, then she crossed her legs and stuck her hands in her pockets. "Just ask Bob. I'd never worked with kids before and used to spend my days behind a computer. I was a programmer, working on a piece of statistical analysis software for one of the big banks."

"Really? I presumed you'd always been a teacher." Although why, V was questioning. It actually stood to reason that she wasn't, or she'd probably have been way higher up the food chain by now.

"I retrained. This is only my fourth year of teaching."

"Holy shit, then there's hope for me yet."

"Exactly." Standing and eye-balling some year eight boys as they kicked their ball against the outside wall of the class-room, Sofia muttered something under her breath in Italian before continuing. "On the first day of term, I was absolutely terrified of having to get up in front of everyone when Bob has been teaching far, *far* longer than I have. I think it annoyed him that they made me acting head instead of him."

"I expect he was livid, and his bald patch went purple." Perhaps that's why he was always such a grumpy sod. "I really can't understand why he doesn't quit and do some-thing else. I don't mean that as a dig, he just doesn't seem at all happy."

Returning to her seat, Sofia let out a long sigh. "Not everyone can be bothered, or knows what else they'd do, or has the means to leave a steady job I suppose."

"True." Which posed the question of why the hell Sofia had done it when she could've been fiddling with computers instead of wrangling gobby teenagers. "I cannot even fathom why *you* wanted to do this. Don't get me wrong, you're a brilliant teacher, but compared to programming I expect the pay's only so-so, and the stress is next level."

Sofia was about to answer, but then shook her head and frowned as she did a double take. "Hang on a second, have you not recently *chosen* to become a teacher too?"

"That's different, I didn't already have a good job. I had no job. This is a significant step up." Although, to be fair to Sofia, V had spent years wanting to do it. Back when she was at university she'd applied because it seemed like a good, steady career with a decent pension. Given the absence of other options whenever anyone asked, she'd latched onto the idea, much to the delight of her parents. When she lost the opportunity, though, it had taken on greater symbolism. It became the job she was going to have to work her arse off to get, rather than fall into. "Okay, so maybe that was a lie..."

"You don't say."

This time when V 'playfully' shoved Sofia's shoulder, she toppled and almost took the chair with her. There was a moment where it perched precariously on only two legs as she lurched sideways, reaching out to steady herself on the desk.

"Shit, sorry!" Cringing and clasping both hands over her mouth, V let out a puff of laughter which blew the hair up out of her face. "Are you okay?" She took them away and gripped around the top of Sofia's arm, gently tipping her back down. The hand slid along Sofia's sleeve and their fingers laced together.

Giving V's hand a quick squeeze, Sofia leant forward and narrowed her eyes as the corner of her mouth curled up. "Yes. Are you always this much trouble?"

"Absolutely not, I only inconvenience the people I really like." Their eyes locked for a few moments, then V cleared her throat and dropped Sofia's hand, wondering if the flutter in her stomach would ever go away. It appeared whenever Sofia did, and sex hadn't got it out of her system. "Anyway, yes I enjoy teaching and I expect you do too, so that was a silly question."

"Most of the time." Sofia returned her hands to the safety of her pockets. "I still have moments where I wonder what the hell I've done and stroke my lovely Mini because I know I couldn't afford another now, but in terms of my career I am more fulfilled than I have ever been."

She would get no sympathy with the first bit, because V hadn't owned a car in many years and during the chat with her spreadsheets, they'd revealed she wouldn't be able to afford one soon, either. Just as she had a bit of money, it would all be going out on rent and bills. "Boo hoo for you."

"I am sensing a startling lack of sympathy."

"Yep." With a defiant nod of her head, V folded her arms. "Sucks to be you."

"Wow. Mature."

"I'm tired of being mature. Want to argue?" When she cocked her head and Sofia pulled out one of those deep, throaty laughs again, it rumbled right through V's core and her clit twitched. Crossing her legs to halt it, she verbalised the first and least sexy word that popped into her head—Bob.

"Bob?"

"Yes, Bob. He's invited me to the pub this week already, you're slacking."

"That is because I was considering having a few people over this Friday, instead of the pub. I'm still working out my guest list, it's always a trial. My house is only small, and—"

"And what? You're deciding between Big Brenda in

finance and that PE teacher with a steak where he was meant to have a brain? Yes, I can see the difficulty."

"You won't want an invitation then? Too busy anyway, I imagine..."

With her eyes settling on the patch of skin to the right of Sofia's shirt collar, V recalled how it felt to kiss there. She went to agree for reasons once again far removed from those that should probably motivate her, like having a friendly chat with her peers and comparing notes. The only person who she really wanted to get to know better was Sofia, and perhaps it wouldn't be such a terrible idea. After all, they'd both proven they could keep things professional. Well, when they weren't shoving each other off chairs. "I might manage to find time."

"Good, because it was partly for your benefit. I thought it might be an opportunity for new teachers to mix with old— so naturally I've invited Bob. Come for six on Friday with an open mind and a bottle of wine?"

"I'll consider it." All of it, in fact, probably in quite a lot of detail. The bell rang and almost instantly the corridor filled with noise, pulling V from her thoughts. "I suppose we should get ready for class." She leant forward to whisper, "After all, I'm still determined to learn your secret."

"Ah," Sofia whispered back. "Then you'd better pay attention for the next fifty minutes."

8

When Friday rolled around, V stood in the living room window willing a silver Corsa into view. The switching of their schedules where Grace had been ill meant her dad was having to collect her off the back of a work trip to Manchester. He'd been stuck in traffic on the M6 and if he didn't hurry, it wouldn't be worth him collecting her until Saturday morning.

"Why do you keep looking at your phone?" Jess tried to peer at the screen, a bottle of beer in hand and a laptop wedged under her armpit. She'd left work early to 'do paperwork' which meant having a few drinks and ordering more baby supplies.

"I'm going out with some people from school." V left it at that, not wanting to get into a discussion about who would be there, or whose house it was at. She'd told no one about what had happened with Sofia, and for now intended to keep it that way. "Where's Grace?"

"She was strangling Hal goodbye last I saw."

Spotting the Corsa turning onto the street, V called to her, and she barrelled in, wearing her backpack and dragging Hal along by his collar. "Your dad's here. Come and give me a cuddle, sweetheart." Grace was still far more interested in making sure the dog knew she loved him and relaying how many treats he would get on her return. In the end, V had to crouch beside Hal to get any attention. "Come on, one cuddle."

Grace kissed the top of his head and then flung her arms around V's neck. "See you on Sunday, Mummy. I love you."

"I love you too."

Once Grace had been bundled out of the door and they'd all had a brief exchange about their week through the passenger window, V jogged back up the path and checked the time on her phone. It was almost six. She grabbed her bag from beside the bed, already packed with a bottle of red wine, and made for the front door again.

"You're in a rush." Jess halted her escape. She leant against the living room door frame as V reached the hallway and went to snatch her jacket. "Must have been a bad week if you're *this* desperate to get a glass of wine."

"Yep." She slid on the jacket and flicked her hair off the collar. It'd had a brush, and she'd sprayed some perfume, but she didn't want to over-do things by getting dressed up. The others were probably going straight from work, so she'd changed into a pair of tight jeans and a clean but casual band T-shirt.

Jess drummed her fingers on the side of the bottle. "So..."

"So what?" V had her hand on the latch now.

"What was so bad? You know I'm always here if you need to talk."

"Nothing, really. Just busy. It's going well, actually, if you ignore the worrying crop of grey hairs." She released the latch and smiled at her friend. Perhaps she had been a bit disconnected lately. Trying to be more independent and less reliant on her may have swung too far the other way. "What are you guys up to this evening? More riveting television, or are you back on eBay?"

"You are so judgemental. As a matter of fact, Melissa is taking me for dinner. She's upstairs getting changed."

"Fancy. Special occasion?"

"Seems to be, but I'm not sure what. We're already engaged and last time I checked she was pregnant." With a quick shrug, Jess let out a sigh and then took a sip of her beer. "Can't imagine what else there is."

"A real mystery. Perhaps she wants to seduce you over candlelight."

"She does!" The interruption came from Melissa as she appeared on the top step in a flowing low-cut black dress. Adjusting the strap, she held out her arms. "What do you think?"

"Fuck me," Jess muttered, audibly gulping. She absently tore a chunk of the beer label away as she gawped.

"Yep, I think that was probably the idea," V concluded. She nudged Jess's mouth closed and opened the door, slinging her bag over a shoulder. "Have fun, kids. Don't do anything I wouldn't."

"That doesn't rule out much."

"No, so don't wait up." Before either of them could ask more, she opened the door and left, half skipping down the path and turning right toward town. It was only a ten-minute walk under normal circumstances, but she did it in eight, making up for the two she'd spent teasing Jess.

Waiting impatiently at the bus stop, she almost gave up and paid for a taxi, but knew she should save her money. She had those spreadsheets nattering in the back of her head, reminding her she was about to be skint again. The move she was slowly reconciling would happen would mean buying furniture, kitchenware, and absolutely everything else from scratch. If it was just her, she'd cope with the basics, but she wanted it to feel like a proper home for Grace.

The bus stopped at the top of Sofia's street. It was lined with much larger houses which had big 4x4's on their driveways, but at the end of the cul-de-sac was a jumble of far less expensive looking cars—a beat up Volvo, a moped, and a Ford Fiesta with eyelashes on the headlights. V laughed to herself, musing that it probably belonged to the meat-head PE teacher.

As the door opened, generating a waft of scent from the familiar burner, she had a sudden thought which stopped the laughter dead—she'd been here before, and people probably shouldn't know that. "What a lovely house you have and that I have never seen before in my life." She raised her eyebrows a touch, trying to put aside her slight discomfort with humour as she held out the bottle of wine.

Sofia took it and stepped aside to let her pass. "Thank you. Did you know there are three floors? I will give you a tour later."

Dispersed throughout the kitchen were at least a dozen other teachers, including the entire maths department, and V circulated this time rather than sticking to those she already knew. It would be rude not to after Sofia had gone to the effort, quickly furnishing her with a glass of wine and a few encouraging words. It turned out to be good fun and even Bob was in reasonably high spirits, probably because the phone signal was poor and his wife couldn't get through.

"I wish I lived on my own," he mused, looking rather disgusted as he peered into the bottom of a lemonade. The

Volvo outside was his, and Sofia had swiftly removed his second beer earlier in the evening.

Having no such problems and now on her third glass of wine, V couldn't resist challenging him. "I'm feeling really sorry for your wife, she can't be that bad."

"She's not. She's a lovely woman, truth be told."

"Then why on earth do you want to live on your own?"

He stopped to consider for a while, frowning as he swilled the leftovers in his glass. "Marriage. Responsibility. All of it, really. It's the death of spontaneity. If I lived on my own, it might bring back a bit of excitement. She could visit, and she might... find me attractive again."

Wondering whether he'd spiked that lemonade with something a little stronger, V peered into the glass. "I'm sorry, Bob." She gave the top of his arm a quick squeeze, not intending to sound patronising but probably falling short.

"Oh, it's alright for you lot," he lamented, gesturing at the twenty-two-year-old as she swooned over the strapping PE teacher with his tiny shorts and a giant beard. "You're young and probably have blokes falling all over you still. Wait until you're fifty, losing your looks, and have been married to the same person for twenty-odd years."

She snorted with laughter. "Bob, remember who you're talking to. There is no orderly queue outside my bedroom door, because it is being guarded by a precocious five-year-old. Yes, I have some fun occasionally, but you're wrong if you think everyone else in the world is living a life of high excitement." More often than not it was a life of high anxiety. She reached behind herself and took the bottle of lemonade from the work surface, refilling his glass as Sofia did the same with her wine. "Listen, if your wife is such a lovely woman, why don't you try talking to *her* about this?"

Was she spending her night counselling Bob now? That

was a twist she hadn't seen coming. He didn't look sure how to take it either, scowling for a second before softening. "I wouldn't even know where to start."

"Here, let us help you." Sofia set down her bottle and gave up on issuing top-ups, then took V's glass from her and discarded that too. She must have put away a few drinks herself because her cheeks were rosy, and she'd gone all glassy-eyed. "Okay, here we go." She took V's hands and positioned them in the small of her own back. Then she cupped V's cheeks and stared deep into her eyes. "Darling. I love you, but there is something I need you to know."

Her voice had become very deep, and V spluttered as she tried to keep a straight face. "Darling, what is it?"

"Darling, I am not feeling as attractive to you as I once was. It is making me miserable to think that you, being so lovely, might prefer another man."

"But darling, it is you I love. Yes, you have gone a little soft around the middle," and with that, V stroked her thumb under the back of Sofia's shirt. "But so have I, and you still find me desirable."

"Oh darling, I'm so glad we could talk this through. Kiss me!" Sofia laughed and wrapped her arm around V's waist, standing to one side and holding out the other. "See? Easy."

Bob shook his head but was thankfully laughing, because he could easily have taken that entirely the wrong way. Not that they meant any harm, they were just pissed. "I know, I know. Talk. Very good." His eyes rolled a little as he chuckled again and wandered off to stuff his face with crisps from the table.

"Have you ever considered amateur dramatics?" V's thumb still stroked the base of Sofia's back, and she hadn't let go. "I think you'd be quite good."

"Quite good?" she leant in to whisper, the tickle of her

breath on V's ear sending a shiver down her spine and right back up again, like one of those funfair strength tests with the little bell. "I'd be a revelation."

"Uhuh, steady Dame Judi. You're a funny drunk, though. I'll give you that."

The PE teacher broke them apart when he needed another drink, strutting over with his hand in his pocket and his chest puffed out. V cleared her throat and scratched her nose, raising the bottle of wine to offer him a top-up.

With a gruff "cheers" he lingered for a second, but the twenty-two-year-old was eye-balling them over a handful of chocolate fingers and V encouraged him to return. That was definitely not something she wanted to get in the middle of, even though she had to admit he was quite cute and exactly the type of person she'd usually have blown off some steam with. Those meaningless encounters had gradually lost their shine, though. Dare she say, she wanted a conversation and a laugh, as well as the sex, and she sighed as she watched them resume flirting.

"What was that for?" Sofia had leant against the work surface and crossed her feet over, a glass of wine back in hand.

"Oh, nothing. I was only wondering when I started having more in common with Bob than these youngsters. Yes, I did just say youngsters. You see how dire the situation is?" She took a step back, standing alongside Sofia. As she mirrored the pose and her palm lay flat on the marble, she reached out her little finger to stroke it against Sofia's, missing her touch. "He's going to take her home tonight." She nodded at the twenty-two-year-old.

"Bob?!"

That thought was enough to douse anyone's sexual desire. Perhaps permanently. "Good god no, don't give me nightmares. The PE teacher. He will have already decided there's nothing better on offer and he wouldn't mind a quick shag. Mark my words."

"How do you know?"

"Because he's me." She turned and shrugged. "It's what I used to do whenever I was let off the leash. I'd go out, get drunk, and hopefully find someone to have sex with." This might be a regrettable line of conversation with Sofia, but wine was a bit like truth juice. She spoke with no access to the 'off' switch. "Haven't done it in a while and I thought it was just about time, but I'm not so sure anymore."

"No?" Sofia cocked her head and smiled. Then she leant forward and lowered her voice. "That's not what I was to you, then?"

"Well... I mean for a start I wasn't even drunk..." They both laughed and V chewed her lip, also wondering if her next comment was a good idea. "No, it wasn't the same with you." She shrugged again, this time with a brief sigh. "I like you. I feel good when I'm around you. I..." She trailed off and laughed again. "Okay, I'm drunk *now* and saying way more than I ought to, especially in a room full of people we work with."

"Why don't you stay and tell me about it when they're gone, then?" Staring down at the floor, Sofia shuffled, then peered up and grinned as she met V's gaze. The sound of the front door slamming shut reverberated through the house, though, and she jumped before getting a reply. "Hold that thought, people are going. I need to say goodbye."

"Oh. Right." It had only just gone nine, but then most of them were driving, and V grabbed the bottle of wine they'd been working through. "Let me help you clean up."

She busied herself eating some crisps to get rid of them, clearing away glasses, and running the sink to wash them.

All the while Sofia laughed and joked with her colleagues as they gradually filtered out. Half an hour later the place was almost empty, and V was wiping down the surfaces, trying to eke out the task so it didn't look odd when she was the only one left and showing no signs of leaving.

"Can I offer you a lift?" Bob called, holding up his keys as he stood in the hall doorway wearing his coat.

V waved her cloth. "Thanks, but I said I'd help clear up. Wouldn't dare leave Sofia's house a mess." As he turned, she yelled after him, "But nice try getting me to come home and straighten things out with your wife!"

There was a laugh which petered out and then the door clicked shut. A few moments later, Sofia wandered back through with her hands in the pockets of her jeans. "So, did you have a good night?" She slowly took a few paces forward, placing a hand over V's as she finished the table. "You can stop doing that now, there's no one else here."

"Whatever do you mean?"

"We both know you were only cleaning so you could stay."

"Ah." After straightening up and flinging the cloth at the sink, V rubbed her hands on the back of her jeans to dry them. "Busted. Just like I'm pretty sure you didn't only arrange this little get together out of the goodness of your heart."

Sofia laughed. "I have always been quite upfront that I wanted you to come back here, but I promise I didn't have an ulterior motive for the party." She held up her hands, now wearing a genuine smile.

"If it were anyone else, I wouldn't believe them..." But V believed Sofia. She laced their fingers together, and they stood palm to palm for a few seconds before she pulled Sofia's arms around her middle, placing both hands in the small of her back. Then she cupped Sofia's cheeks, so they were in the reverse of their positions from earlier.

Hesitating for a moment, she wondered whether kissing Sofia would generate the same electricity as last time, or if she'd built it up in her mind. The jolt of pleasure the second their lips met, the shock of how possessive she'd been, the crackling energy wherever they touched. There was only one way to find out, and her eyes darted up to Sofia's, finding they were already heavy.

V's thumbs stroked along Sofia's jaw as she dabbed her lips, then she dropped her hands and wrapped them low around Sofia's waist as they each let out a gasp of relief. Their bodies melded together while they gently sucked and nipped, the kiss no less exhilarating for being more tender. Then, as it deepened, Sofia pressed her hands lower and drew their hips together.

Feeling her underwear growing damp, V walked them towards the stairs, but Sofia's smile interrupted their kiss. With her lips pressed against it, V whispered, "The mood is taking me towards your bedroom. Is that okay?"

"On one condition."

She hadn't expected any conditions and let out a grunt of laughter. "Dangerous." Her heart thudded, and she hoped she wouldn't regret being so flippant.

"Please stay the night this time."

Sofia didn't sound sure of herself, and V placed a hand in the centre of her chest, feeling it canter. Then she looked her in the eye, able to answer honestly, "I would love to spend the night with you."

9

When V woke it was still dark, and it took her a moment to realise it was because of the blackout curtains. She rolled over, her legs tangling with the sheets, and expected to find Sofia. It was a surprise to grasp and clutch thin air, and an even bigger shock to discover that it was a disappointment. Unwinding herself from the duvet, she shuffled to the edge and reached to tug open the curtain a little so she could see. Then she gathered up her discarded clothes. What she could, anyway, because various items were still scattered in a trail through the house.

Just as she reached the door, it inched open, and she jumped back. "Fuck!"

"Sorry, I have breakfast." Sofia shoved it over the thick grey carpet, causing her tray to rattle. "Presuming you're staying and not about to throw yourself out of the window."

Dropping the clothes in a pile, V stared down at her own naked body. "It depends, will you take your top off?" Sofia was wearing a loose white T-shirt, and it only seemed a fair exchange for not leaping into a freezing canal.

She rested the tray on the end of the bed and then Sofia

unceremoniously pulled off the offending item of clothing. She dropped it on the floor and held out her arms. "Happy?"

"You have no idea…"

Her body was a thing of beauty, adorned by another work of art, and V couldn't resist touching it again. Everything about Sofia was a turn on, even with her hair sticking out at all angles from a night of passion. She stepped closer and inhaled deeply of the spicy, earthy scent, creating a swell of butterflies in her stomach.

"Do you have anywhere you need to be this morning?" she whispered as she trailed her fingertips over Sofia's arse and was rewarded with a spread of goosebumps.

"Besides bed?"

"Correct answer." V climbed back over the mattress, causing the plates to rattle on the tray again. She dragged it closer, interested to see what Sofia had decided would be fuel for more sex. "Toast? Let me guess, did you make the bread?"

Sofia sat on the edge of the bed and then positioned her legs either side of V. She reached over, her scent once again making V's stomach flutter with excitement. "No, but these are homemade jams from my neighbour." She tapped three separate jars, all with swirling handwritten labels. Prizing off a lid, she dipped in the tip of a butter knife and held it close to V's lips. "Here, try some."

She was never one to mess about and took the lot into her mouth. The sugar burst across her taste buds, followed by apricot. "That's amazing." She waited for Sofia to do the same with the next, sampling blackcurrant this time, then picked up a second knife and spread a liberal streak of strawberry over a slice of toast. While not homemade, it was of course a very good quality granary variety, and V melted back into Sofia as she ate. "This is almost better than the sex. No offence."

"Lots taken. You didn't say that about my tiramisu."

"Oh fuck. Say *tiramisu* again," she pleaded, holding a hand to her heart.

Sofia laughed and took a bite of toast as V offered it over her shoulder. She reached around for the tray and strained to push it onto the other side of the bed, almost toppling sideways, then swept up a mass of red hair and began trailing kisses across V's back. "Tiramisu," she whispered, before gently sucking just below V's earlobe and causing her to sink back further with a breathy moan. "See, I am working out what you like."

"I like all of it," V confessed, way past the point of playing coy. She'd spent the entire night confirming, sometimes so fervently that even the jam making neighbour probably heard, exactly how much she liked sex with Sofia.

She moved on, slowly working the kisses across the nape of V's neck from right to left. When she ran out, she tugged gently on the other ear with her teeth and V gasped as she shuddered. Already her nipples were hard, and her breasts throbbed, aching for Sofia's touch. Even after a whole night's worth of attention, she still felt starved of it.

When Sofia repeated the word "tiramisu" with a growling roll of the R, it vibrated against her ear. She did it again, and again, but then stopped abruptly. "Oh." There was a moment's pause and V's heart stopped with fright. Were there only so many times she could say "tiramisu" before evoking a curse which curdled her cream forever more? "Are you sure you can be here? Do you not have to play hockey?"

"Jesus." She held a hand to her heart again, making sure it was beating. "You terrified me then, I thought something was seriously wrong." Leaning over for another slice of toast, V then settled back against Sofia and wriggled to get comfy as she ate it. "No hockey today. I told you, I don't really play much anymore. They let me know when they're short and if I can make it, I do."

"That's a shame."

"Not really. I still keep in touch with everyone, but life moves on... Grace wants to try it when she's old enough, though. That'll be another thing to figure into the schedule." V shrugged and took another bite of toast, dabbing the crumbs on her chest with a finger. It was a bit of a surprise Sofia had let them eat in the bed, given how tidy she was. "At the moment I've capped her at swimming lessons. She's always coming home with a new flyer or something she wants to try, and I feel guilty saying no but needs must."

Besides which, the ballet lessons had only lasted four weeks before she decided she wasn't as graceful as her name might have suggested. Now she just liked to walk around the house in her tutu and attempt the odd pirouette for the dog. They couldn't afford a staged version of the Nutcracker for only a spaniel's enjoyment.

Shuffling back, Sofia propped herself on some cushions. "Perhaps I should take you home if you have a lot to do."

"Don't you dare." Before Sofia could even think of getting up, leaving, or anything else, V slid backwards until they were flush together again, and pinned her to the pillows. "Now I'm here, I'm making the most of having breakfast in bed. Saturdays without Grace are usually an opportunity to complete such riveting tasks as the laundry, ironing her school dresses, hoovering her bedroom, planning our meals for the week, deep cleaning her bag..." She continued to reel them off as a hand clamped over her mouth, then she hooked her fingers around Sofia's forearm to pull it away with a grunt of laughter. "Catching up my professional development folder..." When the hand returned, she laughed again but then the thought of work sent her mind somewhere else. "Do you think Bob spoke to his wife?"

There was a groan, and Sofia's forehead fell against V's back. "I'd forgotten about that." She sighed and propped her chin on V's shoulder. "I hope he didn't pick up on anything last night."

"Like what?

"Like the fact I almost kissed you in front of half the faculty. I'm not sure the fourth glass of red was a sensible idea, I'd been doing a good job of staying away until that point but then I got a little... silly."

V laughed and rubbed Sofia's leg. "I wouldn't worry. I get the sense any sexual chemistry goes whizzing right over his bald patch. Let's just hope everyone on this orienteering trip is the same." Turning over to kneel, she gripped behind Sofia's knees and pulled her down the bed. "Now, tell me more about this urge to kiss me." The muffled strains of her ringtone halted her. "Shit." She sighed and climbed off the bed. "Bets on whether it's Jess or Grace." Fumbling through the pockets of her jeans, she held up the device. "Grace."

"Mummy, I don't feel well again. Can I come home?" A cough accompanied her little voice for added emphasis.

"Of course you can, sweetheart. Can you ask your dad what time he's dropping you home?"

There was a loud exchange between them, and V had to pull the phone away from her ear to avoid losing an eardrum. "I want to see Grandma first so I'm going to stay for lunch. Daddy says I'll be home at three o'clock."

"Okay. Say hi to your gran for me and I'll be waiting. Love you."

"Love you, Mummy."

The phone went dead, and V set it on the side table as she perched on the edge of the bed. "I do love when my point is proven." She sighed again, wondering how she'd ever get everything done now, not that she begrudged Grace coming home if she was ill. "Suppose I should get the bus."

"No, you shouldn't. Finish your breakfast and I will drive you home." Sofia patted the duvet and scooted over.

She didn't want breakfast. She could have breakfast at home. If Sofia had bought them a bit more time, that was not how V wanted to spend it. "Or..." she began, rolling onto her side and curling her fingers into Sofia's hip to pull them together. "We could not eat breakfast, and..." Dipping her head, she took a nipple into her mouth and drew out a moan. "Do you see where I'm going with this?"

Sofia laughed as she was pushed onto her back, her arms pinned above her head. "You have lost me, I'm sorry."

"Hang on, I'll catch you up." On all fours over Sofia's torso, V worked down it with kisses. But then, as she stroked her fingers back up again, and they teased along Sofia's right thigh, she felt her body stiffen. Taking away her hand, V pressed her lips to the inside of Sofia's knee. "It's okay, I remember. I won't." She waited to see if Sofia relaxed, her arse clenched and her hands gripping the sheets. "Do you want me to stop?"

After a few seconds, she released both. "No, don't stop."

Kissing across her stomach, V wrapped her hands around the top of Sofia's legs, so she knew they weren't going anywhere. Then she worked down each thigh again, licking and sucking the tender flesh there as Sofia gradually relaxed. Before going any further, though, she paused, peering up and meeting Sofia's gaze. "I want to know what you like, too. So tell me, honestly, what do you want to happen next?"

It was a risky move, because when she'd asked the same a few hours ago, Sofia had clamped up. She'd quickly revealed one thing that was a complete no-go but had then switched back to pleasuring V all night. There was nothing wrong with that at all. She never saw sex as a tit for tat sort of thing so long as they were both enjoying themselves, but got the sense Sofia was holding back.

When eventually she opened up, Sofia didn't sound at all sure of herself. It was the only time V had ever really seen her confidence waver, watching as she stared at the ceiling and her mouth formed words that didn't issue. "I'm sorry but I can't... I'm not usually able to come first. I need to... be turned on by *you*." She sat more upright on the pillows and wiped a hand across her brow.

"What's the problem with that?" Crawling back up and kissing her now bent knee, V tilted Sofia's chin and smiled warmly. "This seems to bother you, and I'd like to understand why."

Sofia took the hand that was still tenderly touching her face and squeezed it tight, before pressing it to her lips. "Because it is a little difficult, I have not always..." She huffed. "Not everyone *does* understand, is all I'm trying to say, and it is a bit of a mood killer."

"Hasn't killed my mood. Didn't last night, either. What *would* kill my mood is thinking you were doing something you didn't want, or worse still really hated." She shrugged and then laughed. "I'll happily sit and talk about sex for ages. In fact, it's my Mastermind subject." Slipping her hand from Sofia's grasp, she then cupped her cheek, becoming more earnest. "You promised I could trust you, and now I'm promising you can trust me too."

After a few moments, Sofia's smile returned. "I think you're right."

"Good, I often am."

She went to speak again, then paused, but eventually whispered, "It doesn't hurt me... I just don't like it."

V offered her another smile of reassurance. "You don't have to explain yourself. If you need to fuck me to get your kicks, why the hell should I complain? Sounds like a pretty good deal."

As V pushed Sofia back, she sent her rolling into the duvet in a fit of giggles. Sofia quickly climbed on top, pinning V's hips to the bed with a hand either side of her torso and kissing her hard. It created a surge of desire in the pit of her stomach and heat radiated through her core. Wrapping her legs around Sofia's middle to hold her there, she felt her point had been well and truly made.

Sofia's hand slid down the back of V's leg, the lightest of touches then teasing higher. She went to say something but stopped completely this time, a slow smile creeping across her features. They kissed again, then Sofia's lips travelled down V's neck, over her collarbone, and circled her breasts. All the while her fingers delicately explored, slipping over V's swollen clit. Teasingly she slipped inside but then moved on, causing V to writhe.

Only when she was ready did she suck on V's nipple and drive in fully, knocking all the air from her in a long, low groan of pleasure. Immediately splaying her thumb over V's clit, she continued to glide in and out, losing herself. The plates rattled on the tray again, gradually juddering towards the edge of the bed as the evidence of Sofia's arousal flushed down her neck and burst across her chest.

Grasping her arse, V pulled her into every thrust, the weight of Sofia bearing down on her turning a surge of heat into a tidal wave. It stopped though, and she was about to protest, until Sofia ran her flat tongue in one achingly slow movement where her thumb had just been.

Her mouth closed around V's clit and she entered again with renewed enthusiasm, sucking, swirling, and flicking until that tidal wave came crashing down in spectacular fashion and took with it every ounce of strength. With her limbs dissolving into the bed, V cried out something or other which was completely incomprehensible, before closing her eyes and falling limp.

Kissing and nibbling her way back up, Sofia was entirely alert. As V peeked through one eye, she met two which had very definitely darkened. Breathing heavily, Sofia dipped her head to kiss V's neck, and V whispered, "It's a good job I had that toast."

Sofia grunted with laughter, but it stopped as V wriggled down the bed underneath her. Already on all fours, Sofia didn't flinch at all this time when a pair of hands wrapped around her thighs and brought her into contact with V's mouth. Instead, she ground into V's tongue and rested forward on her forearms, letting out a long, low moan of appreciation.

Within minutes she was gripping the sheets, her usually gravelly affirmations pitching higher. When she fell forward, her arms dangling off the end of the bed, V sat up and turned, draping herself over Sofia's back. Resting her ear against Sofia's shoulder, V contented herself stroking along her lover's sides. She smiled, then yawned and closed her eyes. "I like it here. Jam and orgasms in a little oasis next to the canal. What more could anyone want?"

Sofia shook as she laughed. "If only more people knew that this was the secret to happiness."

"Your neighbour might need to make more jam if you're

going to spread it around." V placed a hand on Sofia's arse, giving it a few gentle taps. "Best keep it between us."

"Okay," she whispered in reply. "I will stock up for next time."

They lay like that for a while, their breathing gradually returning to normal, and then V let out a great sigh. "Suppose I should go home soon."

That list of chores was still there, and soon Grace would be too. It had been nice while it lasted, but now she needed to get back to reality.

10

When Sofia dropped her off at home, V felt more relaxed than she had in months. She sat at the kitchen table to work, though, and it quickly evaporated. At the point Melissa interrupted her an hour later, she was glad of the distraction.

"Can I get your opinion on something?" She pulled out a chair and sat, trailing her finger around the rings in the wood.

V looked up from her papers, her eyes widening. If she saw one more quadratic equation, she'd lose the plot. "So long as it's not related to maths or periods."

"Periods?"

"Don't ask." She'd had a year seven girl in tears during lunch on Friday because she didn't know what one was, and they'd ended up on the search for sanitary towels while she had a good cry. They needed to put that sort of stuff on the teacher recruitment ads, and V's mind was very definitely back from Sofia's. "How can I help?"

"Well." Melissa had a familiar look in her eye which suggested this wasn't about an opinion, it involved a favour.

"I've been thinking about how I can use my maternity leave for something useful."

"Besides giving birth and looking after two screaming newborn babies?"

"Yes." She paused for a second and looked puzzled, as if she hadn't really considered that. "The thing is, Jess is stressed and every time anyone mentions the wedding it overwhelms her to the point where I'm not sure it'll ever happen. I thought dinner last night would be a romantic setting in which to bring it up, but things didn't exactly pan out. We both want something low key and inexpensive, but she thinks that my parents will be a nightmare about it, so I've formed a plan."

"You want me to smooth it over with your mum, don't you?"

Melissa inclined her head. "See, you're so clever and pretty. What would I do without you?"

A quick shot of laughter and then V shrugged. Spending a bit of time with Rachel was no hardship, the woman was gorgeous, and they probably needed to speak about the house at some point. It was time to commit. "When's she coming?"

"About an hour."

"An hour?" V's eyes widened again. "What were you going to do if I said no?"

"Try to broach it on my own, but I wasn't thrilled at the prospect. She's such a pain in the arse, but I've accepted Jess cares way too much about what she thinks to do this without her approval. I need her onside so I can start planning."

"Okay, so what exactly is it that we're trying to get past her?" If she was going to do this, V needed details. Rachel wasn't easy to deal with, even though they got along well, and she wasn't going in unarmed. That'd be like sending a baby warthog in to negotiate with a hungry lion.

"Just a ceremony in the registry office and then a little party afterwards with our close friends and family." Melissa shrugged as if that were no big deal, but it would be to Rachel. "I wondered whether we might do that in someone's garden. Mum and Dad's is big enough, although it means she'll probably take over and turn it into something way more extravagant than it needs to be."

That was exactly what she'd do, if she'd allow her only daughter to have her wedding in a back garden at all. Her son's reception was at a fancy spa hotel with about a million guests and while it'd been fun, there was no way that it was Jess or Melissa's style. "Okay." V smiled, trying to offer some reassurance. "Don't get used to me saying this because I'm also on the verge of throwing up, but your idea is pretty cute. I'm prepared to help you, but I have one stipulation."

"Name your price."

"Grace gets to be some sort of flower girl or whatever." They'd probably factor that into the equation regardless, but Grace would love it and V wanted to be sure. It was the perfect way to reassure her amidst all the changes she was about to go through.

Melissa held out her hand. "Done."

Dead on time, Rachel strode down the hallway, all smiles and confidence. She oozed sensuality, and the fact she could be a total bitch sometimes only added to her allure. Not that it was an opinion V could ever voice, because Rachel regularly destroyed Melissa. Their relationship ebbed and flowed. Sometimes they rubbed along okay, but the pregnancy seemed to have created an odd rift between them at a point when they should've been closer than ever.

"Hello, darlings," Rachel rasped. After clearing her throat, she continued. "Sorry, I've picked something up."

The ability to sound even sexier than usual?

V pushed the chair back and stood to greet her with a kiss on each cheek. She also smelled amazing, but the scent differed from usual, with a hint of peach. "New perfume?"

"Yes, a little something I picked up on my travels. Do you like it?"

"I love it." Finally, something V could admit out loud. Getting Rachel onside with a little flattery would help their cause. "Where are you off to next?"

Rachel slipped out of a light trench coat and folded it over the back of a chair, flicking away a wedge of sleek blonde hair. She clearly dyed it, but who cared? For a woman of nearly sixty she looked incredible. "Oh, nowhere for now. We won't make the mistake of going away and missing any more key moments."

It seemed even enquiring about Rachel's holiday wasn't safe ground, and V shot Melissa an apologetic smile. She'd been in Australia and not found out about the pregnancy until she got back, which had gone down like a lead balloon. "What a nice surprise it was to come home to, though."

"Yes, finding my daughter was already sixteen weeks pregnant and hadn't bothered to tell me. Never mind, though. I don't suppose it matters when or how the news was delivered."

"Exactly, and after all that time wanting grandchildren you got two in one go."

Rachel expelled a long jet of air from the side of her mouth and her eyes widened. "Yes, heaven help us all." She opened a cupboard and pulled out a glass, pouring herself some water from the tap. "How are you feeling, darling?"

Melissa shuffled over, her back pressing along the oven

knobs as she moved out of the way. Her shoulders had tightened, and she placed a protective hand on her bump. "Pretty good but glad to be on maternity leave now. I thought I'd want to keep going right until the end but I'm over that, I can't be on my feet all day or they'll explode."

"Yes, well, that's what happens when you work in retail." Rachel turned in time to catch the tail end of V's strangled expression but ignored it and pulled out a chair to sit opposite. "How is your first term going?"

When V glanced at Melissa again, she was rolling her eyes but looked equally relieved to have the heat off her for a minute. It wasn't the first time Rachel had stuck in a little dig about her choice of career, and it wouldn't be the last. "Full-on, but I'm loving it. Helps that I'm working with some great people, I think that makes all the difference. It's a bit like Melissa in the book shop."

It was supposed to help but didn't even seem to have registered with Rachel, who ploughed on with her own agenda. "You've done well. That girl I remember from five years ago who was so lacking in confidence is long gone."

Her smile was warm and genuine, and V couldn't do anything but return it. She needed to switch this to the intended topic, though. "Thank you, but I couldn't have done it without these guys, and now I want to help them in return. The only thing is, I need your help." Another quick glance at Melissa and she nodded approval, watching intently to see how this landed. "They really want to get married next year, but it needs to be something low key. What do you say to letting us have the reception in your garden?" There were very few ways to dress it up, and V waited with bated breath to see how Rachel would respond.

She shuffled on the chair and took a sip from her glass, then wiped the bottom on her palm and set it down. As she leant forward, she looked uncharacteristically uncomfortable. "Is this about money? Because I would pay for the wedding in a heartbeat. I know how hard Jess has had to work for the house and all these treatments."

V chewed so hard on the inside of her cheek that she almost drew blood, the taste of iron flooding her mouth. She knew Melissa would have done the same but couldn't bear to look at her this time. "No, money isn't really a factor. They've *both* worked hard to save and I'm sure they'd do the same again if they wanted a big wedding, but they don't."

"Surely there's a middle ground, though?"

Rachel tilted her head as she looked to Melissa, but it was a big mistake because her daughter was raging. Melissa's entire face was bright red, and it was surging down her throat. "This is the middle ground, actually, because I didn't want to invite you at all." She still had a hand on her bump, the other stroking circles on the underside. "I'd be quite happy if it was just me, Jess, our kids, and our witnesses. Jess won't do that, though, so will you agree and make this as painless as possible? If not for me then for her."

After a few moments of tense silence Rachel was about to speak when the front door opened, and everyone stopped dead again. Jess came through, pausing to give Rachel a quick hug, but her smile was for Melissa. It caused a subtle shift in her body language, the tensed shoulders dropping as she returned Jess's warmth.

Melissa took Jess's hand and pressed it to her bump, then leant in to give her a kiss. "They know you're home."

"Yeah, they do." Jess laughed and kissed her again. "I wonder which one that is." She mouthed something, which was probably the names they'd picked but wouldn't tell anyone. It'd been a secret for the best part of a month, and it was driving Rachel crazy.

She'd been watching them closely and V nudged her arm. "Look at them," she whispered. "Come on, just let them have their wedding."

Rachel sighed and twisted in her chair, hooking her arm over the back of it. "Fine. I would be honoured if you'd have your wedding reception in our garden." Never had the word 'honoured' been delivered with less enthusiasm, but at least she'd agreed. "I'm having it professionally catered, though. I can accept rustic but we must draw a line somewhere."

"What's this?" Jess looked understandably confused, her mouth dropping open as she rubbed Melissa's back.

"We were discussing your wedding. Let me know once you've picked a date and we'll figure the rest. May bank holiday might be nice if we're doing it outside. The weather will be milder by then but not so hot as to make it unbearable." Rachel had pulled out her phone to look at dates. The kraken had been unleashed, and they couldn't return her now.

As she took Jess's hands in her own, Melissa looked a little nervous. "Yeah, I've been getting on with wedding plans. Presuming you still want to do it..."

"Of course I still want to marry you. How could you think I wouldn't?"

She shrugged, staring down at what would've been her feet if there wasn't a beach ball sized obstruction. "You asked me when we found out I was finally pregnant. I wondered last night when you resisted, whether it was just in the heat of the moment." Looking up, she chewed her lip for a second before continuing. "I know you always said you didn't think getting married was that important."

Jess went to hug her, but it was awkward, so she grasped Melissa's shoulders and turned her around, cuddling in from behind and kissing her temple. "I definitely want to marry you. I promise, I still have every intention of annoying you for the rest of my life."

V inclined her head, half mocking but into it. "And I intend to annoy you both for the rest of my life, too."

"I hate to break up this love-in." Rachel sounded genuinely amused by it now, and it was a relief to sense she'd softened. "But I came with a dual agenda. Are you taking this house or not?"

"Yes please, if it's still on offer."

"Of course it's still on offer. I'd love to have a reliable tenant, and if it helps you out then all the better. You know I've always been one hundred percent behind you."

She did, it was just a shame Rachel wasn't always one hundred percent behind her own daughter. They'd probably achieved enough for one day, though. "Thank you. I've got a week off for February half term, so can I move in then?"

When Rachel shrugged and nodded, V stood and joined in with Jess and Melissa's hug, feeling oddly happy and a touch sentimental. She was also terrified, and the happiness was probably more to do with relief at finally having decided than anything else, but there was at least a positive emotion in there. Now she needed to tell Grace, which was rapidly smothering it.

11

On the Monday of half term week, she was wondering how she'd ever naively imagined that volunteering for a residential trip was a good idea. Grace was being clingy ever since she found out about the move, Melissa was huge and ready to take down the entire house in a giant explosion, and V's tranquil vibes were long gone. It was a recurring theme, and she was trying to remind herself of the greater good.

"Are you sure you don't mind looking after her?" She watched Melissa strain to reach for a mug, wincing and hoping she didn't topple.

"Nope, I need the distraction. Besides, a little helper may come in handy."

"On second thoughts, what am I letting her in for?"

Grunting, Melissa rocked her hips, trying to find some comfort. "Funny, I was asking myself the same question. Remind me why I wanted to do this to myself?"

V stalled. "Er, I have no idea. Sorry. I'd like to tell you it's all smooth sailing once you get past the birth, but I had to fish a bead out of Grace's nose last night on top of everything else, so..." She shrugged, hoping a little humour might lighten the mood, but Melissa looked genuinely terrified.

"Well I'm glad you did. Today she's going to help me think happy thoughts, and Jess is coming home at lunchtime because we're trying to spend some time together before we're at the mercy of two cute little dictators."

Grabbing a banana from the side and slotting it into her coat pocket, V patted her jeans to check she also had her phone and purse. It was far too early in the morning and her brain had not yet engaged. "There's also a bumper pack of biscuits coming your way to say thank you, but try to keep those babies in for a few more days."

"Days?" Melissa exclaimed, her eyes widening. "Try weeks. I want them in here for another fortnight at the very least." She looked at her bump and then adjusted the waistband of Jess's old striped pyjama bottoms. They were about the only thing that fitted anymore.

There was a creaking noise on the stairs and Grace ran in, gasping and swiping the hair from her eyes. "Mummy, I thought you'd gone without saying goodbye."

Jess and Hal had both followed her and the entire household converged in the kitchen. If this was the sort of send-off they gave every time there was a school trip to chaperone, she might be more inclined to volunteer again. Not that spending a few days with Sofia hadn't already softened the blow.

V hoisted Grace up into a cuddle. "Of course I didn't go without saying goodbye, sweetheart." Grace's hands pressed into her shoulders and a big wet kiss landed on her neck. "And when I get back, we're going to have some fun together. Okay? Have a think about what you'd like to do on Friday."

Another gasp and her head shot up. "Zoo?"

"The zoo? You only went a few weeks ago. What about something else with animals, like the aquarium?" When Grace's face went blank, V clarified. "Fish and things. We could catch a train to London, and you might even get a trip on the river." She tickled Grace's sides and let her drop to the floor. A day in London was probably a bit extravagant, especially when they needed to furnish the new house and there was both a birthday and Christmas coming up, but it'd been a long time coming. One or two splurges couldn't hurt.

"Can Auntie Melissa come?"

Melissa laughed, ruffling Grace's hair. "I think they might mistakenly try to throw me in the tank." Another blank look, and she pulled open the fridge. "I fancy a bacon sandwich for breakfast. Shall we make one and let Mummy get to work?"

When Grace still didn't look sure, a hand hooked around V's leg, Jess stepped in to help. She adjusted her work trousers and crouched, taking a hold of Hal's collar to pull him over too. "I tell you what, why don't we see if we can take Hal to visit Harry later?" They were brothers, and Harry belonged to Jess's dad. It was a clever move, because the only thing better than one dog in Grace's eyes was two. "We could take them to the lake."

They had played the trump card. Grace loved to watch them swim, and her grip loosened. "Can *we* go swimming?"

"Not in the lake, but I reckon so. Auntie Melissa might enjoy that, too. I keep telling her swimming would be a good way to get some relief, but she won't listen to me so maybe you can try." Jess stood and grabbed a bag of bread from the work surface, helping Melissa prepare the sandwiches.

"Yeah, yeah. I forget you know everything about pregnancy," she muttered as she pulled out a frying pan and set it on the hob. "You must remind me where you trained."

"The school of Google, and I'm only trying to help."

"I know you are, but right now the only thing that's going to help is getting these babies out of me. Let it be known that I have officially hit the point where the pregnancy I have largely enjoyed is the pregnancy I need to be over."

V left them to bicker and bent down to kiss Grace's cheek. "I think you'll be okay with these two," she whispered, relieved to see her looking more relaxed. "I love you."

"I love you too," Grace whispered back with a little giggle. "Have fun, Mummy."

* * *

It was still only eight o'clock when she arrived at school to meet the coach, and Sofia was unsurprisingly perky. She handed out clipboards to all the teachers, so they had a list of their groups, emergency contacts, and an itinerary for the next two days, then organised everyone into their seats. What was also no surprise was who had been put in the very front one with her.

"Hello," she whispered. It was hard to hear over the sound of forty kids, all sharing breakfast and excitedly talking about their latest TikTok videos.

V leant in slightly. "Hello. Please don't tell me we're sharing a room, I wouldn't cope."

"Me either. I promise to take this very seriously but I brought us a little treat for later, to celebrate your new house." She glanced sideways and pulled her bag out from under the seat, unzipping it and showing one of her bottles of red. "No one must know, I'm swearing you to secrecy."

"Miss Pisano," V scorned. She laughed and re-zipped the bag, shoving it back under the seat. "You're supposed to be setting a good example. You know how impressionable I am, and how important it is that I'm not distracted for the benefit of the children. Chaperoning this trip is a purely selfless act."

Sofia let out a short sharp shot of laughter. "Is it now? Bob and I speak, you know. He told me you were looking for ways to make a good impression."

"What a suggestion, I'm hurt. As if I would also have been swayed by the opportunity to spend three days in the woods with my hot new head of department. Take it all back." She lifted her eyebrows and leant in, but then spotted another teacher coming up the steps in front of them and made a hasty retreat. Perhaps talking about her career options was safer ground. "I'm prepared to admit I got a bit carried away. I'll also concede that I need to get through at least my first year before applying for head."

"Of department?"

"Of the school."

With another splutter of laughter, Sofia nudged their shoulders together. "Why the rush?"

"Lots of reasons." V inclined her head, realising most of them came back to her daughter. She wanted her to have someone to look up to, as much as anything. "Grace, mainly."

"Tell me more about her?"

"What do you want to know?" There wasn't much to Grace, besides a whole heap of attitude and a love of biscuits. Well, that and what seemed to be an inbuilt desire to strangle any dog she met with love.

"*Everything*. Start from the beginning."

"We conceived her in a student flat..." As V laughed again, she turned her head in time to catch Sofia rolling her eyes. "Too far back?"

"Perhaps a touch. I know you fell pregnant at university, what happened after that?"

V expelled a jet of air through the side of her mouth. "Let's see. I just about sat my final exams and passed my degree—thank god—but I had to give up the teacher training place I had lined up because it started in September and Grace was due in early November. I'd only been with Matty—Grace's dad—for a few months when I found out I was pregnant, and we were both a bit shell-shocked." Unless there was a bigger word which conveyed the amount of denial, wailing, and general feelings of help-lessness the news brought about.

"I can imagine. I don't mean to be indelicate but did you never..." Sofia's voice trailed off.

"What, consider a termination? It's fine, you can say it." Many others had asked the same question, including her mum. "Yes, of course I did, but I could never have gone through with it. No judgement on anyone who does, I just knew it wasn't right for me." After proceeding to tell the entire tale, including how her relationship with Matty had died with more of a whimper than a bang, she got to the part Sofia already knew and let out an exaggerated sigh. "Finally qualifying is a big deal for me. As is the house because I've never lived alone. And that—as they say—is it."

Sofia laughed. "And Grace fits into your plans for school domination how?"

"Because I want to prove to her that she can do anything she sets her mind to. I've had a lot of help but now I'm trying to stand on my own two feet for both of our sakes. It's a brave new world."

"You think that having people to turn to somehow means you are not brave or doing enough to support yourself?"

V considered for a second. Was that what she'd said? She knew there was no shame in asking for help, it was the amount of it which always seemed disproportionate. "No, not exactly, I just don't think I should need as much as I do and at some point, it should tail off. Does that make sense?"

"It does, but who gets to decide how much support a person should or shouldn't need? Would it have helped anyone if you hadn't accepted the help you needed to train as a teacher, or to raise Grace? Do you imagine that Jess's life would somehow be better if you had asked nothing of her? It is life. Human connection. We also get to share in each other's joy and triumphs."

Sitting in stunned silence for a second, V turned and stared at Sofia, who had propped her head on her elbow as it rested against the back of the seat. Her features were still, but they broke and her eyes glistened when V finally spoke again. "Have you got a secret sideline in motivational speaking or something?"

"No. That was just a long-winded way of telling you to ease up on yourself. Enjoy the job, the success, and the house, but don't think you weren't fine as you were. Trust me, you are strong and brave and have nothing to prove—to Grace or anyone else."

12

Once they'd checked in and assigned everyone to their cabins, there was some free time to unpack before the on-site staff took over. Then at ten they were due to start their first activity, which involved learning how to use the maps ready for a hike after lunch. V was pleasantly surprised to learn she had a room to herself, however small it was. She'd expected tatty bunk beds and mites, but it was tidy and functional, with a single bed and a chest of drawers for her things.

Sofia poked her head around the door. "Is it okay?"

"Well, it's not *your* house, but it's way better than I expected. Where are you sleeping?"

"Next room down." Her eyebrows nudged up suggestively, which was sending confusing signals. Perhaps it was just that she was excited to be here. She had said she enjoyed this annual pilgrimage, and it might not be a joke. The thought was quite endearing.

"You are very cute," V whispered, knowing she was now the one overstepping a line. "But shush, I didn't say that."

Sofia grinned and shut the door, leaving V to her small

amount of unpacking. Once she'd finished, she waited outside with her clipboard in hand, rounding up loose kids as they filtered from their cabins. None of them had been so lucky and were all four or eight to a room.

Each group had a guide from the camp and the teachers were there more to act as marshals than anything else. It meant V could zone out for most of the day, although she couldn't help but be amused while she listened in on some conversations between the kids. Was she ever like this? So worried about boys, or girls, and whether they liked her. Grace had all this to come, and the thought filled her with dread.

When they returned to camp her feet were sore and all that fresh air had left her ready for bed. She did a roll call of her group and then sent them off to get cleaned up for dinner in the canteen, heading to her own room to change out of her hiking boots and into a comfy pair of Vans. Her stomach grumbled loudly as she inhaled the smell of chip grease wafting down the corridor.

Pushing through the double doors at the end, a cacophony of scraping chairs and banging cutlery deafened her, on top of the usual chatter and noise of forty teenagers. Sofia leant against the start of the serving hatch reprimanding a pair of lads, whose eyes were both on their shoes, and V waited until Sofia dismissed them before joining her.

"Were you being all stern, Miss Pisano?" she teased, grabbing a mottled grey tray from a stack on the table.

Sofia smiled and nudged their shoulders together, pushing V in front of the hatch. "Yes, and I've got some for you if you're not careful." Her lips twitched with a smile, but it quickly faded when she was handed a plate of sloppy lasagne with chips on the side. "Chips? You cannot serve chips with lasagne." She was indignant, poking the layers of pasta with a fork and eying the lot with a certain amount of trepidation. "If you could call this lasagne."

"Oh dear. Is the food not up to scratch?" V sucked her teeth, then took a chip and savoured it, making loud noises of appreciation as they wandered to a clear table in the corner.

"No, and after a very trying afternoon."

The little pout made V laugh. "What happened, did a kid get mauled by a squirrel? Did you eat magic mushrooms you foraged from the woods? Did you—"

"No." Sofia cut her off as she set down her tray. "I ended up in the middle of a teenage love triangle."

V laughed again, banging her chest as she choked on another chip. "Excuse me? Then I think you have bigger problems."

"Not like that! But it was very traumatic for me. The first girl is going out with a boy, but he caught her with the second girl over the weekend and now they've fallen out. It all became very confusing, and I didn't know what to say."

"Oh, I see. The plot thickens. Well, we've all been there."

"Have we?"

"Yep." V left Sofia hanging as she ate a few mouthfuls of lasagne, mentally recalling how she'd first hooked up with Jess at the school prom when they were sixteen. It was likely a very similar story given she'd arrived with someone else. They both did, in fact, but had been dancing around each other for months and it spilled over with the aid of some intentionally spiked punch.

Unable to wait any longer, Sofia nudged V's shoulder "You can't say that and then not share."

She shrugged and picked up a chip, then filled Sofia in. "Has nothing like that ever happened to you? I refuse to believe you didn't have people tripping over themselves." V wore a little smirk as she glanced sideways, catching a blush rise on Sofia's cheeks.

"No, never. I didn't even have my first kiss until I was eighteen and went to university, let alone what they were up to at thirteen."

"And what *were* they up to?"

Squirming with discomfort, Sofia leant over to whisper, "He said the other girl was fingering his girlfriend."

V let out a short sharp laugh, covering her mouth and trying not to expel her chip. "They're bound to experiment a bit at their age. Not good if someone's getting hurt, I'm not condoning that if he thought they were exclusive, but..." Clearing her throat, she wiped her hands on a napkin. "You really did nothing like that until university?"

"Never. I was too busy riding my bike and cooking with my Nona. Besides, I was a little... awkward with myself. I'm not sure many women would've given me a second look."

"Awkward?"

She looked out of her depth again, as if the memory were seeping. "Yes. I grew up in a small town where I was a bit of an oddity." A shrug, and she picked at her lasagne. "Twenty-five years ago, I'm not sure there was as much acceptance for those who were different. I have kids in my form now who are openly non-binary or transgender and their peers are supportive. It is less of a big deal."

Sensing they'd strayed from a laugh to something more serious, V set down her fork and gave Sofia her full attention. She'd promised to be trustworthy and now she felt like she was about to deliver. "So, are you saying perhaps you might be either of those things?"

"No." She twisted and hitched up her knee. "I'm only saying that sometimes if you fall too far outside of the norm, whatever the hell that is, it can be difficult. Especially in a place where everyone has very set roles. I'm not conflating gender and sexuality of course, but if you don't feel confident with one side of yourself, it's difficult to express yourself in the other."

Now the one feeling a little uncomfortable, V shuffled in her seat. Not because she didn't want to discuss this, but because she didn't want to get it wrong, especially in a noisy dining hall. They'd really picked their locations for intense chats today. "Is this anything to do with... you know?" She lowered her voice. "Struggling to be upfront about what you like in bed?"

Sofia shrugged. "Sort of. I told you not everyone is understanding. For a long time, I went along with what others expected, even if I wasn't really into it. Not only in the bedroom, but with what I chose to wear and how I acted."

"Not anymore, though?"

"No, I don't want to do that anymore. Everyone is different and we're all entitled to our preferences, regardless of where they come from or what anyone else says. Sometimes it's not that simple in practise, but..." She shrugged again and offered a small smile.

"I think you're right." Reaching under the table with a quick glance to make sure no one was looking, V squeezed Sofia's hand. "And as for worrying that women wouldn't give you a second look, I can confirm that is *not* true. I'd give you a second look any day. And a third... Maybe even a fourth or fifth. You are incredibly sexy, exactly as you are."

That slight blush erupted fully now, as did Sofia's smile. "It may have taken me longer than some, but at thirty-nine years old I am getting there."

V went to reply but then realised what Sofia had just said. "How old?" She scoffed. "There is no way you're almost forty. Are you seriously saying you're eleven years older than I am? Is there a fountain of youth somewhere along that canal? If so, I need you to take me to it."

"It never came up. Does it bother you?"

"No, not even remotely. I'm impressed with myself for pulling a gorgeous older woman. I wonder if this is how Portia felt with Ellen..." Cocking her head, V ripped a chip in half and flung a piece into her mouth.

"How old did you think I was?"

"I don't know. Early thirties, maybe? It wasn't really your age I was thinking about, sorry to tell you. First it was your voice, then your scent, then probably that tattoo..." As she continued, Sofia swiped her leg, and they both laughed.

"Okay, I get the gist."

"I hope so, because have I told you yet how wonderful you are? I'm just going to remind you now in case you forget."

Although she was laughing as she squeezed Sofia's hand again, she meant every word.

Once all the kids had grumpily trudged off to bed complaining that it was far too early, it was only the adults left. Six of them in total, looking bored out of their minds as they stared at their phones and tried desperately to get a signal. V was hoping to check in with Jess and make sure that Grace had been okay after her wobble in the morning, but it was no good. She'd ventured into the foyer and then out the front of the building, holding it up and trying to connect, but there was nothing doing.

"Is everything okay?" It was Sofia, of course, lingering behind with her hands stuffed in the pocket of her jeans.

"Yeah, fine. Just wanted to check in at home but I can't get a ruddy signal. Have you got one?"

She pulled out her phone and shook her head before returning it. "No, but they'll have a landline at reception. Would you like me to ask if you can use it?"

"No, it's okay." V sighed and returned her own phone to a pocket. Nothing *that* drastic would've happened.

"It doesn't look okay, come on." Sofia gestured with her head and held open the door, peering over the dark reception area, which was long since abandoned. "There is a phone here, let's use it." She'd already picked up the handset and held it out, waving it in V's face.

Once she'd checked that Grace had been fine all day, that swimming had gone ahead and she'd managed a full length of the pool unaided, V could relax. She handed back the phone, and they began a slow wander down the corridor. "Thank you. I'm worried about how Grace is coping with the idea of moving. She's been a bit... clingy lately. The twins are due over the next few weeks, too, so I need to keep an eye on her."

"But she is okay?"

"Yep. I over-worried on this occasion."

"Then how about we under-worry you with a glass of wine?" Sofia held open the door to her room. "I know we're not supposed to touch each other on this trip, so we could accompany it with a game of Scrabble. Nothing quite like it to remove all potential for sexual feeling."

"You mean you're not turned on by board games? Then I retract everything I said earlier about you being the sexiest woman on the planet." Pulling out a chair by the little MDF table at the end of the room, V turned back to find Sofia still smirking in the doorway. "What?"

"When did I get upgraded to the sexiest woman on the planet?"

"When you remembered to bring wine on a school trip?" Straining to pick up one of Sofia's walking boots, which was neatly tucked under the bed, V hurled it and Sofia jumped out of the way, laughing as she jogged off down the corridor.

Returning a few moments later with a tatty old Scrabble board, she set it on the table and then pulled out her wine, a corkscrew, and two plastic glasses. A few seconds later they were followed by a packet of chocolate Hobnobs, and she proudly presented them like a Tiffany ring. "For you."

"Okay, that sexiest woman thing is back on." Tearing into the wrapping, V stuffed a whole one in her mouth and then encouraged Sofia to do the same. She had her fancy home-made pasta and tiramisu, and V had this.

"What is it with the British and biscuits? All my exes were the same. Tea, too, although that stuck."

"*All* of your exes? I'm imagining a hareem now." Nibbling on the corner of another Hobnob while Sofia set up the game, V swung back on the chair but quickly gave that up when it let out an alarming creaking noise. In its defence, they probably intended it for children, and not an adult who ate this many biscuits.

"Oh, yes. I'm exactly the love 'em and leave 'em type. Hadn't you picked that up by now." Selecting a couple of tiles, Sofia held up the N and the O.

"On? What were you having lots of sex *on*? Knowing you, probably the kitchen worktop."

"Hilarious." With a roll of her eyes, Sofia threw the tiles into the little green bag and gave it a shake. "I hate to disappoint you, but my love life is not at all interesting. I have had three major relationships, the last did *not* end well, and then

I met this redhead who teases me mercilessly. My poor heart."

V laughed and passed her another Hobnob. "Cheer up. I must be doing something right or you wouldn't be buying me treats and hanging around all the time." She was in a teasing mood now, but only because she knew Sofia was enjoying it. "Like a bad smell."

"Oh, well. If you don't want me hanging around, I'll just pack up my biscuits and wine. You can go back to your little room. Alone." She wasn't helping her cause by doing the reverse of that and uncorking the bottle. Pouring them each a glass, she pushed one across the table and then sat on the opposite chair.

Taking a few sips and then tapping her fingers on the plastic, V got up and scraped the chair out with Sofia still sitting on it. There was a high risk of disaster given how sturdy they were, but she didn't much care right now. Straddling Sofia's lap and wincing as the metal creaked again, she hooked her hands around Sofia's neck. "Do you really want me to go?"

As she shook her head, Sofia ran her tongue over her bottom lip. "No."

"Good. Because I'm still feeling bad that you missed an essential rite of passage."

"What's that?"

V shrugged. "I don't know. Making out at camp?" She raised her eyebrows a touch, looking for just about any excuse. "What did you want to be doing when you were an awkward sixteen-year-old?"

After a few moments of consideration, Sofia wrapped her arms around V's waist and kissed her, far more competently than any teenager. Stroking away her hair, V was gentle at first, but then deepened the kiss. Rolling her hips slowly forward when two hands rubbed into her arse, an urgency built.

As Sofia pulled back, she grumbled slightly and then nipped V's bottom lip again. "Now I am frustrated. This is my teenage years all over again and you are very cruel."

"Oh no," V whispered, kissing Sofia's neck and sucking a little too hard. Perhaps leaving marks was less sensible, and she giggled as she wiped at the red patch. "You poor thing. How can I make it up to you?"

Not waiting for a reply, she cupped Sofia's cheeks and kissed her deeply, their tongues massaging together as they explored and rubbed each other over their thick sweaters. Running her hands through Sofia's hair, she blocked everything else out for a while and enjoyed a long kiss, the simple intimacy of it something she hadn't experienced in ages.

Her eyelids heavy, she eventually opened them to find Sofia was wearing a lazy smile. What could it hurt to have a little fun? They were in a private bedroom, could be called if anyone needed them, and would keep their clothes on... pretty much. V lowered a hand to unbutton her own jeans, then she took Sofia's wrist and guided her under the fabric.

"For the authentic experience you should be a bit clumsy, but feel free to bend the rules," she whispered.

Sofia played, their tongues pressing together as she stroked and explored. Her fingers trailed delicately over V's clit, slow and then fast, fast and then slow. She varied the weight of her touch, smiling whenever V mumbled some affirmation. It was the only time their lips parted, until V straightened and pulled off her sweater, her entire body glowing hot.

She gasped as Sofia's hand smoothed down over her breast. The orgasm built, her thighs squeezing against Sofia as her hips picked up pace. Struggling not to make too much noise, she bit down on Sofia's shoulder and let out a stifled high pitch grunt, then quickly reached to grab Sofia's wrist and let out a laugh as they stilled.

Sitting upright again, she buttoned her jeans and pressed her lips against Sofia's with a smile. "I'm sorry, I've just remembered you wanted to play Scrabble."

Sofia laughed and then there was a pause before she spoke. "I was going to say this was a surprise, but it wasn't at all. We can't seem to keep away from one another."

"I wasn't even trying to. *When the mood takes us* seems to be every time that we're alone right now." Kissing Sofia again, V felt the familiar swell of butterflies. "Is that okay?"

Sofia nodded, her lips hovering as their eyes met. "I won't tell you I want to see you again because you already know that. I will only say... I would love another game of Scrabble some time."

Reaching down to grab one of the clipboards Sofia had issued, which was resting against the wall by the wardrobe beside them, V pointed at her number under the list of contacts. "Text me?"

Taking hold of the clipboard and chucking it at the bed, Sofia tickled V's sides and as she wriggled with laughter, the board went flying, sending letters scattering across the floor. Then the chair let out an almighty creak, and they both stopped dead, trying not to giggle in case they ended up in a pile of old wood and metal with a leg lodged somewhere.

"Is it safe?" Sofia whispered.

"Fuck knows. We seemed to be alright when we were kissing, though. Perhaps that was the answer." She pressed their lips together again, still looking for any excuse.

13

V expected the house to be filled with noise and the smell of dinner when she opened the front door on Wednesday evening, but it was eerily quiet. "Hello!" she called, dropping her rucksack next to the shoe rack and slipping off her Vans. Hal's collar jingled as he trotted up to greet her, and she spotted Rachel at the kitchen table, her heart jumping into her mouth.

"Oh good, you're back." Rachel peered up from whatever she was reading.

"Is everything okay? Where's Melissa? Shouldn't you be at work?" V rattled off her questions, desperately searching for Grace and finding no sign of her.

"At the hospital. Went to be induced yesterday and they called me to come and do a spot of babysitting because Jess couldn't get hold of your mum." Clocking the look of panic, Rachel smiled. "Don't worry, Grace is upstairs. She's been fed, bathed, and is tucked up in bed asleep."

At seven? That was a first. Usually, she eked it out as long as humanly possible. She also, notably, did not have a dog with her, so perhaps Rachel should stay more often. "I'm sorry." V's mind was still racing with questions as she tried to catch up, and she stammered before delivering any more of them. "Is Melissa okay?" She pulled out her phone and tapped it nervously against her palm. She should've been here for this.

"Scared, but yes. Went for a routine check up on Monday afternoon and a few things were off. Rechecked on Tuesday morning and no improvement, so they sent her straight to the hospital. Contractions started in the night and when Jess rang half an hour ago, she'd just moved to delivery."

"Then don't you want to get off pretty sharpish?"

Rachel's smile was far tighter this time. "No, darling. Thank you. She won't want me there."

It was tough to argue when Rachel was probably right. Instead, V pulled out a chair and sat opposite. "She'll want to see you once the babies arrive, but it'll be chaos in there right now. Was Jess okay when you spoke with her?" She'd probably be spinning out because they were early. Either that or have gone into a calm state of denial, which was perhaps why she hadn't mentioned the test anomalies when they'd spoken on Monday evening.

"Tired but coping. I told her to get used to that." A little laugh, but Rachel was in a decidedly maudlin mood. She shrugged and got up, pulling a bottle of white wine from the fridge. "Can I tempt you?" Not waiting for a reply, she grabbed a couple of glasses from the cupboard and nudged it shut. "I could use one."

It was hard to discern what was causing her lack of enthusiasm. She was about to become a grandmother, the one thing she'd wanted in all the time V had known her—besides money and power. "Are you okay? You seem... off.

Are you worried about Melissa? I'm sure she'll be fine; you raised a pretty tough woman."

"Mm," was the only sound to issue in response, and V couldn't help probing. She had a feeling Rachel wanted to talk about this, otherwise she wouldn't be pulling out the booze and offering to share.

"Things seemed to get better between you two for a while. What happened?"

Rachel poured them each a large glass and then returned to her seat, leaving the bottle in the middle of the table. "I don't know, I just... worry?"

"About what? Because from where I'm sitting, Melissa seems to be fine, if you ignore the situation between the two of you."

Rachel's eyes shot up and for a second V thought she was going to get an earful for confronting the topic so frankly, but then her features softened. "I worry that she's making a terrible mistake, committing to this relationship so young. And I worry that she'll regret not making more of a career for herself before having children. It's a struggle. You can do it, but my god do you have to work. We both know that, and I want her to have a full life where she doesn't have to make those compromises."

That was far more honesty than V was expecting, and she slumped back in her chair, taking the glass. Rachel had been right, and alcohol was needed. "She is happy, I genuinely believe that."

"Is she, though? She came straight out of university into that bookshop job, settled down with the first person she fell in love with, and—" There was a pause and Rachel's eyes darted up again. "I wondered whether she only got together with Jess because she showers her with affection. Not at first, but when I gave it more thought. That girl loves

Melissa without equivocation, she always has, and if you don't feel anyone has ever done that..."

V shuffled, feeling suddenly uneasy. There was also a flare of anger or something and she felt compelled to jump to their defence, regardless of the consequences. There would be other houses, but Rachel couldn't get away with saying that. "Jess loves Melissa, but I really don't think it's one-sided. Did you know she spent almost a year sitting with her feelings before they got together because she worried about ruining their friendship? And before they had kids, they went to couples counselling to make absolutely sure they were in a good place and ready for this."

It was a complete over-share but right now V was being driven by a compulsion to protect them both and couldn't stop herself. The phone vibrated against her leg and she pulled it from her pocket, finding the interruption a useful tension breaker. She scrolled through to the message, seeing it was from Sofia and unable to resist a small smile. She'd clearly jotted down that number after all and had asked if Grace was okay.

"A friend?" Rachel peered across the table.

V glanced up for a second. "Work colleague." She tapped back a reply to say she was fine but that the babies were on their way and was very quickly rewarded with a series of heart emojis.

"They've certainly put a smile on your face."

"Yeah, they have."

"So, not just a colleague?"

"No, not exactly."

"Well, if you want my opinion, I'd say tread carefully. Your career is too important, you don't need any distractions right now. Especially not within the workplace. That sounds like a recipe for disaster."

V tucked the phone back into her pocket. She didn't remember asking for Rachel's opinion at all, but would rather talk about this than continue with their last conversation because she was about to say something she might regret. "It's fine. There's technically nothing to say we can't hook up."

"Hook up? My darling, if it's fun you're after, use an app."

It was hard not to laugh. The idea of Rachel anywhere near 'an app' was hilarious, even if she hadn't been married since the beginning of time. "Thanks for your concern, but she's an actual grown-up who I have a real connection with. Going to bed with someone whose housemates don't insist on bursting in to steal weed has a certain appeal." However ironic that was, given her own living situation. Not that there was any weed stealing in their house, it was more likely to be ice cream.

"I once had a liaison with a colleague," Rachel mused, leaning back in the chair and taking a sip of her wine. "His name was Henry, and he was a complete disappointment. I met Paul shortly after and the rest, as they say, is history."

"Wow... wild." V tried to smother another laugh, but it was no good. It was easy to see where Melissa got her penchant for books and early nights.

"Excuse me, but I had some wild moments. Not many, granted, but they're overrated. Passion is fleeting and overrated. What's important right now is your career."

"Here's where we're *really* going to disagree. Passion is not overrated. Trust me. If you met Sofia, you'd understand. I would also argue that you don't need to be wild to have passion." This was, aptly, a subject she was very passionate about. More so than she'd realised until now. She never wanted to be like Rachel, so focussed on her career that it shot her relationship with her kids to pieces.

"Sofia? Is this the colleague? Well, I hope she's worth it..." Rachel shook her head, her disapproval clear.

It was hard not to reverse that question, but V really didn't want a full-scale argument. It wouldn't help anyone, least of all Jess and Melissa. Instead, she went with a softer approach. "All I'm saying is that your daughter has passion. She has genuine love. They are the most boring people on earth, but they love each other passionately." V shrugged, the wine going to her head. She took another sip and sat back again, challenging Rachel to argue.

She was about to when her own phone buzzed across the tabletop. As she picked it up, she pressed the other hand to her mouth, her eyes welling with tears. "Oh, I'm a grandmother. I don't look old enough, but I'm a grandmother." She turned the screen to show a picture of baby number one. There was still no mention of a name, but it was probably too soon for that. "My baby had a baby. It's so surreal."

"Two of them soon. Congratulations." V raised her wine glass and Rachel wiped under both eyes before grabbing her own.

"To their health and happiness."

She echoed Rachel's sentiment and grabbed her phone again, first texting Jess, and then dropping another to Sofia. She replied immediately, asking whether this made V an auntie, and she laughed, replying with a defiant 'YES'.

"You know, they're going to need us both when they bring those babies home." This was her last shot, and if it didn't work, there was nothing more she could do. "I don't want to speak out of turn—and not only because you're about to become my landlady, I do also respect you—but I'm not sure you realise the amount of damage you cause. Melissa cares what you think, and she needs you on her side. Especially now, which is probably why she's backed off. It's self-protection because she's feeling vulnerable."

She left Rachel to stew on that for a minute, texting back to Sofia. Setting her phone down and folding her arms, her mouth dropped open when she saw Rachel was crying again. She hadn't meant to go that far.

"I'm sorry, darling," Rachel whispered. "It's just been a big day." She let out a long sigh and her lip quivered as she stared at the wall of pictures at the other end of the kitchen. "And I have two granddaughters who I'm not sure Melissa even really wants me to see."

"Haven't you been listening?" V was gentle as she leant forward, taking Rachel's hand on the table. "She absolutely wants you to be part of all their lives, but she needs you to support her choices. Even if you think they're the wrong ones, that isn't your call. Accept what you have, which is a bloody lot, and join in rather than putting yourself on the outside. Melissa is fine as she is, and she shouldn't need to keep proving herself or trying to live up to your expectations."

Rachel nodded and V squeezed her hand before slipping away. She was considering Sofia's words on the bus again and wanted to see her own daughter to give her a big kiss, even if it woke her up. Carefully climbing the stairs and inching back the bedroom door, she found Grace propped on her pillows reading a book to her teddy.

"Mummy!" She gasped as she dropped it and held out her arms.

V sat on the edge of the bed and hugged her tight, then shuffled to pull back the duvet and climbed in with her. "Shall we have a cuddle, sweetheart? I've got some good news for you. The babies are here."

"The babies?" Grace's mouth hung open and her eyes widened as she sat bolt upright. "Can I see them?"

"Not here in the house, but they've been born. I expect given they're a little premature they'll be kept in the hospital for now. I promise as soon as they come out you can see them."

Grace leant back and V kissed her head, stroking the hair from her eyes. "Did you bring me anything?"

Of course that was the next thing she was going to ask, and V let out a gentle laugh. She wriggled to reach into her pocket and pulled out a packet of sweets she'd stolen from the canteen. Grace wouldn't want much, just something to know her mum had thought of her.

"You can have them tomorrow." V's phone had fallen out into the bed and she fumbled to retrieve it, patting around her legs until she found a cool lump of plastic. There was another message from Sofia, this time with a picture attached. It was her on the sofa, pouting because she was lonely after having so many people around. "Say cheese for my friend." V held up the camera and took a photo of them both as Grace pulled out the cheesiest grin she had. "Thank you."

"What friend?" Grace tried to peer at the screen as V sent it over.

"Someone I work with. She was on the trip with me."

"Would I like her?" You had to admire the arrogance of a five-year-old, making it all about them.

"Yes, you'd love Sofia. She's kind, and funny, and always smiles."

"Does she like aquariums?"

V laughed. She could see where this was going. "I'm sure she does, but Friday is only for you and me." She tapped out another message, deciding that didn't mean there couldn't be time for Sofia, too. Quite when, she hadn't yet figured out, but she would.

"What are you doing now, Mummy?"

"I'm asking Sofia if she wants to meet up for a game of Scrabble." Her thumb hovered over the send button. Despite what Rachel had said—in fact, probably because of it—she couldn't let Sofia go. Her career was important. Grace was important. But the type of connection she had with Sofia didn't come along all that often and she needed to explore it. Before she could press send, though, Grace gasped and sat bolt upright again, sending V's pulse skyrocketing with panic. "What's wrong?"

"Will I still be able to have *my friends* over this week?"

V's shoulders dropped. For a second, she thought the apocalypse was coming. "I should think so." She read her message one last time and then sent it. When a reply came back almost immediately asking if she wanted to spend the weekend, she slid the phone back into her pocket and wriggled to get comfy. "After all, I'm seeing my friend and fair's fair."

14

"When will they be here?" Grace had been standing in the window for almost an hour, staring down the drive. It was five o'clock on Friday evening and V had got out in good time to collect her from the babysitter so she could meet the twins before going to her dad's, which had also been pushed later. There was no way in hell she'd have forgiven anyone otherwise.

"Why don't you come and pick something for dinner?" It was a vain attempt to move her. Nothing was going to shift that kid until she'd seen two babies carried up the path. "Or we could bake them a coming home cake?"

"That's a good idea. I'll wait here while you make it and then we can ice it together."

Great. Now there was a cake to bake, and she was still leaving smears all over the glass. V gave up and headed back into the kitchen, pulling out the ingredients and a bowl. Ten minutes later, when the tins were being slid into the oven, she heard a car pull up outside and took a deep breath, mentally preparing for what was about to ensue.

"They're here!" Grace jumped up and down, her palms

flat on the windowsill and her school dress billowing around her bum. She'd usually have changed straight out of it when she got home but had decided it was more important to begin her vigil at the window.

V quickly bundled the cake making equipment into the dishwasher and tried to calm her down. "Okay, sweetheart," she soothed. "They'll probably be asleep, though, so let's try to chill out. Remember your indoor voice and don't crowd them." Stepping through to the hallway, she opened the door and hoped to catch Jess before Grace did. They'd all be tired and need some warning. With one car seat in each hand, Jess walked up the path, and V stood aside to let her pass, whispering quickly as she slipped off her shoes, "I'm sorry if Grace is a bit much, she's very excited."

"That's okay, I figured she would be. Any chance you could grab the bags from the car?"

Stealing a glance at the tiny sleeping bundles, V jogged down the front garden and took a small case from Melissa's hand. "Sorry, orders from the boss. I'm carrying."

"You'll get no arguments from me." Melissa smiled as an arm wrapped around her shoulders and they ambled back up the path.

"How are you doing?"

A grunt of laughter and she shrugged. "I feel like I've been in that hospital for months rather than ten days."

They'd been kept in to monitor the girls. Jess had been back and forth to the hospital every day which meant V and Grace had the house largely to themselves. It was an interesting insight into what life would be like in a few months, and Grace's reaction to having them back was causing V a little concern.

"Grace has missed you. She's so excited to have you home." While V had already been to visit and meet the babies, they'd kept Grace away because she was a walking germ. She'd spent every evening when Jess got home from the hospital looking at whatever new pictures had been taken, or making them cards to send in.

"I've missed her too. Even the biscuit stealing. It was worth it to make sure the twins are healthy, but I am so glad to be back in my own house, sleeping in my own bed, and snuggling with my own dog."

"Ah. About that." V's face scrunched as she sensed the start of an argument. "Your mum insisted on taking Hal for the night so you could introduce them tomorrow. She said she ran it past you."

They reached the entrance hall and Melissa took off her coat, hooking it over a peg. "For once, she did. I forgot. Too much has happened over the past few days, my brain has turned to mush."

And it would stay that way, but it didn't seem the time to point it out. Instead, V left her to sit down and went to put on the kettle, hoping Rachel's unexpectedly considerate communication was a good sign. She peered through the archway into the living room while Grace sat patiently on the sofa, a pillow under her arm as she waited to be handed a baby. She looked a little nervous now rather than being a bundle of excitement, and V smiled. "Are you happy, sweetheart?"

She nodded furiously and then her mouth hung open, showing off the gaps in her teeth as Jess slowly lowered one of them into her lap. "Hello, baby."

"This is Izzy." Jess knelt in front of her, keeping careful watch.

"Oh. Hello, Izzy." She watched the little pouts with intense fascination, enraptured and finally quiet. For a few moments, anyway, but then she was distracted by the other baby. "Can I hold them both?"

"No, just one at a time."

Melissa sat next to her, cradling baby number two. "This is Ruby. Or at least I think it is, presuming we put the right hat on her. They look so similar and I know I should be able to tell my own children apart but..." She laughed and stroked a finger over the bridge of Ruby's nose.

It would not go down well to part them, but V was intensely aware that Grace needed to go to her dad's in half an hour and he thought she was being fed first. Sofia would also be on her way over soon because this was the weekend they'd chosen to spend together. Not just a night, but two of them. Quite what they'd do with all that time, she wasn't sure, but they always had the sex to fall back on, and it'd worked well because it'd give Jess and Melissa a chance to settle in.

She delved in the fridge for some pasta sauce and filled a pan with water, hoping to at least chuck some of that down Grace's neck without causing World War Three to erupt. "Sweetheart, you need to get ready in a minute because Daddy will be here soon." V preemptively winced, expecting a torrent of protests, but Grace was talking softly for the babies. Perhaps they were going to be useful allies.

"I don't want to go to Daddy's today."

That was unexpected. She'd never once said she didn't want to go, and V stood completely immobilised. "What do you mean? Daddy will already be on his way over and he'll be looking forward to spending the weekend with his favourite girl."

"Not today. I want to cuddle Izzy and Ruby."

Jess shot V a quick look of reassurance. "Izzy and Ruby will go to bed soon, so you won't be able to cuddle them, anyway. Why don't you see Daddy, and then on Sunday they'll be up for more attention?"

Grace still didn't seem sure, her gaze fixed on Izzy's face. They'd never forced her to stay where she didn't want to, and V had no idea what she'd do if she flatly refused. She was unprepared to drag her kicking and screaming and hoped this wasn't an omen of things to come.

"If you help me ice this cake, you could take some with you, too. Daddy would like that," V added. It was still warm, but that didn't matter; she'd made worse. A bit of runny buttercream never put them off. Hell, even a smattering of arsenic was unlikely to stop anyone from this household digging in to cake.

"I think Daddy would like pink icing."

This was progress, and V went along. "Yes, you're probably right. He has always loved pink." She grabbed the ingredients and a handful of dried ravioli from the fridge, chucking the pasta into the pan as it came to the boil. It'd be nowhere near the standard of Sofia's, but Grace would never know that. "Let Jess take Izzy then and wash your hands."

Jess scooped the sleeping baby from Grace's arms and sat on the sofa with her, then Grace jumped down and ran up the stairs. There was a collective sigh of relief, and Melissa laughed. "That was tense."

"I know. My friend is picking me up soon and I'd have had to send her away."

"Who is this friend you're staying with?"

V busied herself weighing out the butter for her icing and pretended not to hear. She still hadn't told either of them what had been going on, and she wasn't sure why. It was probably that she knew Jess would ask questions about how serious they were, and she was a little hazy on that right now. When probed again, though, she spilled enough to keep them off her back. "Oh, do you remember I told you about that woman from work?" She kept it casual, moving on to pour in icing sugar which plumed and settled on her sweater leaving a big white mark. "She said I could chill at her house when Grace is away. Give you guys some space, you know." A little shrug, but she wasn't sure if they'd bought it.

"Woman from work?" Melissa looked to Jess, who shook her head.

Perhaps they were both suffering from a little baby brain, but at least they dropped it.

* * *

It was an hour before Sofia arrived, having gone to the pub after work. When she pulled up, Grace had not long left because she wanted to show off Izzy and Ruby first. She'd still been reluctant but had agreed to at least one night, and V was feeling a little fragile as she slipped into the passenger seat of the Mini. Part of her wondered if they should've let Grace stay home rather than cajoling her into going.

"What is this?" Sofia enquired, pointing to the tub on V's knee.

"Um, cake. Grace made it and I brought you a slice. Don't worry, it's sealed. No crumbs in your car."

She must have sounded more pissed about that than she was because Sofia cut the engine and twisted in her seat so they were facing. "Tell me what is wrong."

"Nothing, I'm fine. Just tired." V sniffed into her sleeve, knowing that was fooling no one, and then burst into tears. It wasn't like her at all, but tonight had really been an emotional curveball which she felt she should've expected.

Sofia unclipped her seatbelt and leant over, pulling V

close as best she could over the gear stick. "Please tell me what has happened," she whispered, a hand gently stroking V's hair.

"It really is fine; Grace didn't want to go tonight. I'm worried about her still, but it'll be okay. If needs be, she can come home, and we agreed she only has to call."

"Of course she can. We can go to collect her any time of the day or night. Keep your phone with you, I won't drink tonight, and—"

Her cheeks warming, V pressed her sleeve to her nose again. She was about to say she wasn't in the mood for this anymore and they should postpone but quickly changed her mind. "I meant more that he'd drop her back but thank you for offering."

"Well, of course, I just meant..." Sofia pulled away, rubbing her palm into her forehead. "Sorry."

"Don't apologise, it's very sweet." After wiping under her eyes, V managed a smile. "I've been looking forward to this weekend, but I'm not sure I'll be the best company tonight, so I'll understand if you want to cancel."

With something between a laugh and a sigh, Sofia turned on the ignition and pulled onto the road. "I don't want to cancel. Even if we curl up and watch films all weekend, that's fine by me. Okay?" When V nodded, she continued. "Do you want to know what we're eating tonight?"

"Besides melted cake?" V rattled the mess in her tub, and it thumped against the edges, leaving splatters of pink icing.

"Yes, besides that. I have prepared you a proper lasagne and guess what?"

With a grin, V whispered, "No chips?"

"Precisely. I am righting a wrong, and while we wait, I am now planning to take all that tension out with a relaxing shoulder massage. What do you think? Too much spoiling or not enough?"

"Mm, we'll see." Biting back another smile, V sunk into the seat. "How are you with foot rubs, peeling grapes, and catering to my every need?"

"Can the grapes already be peeled in the form of wine?"

There was a moment of consideration before a definitive nod. "Yes, I believe that would be acceptable."

When they pulled up at Sofia's house, V headed inside and shut the door on the world. She took off her Vans and padded through to the kitchen, taking a bottle of wine from the rack. Holding it up for Sofia's approval, she poured two glasses while Sofia pulled their lasagne from the fridge and shoved into the oven.

When she ran upstairs to get changed, V took their wine and followed her up. There was a grey fleece throw over the back of a chair and she snagged that too, getting comfy underneath it and waiting for Sofia to come back in a pair of black tracksuit bottoms and a loose T-shirt.

"Do you fancy that film?" She lit a selection of scented candles as she passed the sideboard on the far wall.

As Sofia settled in behind her, V reached for the remote. "Sure." She smiled as a hand stroked her hair again and kisses pressed to the side of her head, then Sofia got to work on a massage. "Oh, you were serious." Flicking through the channels and finding nothing but reruns of game shows, she finally hit the button to take them to Netflix and selected the first romantic comedy she found. She wasn't really watching anyway and closed her eyes, suddenly overwhelmed with exhaustion. "Not that I'm complaining."

"I am always serious," Sofia whispered, as her thumbs rubbed the tight knots tied across V's shoulders. "You should know that by now."

When her phone buzzed in her pocket, V fumbled to yank it out, worried that it would be an SOS from Grace. "Shit, shit, shit," she muttered. Pulling up the message, she smiled to find it was only a photo of her enjoying cake with her dad and his girlfriend. "Okay, panic over. Sorry." Sofia resumed while V typed out a reply. "She's fine."

"Please stop apologising. Grace is your daughter, of course you worry."

"I know but I can't help feeling this isn't what you signed up for. It's not exactly sex and jam, is it? Or Scrabble for that matter..."

Sofia stopped again and reached around to drop V's phone in her lap, then clasped her hands and held her tight. "I signed up to spend the weekend with you. Sex was never mentioned. Nor was jam." She pressed another kiss to V's temple. "Perhaps Scrabble was, but let's overlook that for now. I enjoy your company a great deal, even when you have all of your clothes on. If sex happens, it happens, but it will never be why I invited you to spend time with me. Do you understand that?"

After laughing because she'd gone all teachery, V then sighed and moved her phone to the coffee table. "Yes, miss. Understood." She hooked her hand under Sofia's knee and wrapped it around herself. "Although I definitely *do not* act this way with my other friends. Perhaps you do, but..."

"Shush." Sofia playfully shoved V's shoulders and then carried on rubbing them. "I am a very special friend."

"The *special*-est," V whispered, her heart swelling. "But don't tell Jess."

15

When V woke the next morning, she was swiping fresh air again. This time, though, there was no interruption with breakfast. Pulling on her pyjamas, which were still neatly tucked away in her bag, she trudged downstairs to find Sofia sat at the kitchen table. She wore only her black boxers and a matching T-shirt, slumped in a chair with a book in hand and a pot of tea in front of her.

"What are you doing here?" V probed, scratching the back of her neck and yawning. She poured a quick glass of water from the tap and took a few sips.

"I live here."

"Funny." Wrapping her arms around Sofia's neck, V peppered her cheek with kisses. "I enjoyed Scrabble last night. Fancy another game later?"

"I would love to, but first I need to shop for my neighbour." Flicking to the next page, she slotted in her bookmark and set the book down.

"The jam neighbour?"

Sofia laughed and picked up her tea instead, blowing over the top. "Yes. If you're lucky, there will be more. She doesn't have a car, so I collect her shopping occasionally. She sticks a note through the door when she's low and I got one this morning."

"Well, aren't you an overall good Samaritan? I'll go get dressed."

With a little shrug, Sofia whispered, "She reminds me of my Nona."

Bending down to kiss her cheek again, V ruffled Sofia's hair. "Stop, you're sending me all mushy."

She held out her hand and Sofia set the tea back down, lacing their fingers together. V led her upstairs where she was stripped, showered, and covered in more kisses to tide them over. Then Sofia grabbed her keys from the hook in the kitchen and drove them to the supermarket. With the list on the back of the note, she put together a basket consisting mainly of heavy tins and then they drove back, but as V went to knock on the house next door, Sofia grasped her wrist.

"Not that neighbour," she corrected, holding V's hand and leading her past the car onto the towpath. She stopped again about two hundred yards away, outside a tatty narrowboat with plastic flowers along the top, all covered in green slime. As they stepped onboard, the rest of the boat was in mercifully better condition.

A call of "Sofia" came from inside, followed by a "Ciao!" as they stooped and entered the kitchen.

Sofia smiled cheerily. "Ciao, Angie. I have your shopping, where shall I leave it?"

An elderly woman in a brightly patterned floral dress peered up from the sofa where she sat crocheting. "On the counter." Then she glanced back at V. "Ah, Anya. Hello, my love."

"No, this is V, not Anya. You know that we're not together anymore, I told you that."

"Of course you did. Good. Never liked her anyway. Come and sit down. Sofia will make us tea." Something moved next to Angie and V jumped for the second time. The first slight jolt had been at the mention of Sofia's ex, who she never talked about, and the second was because the blanket had a tongue. "Oh, don't mind Percy. He won't bite, and I can't until I put my teeth in."

Squeezing behind Sofia as she put on the kettle, V sat next to Percy and scratched his head. He was a little Westie with wisps of brown fur around his eyes—just the type of thing Hal liked to chase. "My daughter would love you."

"He's an old boy now." Smiling at V, Angie then diverted to address Sofia. "She's a pretty one. Young too. Good girl."

Letting out a splutter of laughter, Sofia turned and wagged her spoon. "I hope you're going to behave, seeing as I brought you company."

"When have I ever behaved? Now, be a love and take him for a quick walk, will you? I've left your jams by the bread bin, and this new blanket is almost finished. Perfect for your little one."

"What little one, Angie?"

She faltered and patted the blanket across her knees. "You and Anya... no. I'm getting mixed up again. Sorry."

"You were making that blanket for your grandson, weren't you?"

Pressing her hand to her head, Angie let out a sigh. "Of course. Yes. I've made so many of them, I lose track."

Passing her a steaming mug of tea, Sofia then grabbed a pink lead with a roll of black bags attached to it. "Come on then, Percy."

"Let me do that." V took it from her and clipped it onto Percy's collar, then picked him up and carried him to the back of the boat. "I am an expert, after all. Be back in a few minutes."

She stepped off and set Percy on the ground, ambling down the towpath. It was a far gentler pace of walk than with Hal, who was good on a lead but a lot more boisterous and wanted to be let off at the first sight of a field. Percy only wanted to sniff about a bit and then cocked his leg a few times before stopping and turning to peer back at the boat.

When they returned, Sofia and Angie were laughing over something on the sofa, then Sofia got up and kissed her cheek. "Thanks for the jams. V here is a big fan."

"That's how you get the girls, my love. Take some money from my purse for the shopping on your way out."

Ignoring her and taking only the two jars of jam, Sofia bent to ruffle Percy's ears as V unclipped his lead. He settled back in, needing a hand onto the sofa, and they all parted. When they were back on the towpath, V looped her arm through Sofia's.

"Do you miss your family?"

Sofia shrugged. "Of course. I will go back at Christmas, and I visit every summer, but I miss them all—my Nona, my parents, my nieces. We are a close family."

"Why did you come over here, then?"

"It was meant to be temporary, for study, but you know how it goes. You make friends, get into relationships, have job offers. Soon somewhere else is your home."

It sounded lonely, but that didn't seem a very kind thing to say, so V only nodded. "And Angie?"

"Ah, well she came with the house. When I bought it, the previous owners used to help her out. I agreed to take over. I enjoy it, she's become a bit like family. I suppose you know all about that, so I won't explain."

V laughed. "Yep. I know that feeling well."

"Her mind isn't what it was, and I worry for her, being on that boat on her own. She refuses to move, though, so what can you do? Anya—my ex in case you hadn't already worked that out—always used to say if I kept propping her up, I was enabling her when it isn't safe, but..."

"No wonder Angie didn't like her."

And she wasn't the only one, because Anya sounded like a right pain in the arse—not that V wasn't a bit biased.

They left the jams in the kitchen and then spent some more of the morning walking the canal while Sofia explained the entire structure of her large family, and V offered the history of her own small one. The weather was turning, though, so they were back by eleven and in need of other ways to occupy themselves.

"Is this it? The secret to your innate calm and gentle aura?" V held up her hands, which were covered in a sticky mixture of flour and water and wriggled them in Sofia's face. She'd made the mistake of asking Sofia what her greatest passion was. When she'd been led to the kitchen, she'd expected another orgasm but been draped with an apron and handed a mixing bowl.

"Gentle aura?" As Sofia looked up from where she crouched in front of the fridge, she shook her head.

V shrugged. "You know what I mean. You're so in control, relaxed, whatever. I still can't work out how you do it. I try hard but I'm always worrying about something, it's like my head is constantly swirling with what ifs, maybes, and potential catastrophe. I spend a great deal of time trying to assure myself that everything will be fine." And it'd been that way, she realised, since she picked up that pregnancy test almost seven years ago.

"Choice." Sofia stood up, a jar of homemade ricotta in one hand and a loose bag of prosciutto in the other, and V pointed at both again.

"As ever, please combine."

She laughed. "No—choice. Everything is a choice. Realise that, padawan, and freedom will be yours." With a gentle bow, she placed the cheese and ham on the work surface and began unwrapping it.

"Ahh, okay." Needing a moment of consideration, V went back to kneading her dough. "You don't *always* have a choice, though... I will never be free of my responsibilities towards Grace—not that I'm saying I want to be—but that isn't something I get to choose anymore."

"Of course it is. You could put her up for adoption tomorrow, or at least not bother as much as you do. You choose not to, though. That's how I approach life these days. If I'm unhappy with something or I want to make a change, I know there is always a chance to do so. Sure, it may not be easy and there could be repercussions, but I still always have a *choice*."

V nodded slowly, the analytical part of her brain working overtime like it did whenever she was presented with a big maths puzzle. "Are there any other variables?"

Sofia pursed her lips and pulled out a chopping board. "Yes. I think perhaps if fear clouds your choices then you are not truly exercising your freedom. That can be tricky and sometimes requires trying to dig deep and look past whatever is causing you to fight against what you would truly want if the fear wasn't there. Make sense?"

"A surprising amount. What I want to know, though, is where do you come up with these pearls of wisdom?"

With a gentle laugh, Sofia grabbed a terrifyingly sharp looking knife from the block and waved it absently so that V stepped back. "Ah, well that one was Angie. When I was in a swirling hole after my break-up, she was an excellent listener. Don't be fooled by how she was today, because often she is entirely lucid and a very interesting woman to talk to." She seemed to realise what she was doing and cringed apologetically, setting it on the chopping board.

"Noted. I will consider this all and let you know my final thoughts in due course, but for now..." V held up her ball of pasta dough for Sofia's inspection. "What do you think? Would your Nona let me in her kitchen?"

She stepped behind and reached under V's arms, taking the dough and rolling it into the work surface. "It must be smooth; this still has lumps and bumps."

As V placed her hands over Sofia's, she swayed and hummed through a few bars of 'Unchained Melody', then tipped back her head and burst into song. This was the first full day off she'd taken in a long time, and she was enjoying it. Not that taking Grace to the aquarium the previous Friday hadn't been fun, in fact they'd had a great time, but she was still having to be a responsible parent. Today, she had adult conversation, there wasn't a stingray in sight, and she could cut loose.

Sofia pressed a kiss to V's temple. "I love to see you so happy. How can we ensure it continues?"

"More days off? Not really practical, though."

"Forget practical. Take them. Come here when Grace is with her dad and spend weekends with me."

Twisting and stretching her hands out over Sofia's shoulders, V frowned. "What, like a regular thing? You realise that's every other weekend?"

Suddenly looking less sure, Sofia shrugged. "Yes. Why

not? We have a good time, don't we? You can always bring some work with you if you really need to, and you said you wanted to give Jess and Melissa some space."

"We have the best time, but I thought we were just... how do I say this without sounding like a complete dick? Um, having sex and enjoying each other's company?"

"We are." Sofia laughed and then pressed their lips together. "I understand Grace comes first, but I'm here. No expectations or grumbles if you have to cancel; any weekend you want to spend with me I will take."

It still felt too good to be true and V narrowed her eyes as she went in for another kiss. Sofia had never lied to her yet, though. If she said she didn't have any expectations, perhaps she meant it. "You'd really be okay with that?"

"Yes." She grinned and raised her eyebrows. "It is my *choice*. Things with Anya were difficult, so it isn't entirely selfless. It works for me too. I can be with someone I care for, but it's a little less..."

"Risky?"

"Well... yeah. Who knows what will happen down the line, but so long as we are both happy, does it matter?"

V shook her head. Sofia was right. It didn't matter one bit.

16

Life became a carefully organised series of compartments. Grace always needed something. Jess and Melissa had taken literally her pledge to support them with encouragement and often more practical tasks. Bob, even, was constantly on her back about something or other to do with professional development and teacher standards. Sofia, on the other hand, wanted very little if you discounted wonderful food, sex, and the occasional hand with Angie's shopping or walking Percy.

She'd be waiting outside in the Mini every other Friday night with dinner prepared, and they'd ensconce themselves in their own world for two days. As the final day of term mercifully arrived, V was about three pounds heavier and finding her jeans were a little snug from all the pasta, but a whole load lighter in other areas for having some space—and some fun—even if it had meant a few late nights doing work and chores to make up the time.

"Mum, can I wear my Rudolph jumper today?" Grace already had it on and stood in the doorway flicking his red bobble nose. She'd paired it with jeans and the Converse

Jess and Melissa had bought for her birthday. It had become a sort of annual tradition that they got a new pair, always in pink, and she loved them even though they clashed with the red sweater.

"You can wear whatever you like, so long as you hurry." As V shooed her along the hallway, she tried to squeeze the button of her jeans at the same time. Both schools were having a casual clothing day as part of an entire district charity event. You paid a pound to wear whatever you liked, and it was coinciding with the end of term Christmas meal. V tucked a coin into the pocket of Grace's trousers and made sure she had one for herself, then pulled her winter coat from the peg. "Do you have everything?"

"Yes. Don't need a lunchbox, I'm having turkeeeey." Grace tilted back her head and carried on until she was out of breath. She was already ridiculously excited about Christmas and today was pushing her towards the edge.

V smiled at her, relieved to have made it this far. It'd been touch and go over the past couple of weeks, especially when she found an entire section of her professional development folder that hadn't been completed. After a panic and near meltdown she'd ended up taking it to Sofia's on their last weekend together and used the peace of her kitchen to rectify the situation. They'd successfully kept their personal lives out of work but not quite managed to do it the other way around.

Calling a quick goodbye to Melissa, she gently closed the door so as not to wake Izzy or Ruby and bundled Grace into Jess's waiting car. She already had the engine running so she could defrost the windscreen and rolled down the window. "Are you sure I can't give you a lift, too?"

Zipping her coat and pulling a pair of thick gloves from the pocket, V turned and waved them. "No thanks, the walk will wake me up a bit. I'm struggling to keep my eyes open this morning." There had been many fraught moments of interrupted sleep over the past few weeks owing to babies and work, and that was another thing Sofia's house was good for—catching up. "I'll see you back here this afternoon before Grace's concert and then we can start the celebration."

She did a little shimmy as she turned to continue down the drive. They'd planned the next few days. It was Christmas Eve on Monday. That meant three days of intense shopping and wrapping, then Jess had somehow convinced Rachel to let them all spend Christmas Day together, given it was their last one as a complete household. There was a stash of booze and food already in the fridge, and V had even splashed out on a bottle of Champagne. It was a complete extravagance for her and Jess, given Melissa didn't drink even when she wasn't breast feeding, but getting through term one called for it.

As she reached the school gates, she was in an upbeat mood, stopping to smile and greet the kids who were filtering in. There was a sea of red hats and girls with tinsel strung through their hair, and it would've been hard for anyone not to get in the spirit—tired or not. As her eyes locked with Sofia's, her smile widened.

Sofia opened her coat and peered down at a light-up Christmas tree jumper as V approached. "What do you think?"

"I think that would impress Grace a great deal. She went off in her Rudolph one this morning."

"Then we are kindred spirits." Leaving the coat open, Sofia slammed shut the car door, hitting the remote so the lights flashed. Then she thought again and pressed the fob a second time. "That reminds me, I have something for her."

She looked up and faltered. "I hope that's okay. I couldn't resist when I was buying this jumper." Pulling out a paper bag from the back seat, she then held up a navy sweater with a pack of huskies pulling Santa's sleigh sewn to the front. It also lit up as she pressed a button under the hem.

"She'll love that, thank you."

"You don't have to give it to her." The sweater was neatly refolded and slipped back into the bag. "Just me being silly."

"It's not silly, it's lovely. Can I get it from your car before we leave?"

Sofia nodded, and they wandered into the warmth of reception, past the front desk and into the staff room. It was bustling with activity, mainly because someone had placed big tins of chocolates on all the coffee tables and everyone was excitedly rifling through them. Give sweets to a bunch of adults before nine o'clock and they all thought Christmas had in fact come early.

They carried straight on to the maths block, parting at the door to Sofia's classroom. She lingered in the doorway, hooking her satchel over the peg. "See you at lunch?"

"Are you sure you're prepared to eat from the school canteen? We both know what happened last time."

Sofia raised a finger. "Ah, that was different. I expect the turkey here to be dry, it's a tradition and it wouldn't be Christmas otherwise."

"You are an enigma."

"But that's part of the fun, right?" She grinned and disappeared into her room, turning back to light up her Christmas jumper again, and V laughed as she walked past the window and saw her dancing. Turning sideways to imitate Sofia's moves, V banged into something soft and plump, knocking a ream of yellow papers to the floor. "Shit, sorry," she pleaded, crouching to pick them up. It was Bob, and he didn't look happy.

"I still need to see your folder. Do you have it?"

"Absolutely, all done as promised." She'd put the very last touches on it the previous night and tucked it into her bag so she couldn't forget.

"Jolly good, makes my life easier." He tapped his foot as he waited for her to continue returning his worksheets to order, and Sofia came out to help her. When they were both upright and Bob had his papers back, she appeared almost as nervous as V to see the folder handed over—probably because they'd fudged a few bits. "I'll look at this and get back to you. Are we all heading to the pub later? Lord knows I need it." He only seemed to have become gloomier as the term progressed, and V hadn't dared enquire about the situation with his wife. "Two weeks with our families, heaven help us all."

"That's the spirit, Bob." Sofia slapped his shoulder.

"It's alright for you, jetting off to Italy. I'm in Rhyl with the in-laws for three bloody days. Tell me which you'd prefer?"

He'd directed the question at V, and she squirmed even though the answer was an honest one. It was perhaps just not for the reasons he'd assume. "Italy for sure, although I love Wales. We go on holiday every year."

"Is that so? Well, you won't find anyone here who shares your enthusiasm there, that's for sure."

"Why, what's Wales ever done to this school?" It had to a joke, but she couldn't figure out why or how. They were a hundred miles away, and while she could understand his reticence about spending Christmas with his in-laws, didn't think the rest of the school would care that much.

"Ask Sofia." He nodded and trotted off, leaving her more confused than before.

"About Wales?"

Sofia dug her hands in her pockets and shrugged. "Yes. Anya is Welsh, and I'd happily never go back there again in my life." She grimaced and lit up her jumper a third time.

"Ugh, *that* bitch." V laughed and playfully nudged Sofia's shoulder. "I hope you haven't been taking relationship advice from Bob, because that may have been the problem."

There was a big gaping silence, and then Sofia let out a long "nooooo". She shuffled and ran a hand through her hair. "Anya actually worked in the finance office, and my entire car crash of a relationship played out for the whole faculty."

"Ah." Now her hesitation made a bit more sense.

"Yes. Ah. We met when I first started working here. I was lonely, and out of place, and probably jumped in a little too fast when she showed an interest in me..." She was beginning to ramble and stopped herself. "Anyway, I really don't use this place as a dating pool. I promise."

V shrugged. What else could she really do or say? Although her interest was piqued by hearing the name 'Anya' again, she could hardly blame Sofia for sleeping with her colleagues when her very first thought on entering the building was how she wanted to bed the head of department. Heeding that warning of Bob's about gossip getting around was seeming like it had been a wise move, though.

* * *

V was hanging around her classroom again with her jacket on hoping to catch a moment alone with Sofia. They wouldn't have another weekend together for four weeks and she wanted to say goodbye properly. Lining up all the pens on the desk, she was lost to her task and hadn't heard anyone come in when an arm slid around her back.

"Hello," Sofia whispered. "I have Grace's sweater here and there is a little something in the cupboard for you too." She took V's hand, the paper bag in her other, and led her towards the door in the far corner wearing a smile almost as bright as her Christmas jumper.

"A surprise?"

"Mhm." Sofia produced a sprig of mistletoe from the bag and held it over her head.

"Are you bending those rules?"

"Mistletoe has its own rules, and school is over. Term is over. There are no kids left on site and even Bob has gone to the pub." Sofia nipped on V's neck as she spoke, then worked up to kiss her. When she put a hand out to close the door, it plunged them into darkness and V gasped as Sofia backed her against it. The bag rustled as it was dropped, with the mistletoe in hot pursuit.

"Does Christmas always have this effect on you?" she whispered. "Because you are being generous, even by your own high standards."

She stroked her hands up Sofia's sweater, quickly deepening the kiss. They wouldn't have long before the cleaners came around and she didn't want to be caught out, but she also couldn't resist the chance to play out at least a little of her fantasy from the first day of term. "Do you always bring women here to seduce them?" She laughed, but Sofia went rigid in her arms. "Sorry, I guess we can't joke about that."

The cupboard filled with Sofia's sigh. "No, I'm sorry. It was just a bit... overwhelming. I'm usually a very private person and I didn't enjoy being the centre of everyone's gossip."

"Then should we really be kissing in a cupboard?"

Sofia laughed now. "No, probably not. You'd think I'd have gone off having affairs with colleagues altogether, but..." Stepping forward again, she placed a gentle kiss on V's lips which tingled to her toes.

"But that, huh?"

"Yes—but that." When Sofia cracked the door, a shaft of light blinded them both and they recoiled. "Now I must give you your gift."

"You mean that wasn't it? I'm struggling to think what else there could be... Diamonds? An expensive watch? A beach villa in The Bahamas?" V snuck out, tidying her hair.

"No..."

There wasn't any follow up and by the time they'd reached the corridor, their things collected, V was becoming bored with the suspense. "Well..." She prodded Sofia's stomach, hitting the lights again, and then ran her finger from one LED to the next in a trail. "What else did you want to give me?"

Sofia reached into the pocket of her jeans and pulled out a key, and for a moment V's heart was in her mouth. She quickly swallowed it down when Sofia explained. "I won't be at home for two weeks, but I thought perhaps you could still use the sanctuary. You are free to visit whenever you like over Christmas. Consider this the gift of peace and quiet."

"Are you serious?"

"Yes, why wouldn't I be?" As Sofia tucked the key into V's pocket, she shrugged. "You can't keep the house of course, or run any sort of illegal enterprise from there, but if you want to get away for a few days, then you are very welcome." She averted her gaze and wore a little smirk. "And if you happened to water my plants and check on Angie while you were in there..."

"Oh, I see." V folded her arms and kicked Sofia's foot. "I'm taking no responsibility for any plants which die while in my care." Or anything else, for that matter. She peered around to make sure they were alone, then snatched a kiss. "Now tell me you're going to miss me."

Sofia pouted and leant in for another. "I will miss you, miele. So much."

"Miele? Is that Italian or just a brand of vacuum cleaner?" A warm blush filled V's cheeks, matching Sofia's, and her heart skipped a few beats. Sofia wasn't usually this soppy, but the holidays seemed to have turned her from cool and in control to an enormous pile of slushy half-melted snow.

"Yes, it is Italian, although if my mother caught me saying that she'd tell me I was too English." Stroking the loose strands of hair away from V's face, Sofia kissed her again, more tenderly this time. "It means honey. You are my honey."

"Am I?"

She nodded. "Yes, it seems so." There was a burst of laughter and she drew V into a hug. "Have a wonderful holiday and try not to throttle any family members."

V sighed and held on a while longer. She'd try, but no promises were being made.

17

"It's Christmaaaaas!"

When V opened her eyes, a wide pair of blue ones stared back, and she was so startled that she jumped and almost fell out of the bed. Grace had wriggled in with her the previous evening and was as awake as she'd been at midnight. Grabbing her phone from the bedside table to check the time, V rubbed her eyes and tried to return her heart to a normal rhythm. "Sweetheart, it's only five-thirty. Even Izzy and Ruby won't be awake yet."

Almost on cue, there was a loud cry from the next room, and she slumped back against the pillow. This was going to be a long day, and the mattress creaked as Grace bounced up and down, causing V's head to bang against the headboard and generate a dull headache.

"Can we get up, Mum?"

She pushed back the covers and swung her legs around. "It might be for the best, yeah. Don't disturb Melissa and Jess, though, please. They need to feed the twins and you'll have to be patient. Wait until they come out of their room."

Grace did at least do as she was told, so worried that she

might not get her presents that she was completely compliant. An hour later she was still sitting on the sofa with Hal's head in her lap, watching television. She'd dressed herself in the new sweater from Sofia and her favourite sparkly skirt. There was even tinsel tucked into the dog's collar to give him a bit of Christmas pizzaz.

When Melissa did finally come down, she had a baby in one arm and her phone in the other hand, pressed to her ear. It looked like her day had started even more abruptly than V's, and she didn't even have the benefit of an empty canal-side house to go to when Grace went to her dad's later. He was collecting her mid-afternoon in order that they each got to see her on Christmas Day.

"I thought we agreed to Boxing Day dinner." Melissa's eyes widened as they met V's and she mouthed something about her mum being a nightmare. "Yes, I know you want to see them but... that was the point... if you're coming can you just make sure it's not dead on dinner time?" Her grip tightened around the phone. "Fine, yes if you insist. We won't open anything until you get here." She thrust it into a pocket in her pyjamas. "Give me strength. Mum is on her way over; she wants to bring everyone's presents today because apparently it can no longer wait until tomorrow."

V stretched out her arms. "Want me to take her while you get ready?"

She was glad she didn't have to go through this with her own family, who were far lower maintenance. When Grace got back on the twenty-eighth, they'd spend some time together, giving her a third Christmas. V's mum and dad always went abroad until then, though, so there was no tussle over who was going where. Ironically, it was Italy this year. The thought had V wondering what Sofia would be up to. Whatever it was, she imagined it would be more sedate and that no one had woken her at such an ungodly hour after repeatedly kicking her through the night.

Half an hour later, both babies were dressed in matching elf suits and screaming at the top of their lungs because Jess had come down in a full Santa suit. Even Grace's bottom lip was wobbling as she peered up in horror at the giant belly and white beard, wondering if a predator had broken in. The only person who looked disturbingly into it was Melissa.

When Jess had changed and they'd settled, the household assembled in the living room, waiting to open presents. Rachel breezed in with full bags but was notably on her own. She noisily rustled through her bags as they questioned her about it. "You can't get Paul out of bed this early for anything other than golf." She stood with her hands on her hips and blew a few errant strands of hair off her nose. It was a wonder they dared slip out of place. "Now, how do you want to do this?"

Grace tugged on Rachel's dress. "Is there a present for me?"

"*Grace*," V hissed. "That's rude, sweetheart. Come and sit down."

"Of course there's a present for you, my darling." When Rachel pulled out a box and handed it to Grace, it required V clasping her hands to stop her immediately tearing into it. "And one for you." Another box was passed to V, and when everyone had their gift, she wafted her hands to hurry them. "Open, for goodness' sake."

Grace didn't need telling twice. The paper was instantly shredded onto the floor, and she held up a pair of pink roller skates. "Look, Mummy!"

"What do you say?" V whispered in her ear, grabbing

her before she could get her feet in and fall straight on her arse.

"Thank you."

It was hard to generate the same enthusiasm for a toaster, however generous. As they moved on it seemed everyone had the same idea, because each present this year had a distinctly practical theme. Her parents had gone for a microwave, Jess and Melissa had bought a set of crockery, and even Grace had got in on the act. It would've been courtesy of an online shopping trip with her dad, but she'd haphazardly wrapped a clock which was printed with a picture of herself and Hal.

Once presents were out of the way, Melissa made various subtle attempts to evict her mum, but she was playing dumb and pretending not to have picked up on any of them. At one-thirty when V and Jess were getting ready to serve the dinner, she was still loitering and ended up perched at the end of the table tending to the twins while everyone ate. Apparently she wasn't cooking until later in the day and didn't need to rush off, but when she was finding more reasons not to leave at three o'clock as Grace went and V wanted to head to Sofia's, it was getting a bit ridiculous.

"Are you alright?" Cornering her in the living room while Melissa and Jess did the second load of washing up, V was trying to move things along a bit.

"Yes, darling." She wore a tight smile and glanced at her watch. "I suppose I should leave."

"You don't seem to want to, though..."

Rachel sniffed and wiped under her eyes, and V glanced back into the kitchen before pulling her into the hallway and shutting the doors. "Why don't you give me a lift to Sofia's house, and we can have a chat? Okay?"

She nodded and grabbed her coat from the peg, while V

retrieved her overnight bag from upstairs and said goodbye. Jess and Melissa thought she was house sitting for someone who was away over the holiday, which wasn't strictly a lie.

They both got into Rachel's Mercedes, but she didn't start the engine, her hands firmly gripping the steering wheel as it sat stationary. "I've done something," she whispered.

"Okay..."

Rachel closed her eyes and tilted back her head. "I contacted my sister about enrolling the twins in private school. Paul won't speak to me, he's furious, and I'm dreading going home."

"Oh, for fuck's sake..." V's head dropped into her hands. "Why on earth did you do that? If Melissa and Jess find out, they'll never forgive you."

"I know, darling. It was only a quick enquiry, but I shouldn't have done it." She started the engine, gliding off the verge. "Please promise you won't tell them. I've told her to forget all about it and I'll smooth things over with Paul."

Letting out a deep sigh, V tapped her fingers on the chrome door inlay. She had no intention of telling them, it served no purpose. Melissa had hated that school and her feelings weren't much warmer towards her aunt Penny who was head teacher there. If she found out her mum wanted Izzy and Ruby enrolled there, she'd go nuclear. "Your secret is safe, and at least you realised you were in the wrong."

Rachel nodded her thanks. "Where are we going, anyway?"

"Sofia's house is by the canal; I'll direct you." They travelled in silence for a few minutes, V pointing the way until they were on the edge of the village. Rachel glanced sideways, clearly considering saying something, and V had to ask. "What?"

"I fear I'm at risk of overstepping the mark twice in one day, but Penny also asked how you're getting on. She was impressed by your determination when you first met—you know that—and said she thought you'd make an excellent teacher. When I filled her in on progress yesterday, she commented you were exactly the type of character she looked to employ."

"Really?"

Rachel glanced sideways again and smiled. "Yes. You should make sure you have another word with her at this wedding. Career progression is always as much about networking as anything else and she is a wonderful contact if you'd ever like to move into the private sector."

They'd discussed that before, on the down-low. She knew what Jess and Melissa thought of the idea but their view was coloured by a bad experience relating to boarding, and V could see many benefits in working at a private school—better pay, smaller class sizes, kids who all wanted to learn. "That's good to know. Maybe in a few years, it's something I can look into properly."

"Why wait, darling? I thought you wanted to get on."

V laughed. This was Rachel all over. "I do, but I've had a bit of a re-think. There's plenty of time, I'm still only twenty-eight. I don't want to run before I can walk."

With a quick huff, Rachel pulled up in Sofia's parking space. "If you're sure."

"I'm sure."

* * *

It was strange being in Sofia's house without her. V almost felt like an intruder, worried she'd stumble across some secret stash. Truth was, though, it would only be pasta. It was hard to imagine Sofia had anything mysterious hidden in her cupboards. She was always completely open, and there never seemed to be an agenda, if you discounted wanting her plants and neighbour watered.

Pulling a little pink watering can from the cupboard under the sink, V decided to get the practical stuff done. That way there was less chance she'd get drunk and forget, leaving herself feeling horribly guilty that she hadn't followed through on the one thing Sofia had asked of her. She filled it from the sink and made her way around the house, ending in the master bedroom.

When she opened the door, she let out a sharp shot of laughter. There was a square gift box in the centre of the bed, wrapped in white paper with a red ribbon tied around it, and a card on top. She set the watering can on the bedside table and took it, reading the note out loud. "Just a little something to enjoy while you miss me. Call when you get here, I want to wish you Merry Christmas."

She laughed again and ripped into the paper, sending fragments twirling onto the duvet. Inside was a gold box of Champagne truffles. Not even supermarket ones, but the fancy stuff from a proper chocolatier. Carrying them downstairs and settling in on the sofa, she pulled the phone from her pocket and felt a little apprehension swirling in the pit of her stomach at the idea of phoning Sofia. They never spoke on the phone; it was either a text or they saw each other in person. In fact, she didn't call anyone if she didn't have to, and she was suddenly struck with fear that she wouldn't know what to say or it might be awkward.

After furnishing herself with a glass of wine to combat that, she tucked herself under the grey fleece from the back of the chair and opted for a video call. It'd be easier if they could see each other. When Sofia answered, she was in another Christmas jumper—this time one which had miniature baubles sewn to it.

"Do you have a separate wardrobe for those things?" V laughed, grateful for the ice breaker.

Sofia grinned and moved the phone to provide a better look. She was lying on a bed, with a selection of cushions scattered around her. "No, but that is a good idea. Do you think they're sexy?"

"Oh, definitely. I have never wanted you more than I do right now." There was some truth to that, and V wished she had Sofia cuddled in behind her. "Are you free to talk?"

"Yes. I was just taking a break from my nieces."

"You mean you were having a nap."

For a few moments, Sofia laughed and tried to profess her innocence, but it wasn't convincing and eventually she gave up. "Is the place okay? Did you water the plants?"

"I did…" Sort of. The job would be finished later, it was only paused in favour of chocolates and their call. She'd check on Angie tomorrow when it was light and maybe take her some mince pies. A bit of company would actually be nice by then, because as much as she always told herself she wanted peace and quiet, she soon got bored with it. "I found the gift you left for me. You have no idea how pleased I was to see something frivolous after receiving only practical house related presents, but if you carry on like this, I'll be the size of a house by the end of the academic year."

"Rubbish, and you would still be gorgeous. Do you want me to stop?"

V sucked her teeth as if she were considering for a moment. "No. I like it. I think I'd miss having you cook for me."

It wasn't quite the same as admitting she would miss Sofia, but she was struggling to say that. She did miss her.

She couldn't wait for their next weekend together. They hadn't discussed the status of their relationship again, though, and she feared saying anything which might rock the boat. If she lost this—no, if she lost Sofia—she wasn't sure she'd handle it very well. That thought was a little daunting to someone who hadn't been close to a relationship in the best part of five years.

"There are some frozen meals if you want them. How long will you stay?"

V shrugged. She'd only brought two changes of clothes, but she supposed she didn't have anywhere to be until Grace got back in a few days. "I don't know. Depends how much food you've left." She laughed and then leant the side of her head against the back of the sofa. "Was Christmas dinner up to scratch?"

"It was exceptional, and I got to cook with my Nona." Her face lit up, written with affection for her family. "How was your day?"

"Long, and fraught in unexpected ways. I ended up counselling Melissa's mum."

She filled Sofia in, and she laughed. "What did you advise her?"

"Nothing, I'm not getting involved. In fact, I'm pretending I know nothing about it. I've got enough going on in my own life. Thank Christ we're so uncomplicated, although she gave me a little confidence boost. Her sister is the head of a private school on the south coast and she gave me some advice when I was first looking to train. I'm not interested just yet, but apparently, I've impressed her."

Sofia laughed again. "Of course you have, miele. You're an excellent teacher."

V's cheeks warmed more at that than with any compliment Rachel could throw her way. "You're just biased because I sleep with you."

"Probably. What has spurred this turnaround, though? I thought you were hell bent on that headship by the end of the year?"

"Oh, I don't know. Partly some things this wise *old* Italian bird said to me." And partly another old bird she could never get away with calling that. Rachel would slit her throat.

There was a knocking sound, and the screen went dark for a moment as Sofia called something in Italian. When she came back, she was shaking her head. "I'm sorry about that, my cousins have arrived to torture me with yet *more* food. I will need to go shortly, but first there is something I want to speak with you about."

Her face had turned serious and V's stomach lurched with what was probably an undue amount of panic. She'd give herself a real talking to if she'd tempted fate by using the word 'uncomplicated'. "Oh?"

"I've been asked to stay on as head of department until the end of the academic year, and there is a good chance it will become permanent. I'm afraid it changes things for us a little, and I wanted to discuss this in person, but they need an answer before we can do that."

V's heart pounded, the panic well and truly back. She shuffled to sit upright, preparing herself for what was coming next. "I see. Congratulations, you're a brilliant head of department."

"Then you don't mind me informing the senior leadership team about us? That we are... intimately and yet *uncomplicatedly* involved? It didn't seem a problem before, but I think it might be better if we're transparent. I know we agreed not to tell anyone..." She trailed off and shrugged.

When her cheeks flooded with warmth again and her hands tingled, it was at least relief this time, and V laughed. "Oh. Right." She rubbed a hand over her heart. "No, that's fine. If you think they need to know, I'll trust your judgement."

"It would only be the head and assistant head." Sofia held out a hand, as if she needed to make that clear. It wasn't necessary, though. V was just glad they wouldn't need to stop seeing each other. She quickly realised it would've been a bigger Christmas clanger than Rachel's meddling.

18

"Fish and chips!" Grace yelled, her feet slapping against the floor as she jumped up and down.

She snatched for the sweaty vinegar-soaked bag before V had even crossed the threshold and ran into the kitchen with it. Jess and Melissa were already at the table, each holding a baby and looking like they might nod off. It had been a long first week back for everyone except Grace, who thrived on the routine. Not to mention the attention from her classmates.

How V would love to share her enthusiasm. It was dark, cold, and miserable as she arrived and left the school premises, and there was still another week to go before she could see Sofia properly again. They'd caught up on her trip briefly but that was the limit. Besides a few snatched moments, it'd been a case of trying to get back into the right headspace for work while simultaneously panicking that there were only a few weeks to go before the move. It'd seemed a long way off when they'd made the agreement in October, but now Christmas was out of the way it was suddenly looming.

She sidled up to Grace, kissing the side of her head as she started ripping into the paper, and tried to get the food onto plates. Their chips would end up spilled across the kitchen floor being hoovered up by a greedy spaniel otherwise. "I thought after this we could look through your old toys to see which you want to give to Izzy and Ruby." They needed to pack and framing the clear out as a gift was probably a good shout. "What do you think?"

"No thank you."

She was a clever kid, and V nodded with appreciation. Being polite was not getting her out of this, though. "Let's pack up some of my clothes, then. We're moving soon and we don't want to leave it all to the last minute."

"Okay. You do that while I read a book."

This was not going to plan at all. Thankfully, Jess joined in, offering some support. "Come on, Monster. I'll help go through those toys. I also got some paint samples at lunchtime so we can pick out a colour for your new room. What do you reckon?"

It seemed to have piqued Grace's interest, and she showed the first sign of a smile before quickly quashing it. "Could I do it... pink?"

"Funny..." Jess twisted to pull a card from her back pocket. It was a set of swatches for pink paint, and Grace's eyes lit up fully this time. "That's exactly what I was thinking. So, what do you reckon?"

There was a tense few moments as V looked from Jess to Grace and back again, praying this was the start of her coming around to the idea. They'd had another conversation about it over the Christmas break and she'd still not fully understood why it was necessary. Just as she was about to deliver her verdict, a loud knock on the door startled them all.

"I'll get it." Grace ran down the hallway before anyone could stop her or say anything, standing on tiptoes to reach the top latch and inching open the door. "Who are you?"

I muffled the voice until she pulled it back fully. "I'm sorry. Are you Grace?"

"Depends who's asking."

"I have your mum's phone. Could you give it back to her please?"

As V craned over, still plating up their food, she could see Sofia stood looking somewhat uncomfortable on the front step. She shuffled from side to side, wrapped in a thick coat and squinting against the cold, then waved when their eyes locked. V jogged through, gesturing Sofia inside. "Come in, it's freezing."

"Are you sure?"

Was she? Yes, she was. Reaching the end of the corridor, she put a hand on Grace's shoulder to move her out the way so Sofia could get past. "Don't be rude, sweetheart." The dog had also joined them and sniffed around Sofia's feet, waiting for her to reach down and pat him. "Where did I leave it?"

"Your desk. I didn't think you'd want to go the whole weekend without it."

"Well, thank you." She'd spent more time than she probably ought to admit hanging around her classroom in the hope of them seeing each other properly because next weekend seemed too long to wait, but it turned out Sofia was in a meeting after lessons finished. "Will you stay for a cup of tea?"

Grace was still gawping at the newcomer, Hal now sat at her feet. "I like your scarf."

Sofia unwrapped a thick bright pink scarf and wound it around Grace's neck, then crouched to admire it. "You look very stylish."

"Your voice is funny."

"I'm Italian. Have you ever been to Italy? We have very good pizza and gelato."

"What's that?"

"Ice cream."

"I love ice cream. Mum, can we have ice cream?" Grace tugged the bottom of V's sweater but didn't wait for the answer, running back to the kitchen with Sofia's scarf still around her neck. It was far too long for her and she almost tripped, whipping the offending length back with a flourish.

Sofia stood and leant closer, lowering her voice, and it was all V could do not to back her up against the wall and kiss her. Just the smell of her perfume had caused a familiar fizz of excitement. "Is it okay that I'm here?"

"Mhm." She tried to hide quite how okay, as the phone was tucked into her pocket and Sofia's fingers rubbed over her leg through the denim. "Would you like some dinner? There's plenty, I went a bit overboard. First week treat."

They wandered into the kitchen where Grace was swinging her legs on a chair and busy stuffing chips into her mouth. Sofia still looked nervous, which was odd to see. Usually she was unflappable, but she was wringing her hands and didn't seem to know where to put herself. "Would you mind if I used the bathroom?"

"No of course not. Upstairs, second door on the left." Grabbing another plate from the cupboard, V finished dishing up their fish and chips. She'd set the plates on the table and sat down, picking up her fork and spearing a chip before she realised everyone but Grace—who was completely oblivious to anything but her food—had stopped and was staring at her. "What?"

"Who the hell is that?" Melissa had an excited grin on her face.

V shrugged, trying to look more casual than she felt about the situation. "Sofia from work. She's another maths teacher."

"Holy hell, maths teachers have changed since I was at school. I might have realised my sexuality sooner if I'd had her to stare at every day."

When Melissa let out a long jet of air and fanned herself, it caused Jess's eyes to widen. "Excuse me, are you ogling that woman in front of me?"

"What? I'm just acknowledging she's hot."

"I know, but..." Faltering, Jess shook her head. "You never look at other women, or men, or anyone. Do you?"

As she laughed, Melissa stroked a hand across Izzy's head. "Not seriously, no. I am only human, though. Despite the appearance that I am in fact a milking machine these days. Why, are you jealous?"

"Yes, horribly."

"Well don't be." She repositioned the baby, putting her over a shoulder and rubbing her back. "I only take my clothes off for you. With the others, I insist we keep them on and just do it through. You know the sort of thing."

"Oh, very funny." Jess did the same with Ruby, putting her bottle down on the table and turning her over to be burped. Then she picked up a chip and threw it at Melissa's head before resuming.

As Grace was about to do the same, V grabbed her hand to halt it. "Hey, settle down kids. You're meant to be setting a good example."

Sofia appeared in the doorway. "Once a teacher, always a teacher."

She wiped her hands on her trousers, her eyes darting around the table. It took a moment for V to understand her hesitation, which was because there were no seats left. She leapt up and pulled out her own chair, then gestured for Sofia to take it. "Come and sit."

"But then where will you sit?"

"Oh, I don't—"

"I'm finished," Grace interrupted as she slid off her chair and ran into the living room. "You can bring me my ice cream while I read my book."

"Can I?" V called after her, trying to halt an eye roll. "Thank you, sweetheart. That's very kind." She shook her head with exasperation but didn't have the heart to argue. Not right now, anyway, because it had done her a favour. She sat back down while Sofia took Grace's seat next to Melissa, sliding her plate across the table.

An awkward silence fell over the kitchen as they all ate, Melissa and Jess both managing one-handed while they each held a baby with the other arm. It was Sofia who broke the deadlock. "They're gorgeous. I saw a picture when they were first born, and they've grown so much."

"Did you indeed?" Melissa smirked, peering up as she kissed Izzy's head and tried to make eye contact with V. "You know each other well, then? Because she hasn't mentioned you at all."

Squirming with discomfort, V cleared her throat. "I mentioned Sofia to Jess."

"Nope. You didn't. Keep telling me stories about that Bob bloke but I've never heard of a Sofia." Jess shot Sofia a warm smile. "Sorry, we're talking about you like you're not here. She probably did but we've both been a bit preoccupied with handing our souls to these two. No offence intended."

"None taken, I can assure you. And yes, we know each other quite well." After pushing back her chair and setting down her cutlery, Sofia held out her arms. "Would you let me have a cuddle?"

Fully smirking at Jess this time, Melissa went to get up and move over. "Of course, Sofia. You can have a cuddle any time." Then she sat back down and laughed. "Only kidding." She passed over Izzy and settled in, resuming her dinner unimpaired.

"Ignore her." Jess let out a soft grunt of laughter. "She thinks she's funny, and she was just saying how hot you are. Weren't you, pumpkin?"

It was her turn to wear a satisfied smile as Melissa's face went bright red and she hurled another chip. Sofia had ignored everything that'd happened since Izzy landed in her arms, though, rocking her gently and whispering to her in Italian. When she finally looked up, she was ready to burst with adoration. "You are very lucky."

"Yes, they are. And they should stop bickering." Hal came along to snaffle two chips from the floor as V hurled one in each direction. She cared less now Grace wasn't watching, and they both deserved it.

"I can see why you love living here. Being at my house must be very lonely and cold when you are used to this."

It'd never once felt either of those things, but V didn't have a chance to argue because Melissa was kicking her under the table. She was mouthing something indistinguishable and gesturing to Sofia with her head so furiously that it looked like she'd developed a nervous tic. "She spends a lot of time at your house, does she? That's interesting. Are you the mystery weekend friend?"

"There's no mystery," V protested, clearing away Grace's plate.

With a little hand hooked over her lip, Sofia mumbled, "Sorry, I have embarrassed you."

"I'm not embarrassed." She *was* embarrassed but didn't know why. It was her choice to let Sofia in and she should've known what would happen. She was just so pleased to see her. "I'm getting Grace some ice cream, does anyone else want dessert?" Sticking her head in the freezer to cool it, V let out a slow, calming breath and grabbed the chocolate.

"Would you like me to leave?"

"No, I don't want you to leave." She dumped a scoop into a bowl and then put away the tub, calling for Grace to come and take her ice cream. There was no chance of her getting waitress service. She barrelled in, grabbed it with a quick "thank you", and was gone again, Sofia's scarf still around her neck and billowing as she ran. "Now, can I get anyone a drink or something?"

"Finish your food, miele. Everyone else can wait."

As V sat, stuffing a chip in her mouth, she wondered how Melissa and Jess would next show her up. Once they got in a playful mood, the possibilities were endless. It would require carefully managing the conversation onto a more mature level. "How are the wedding plans coming along?"

Melissa looked at Jess and let out a long "umm" before stabbing her fork through the centre of her fish. "Good question, we've been a bit busy. Who knew twins were so much work?"

V's eyes widened. "How about everyone?" She laughed and took Ruby's hand, feeling four tiny fingers curl around her own. "Worth it, though. I must admit they're quite cute, when they're not waking me up at three in the morning. Do you need a hand with any wedding stuff?"

"What, you mean in all the free time you've got?"

She shrugged and sat back in her chair. "I have a child who's proficient at cutting out. She could make you some invitations, for a price. What about outfits? I'm *very* good at shopping."

"Oh, I've found a gorgeous dress." Their plates rattled as Melissa jumped up and grabbed her phone from the work surface, frantically tapping at the screen. She held it in front of V's face to show a cream lace dress, then turned it so Sofia could see. "What do you think? It's that or a tuxedo, just to give Mum a heart attack."

V shook her head. "Go with the dress, I'm not sure tuxedos are for you."

Melissa sat again and scraped her seat forward. "No, you're right. I tell you who would look great in one, though." Her eyebrows lifted as she glanced at Sofia, nudging V's foot under the table.

She had a point. V's eyes roamed conspicuously over Sofia's body, imagining her wearing one. Perhaps not the full ensemble, and it would need to be properly tailored, but dear god if it were... The thought brought a warmth to her cheeks again, and she fanned herself with her hand, realising Melissa was doing the same to wind up Jess. They smiled at each other playfully across the table, then Melissa got up again and wrapped her arms around Jess's neck from behind, kissing her cheek and whispering something in her ear.

"I had a tuxedo once," Sofia cut in. She shot V a bashful smile, then returned her attention to Izzy, still bouncing her gently. "It was of course Italian."

V rolled her eyes. "Naturally. All the best things are Italian. Did you have little cufflinks in the shape of the Leaning Tower of Pisa by any chance?"

"As a matter of fact..."

They both laughed, and Jess was looking from one to the other with Melissa's hand still rubbing into her shoulder. "Italian? You're Italian..." She trailed off, and you could almost see the penny drop as she glanced at the ceiling and nodded. "Sofia, I knew I'd heard the name."

"So, she *did* tell you about me."

"Mm, she mentioned one or two things." It was Jess's turn to kick V under the table. If this continued, her shins would be black and blue.

Becoming flustered again, V grabbed another chip and chewed on the end. She really didn't want Sofia to know how much she'd gushed on her first day, or any other day after that, and prayed Jess would keep a lid on it. There had to be a first time for everything.

* * *

When everyone had finished eating, Sofia insisted on helping tidy away while Melissa and Jess took the twins upstairs for their bath. Grace had been intent on heading up with them to help—or hinder—and V didn't know quite what to say now they were alone. Eventually, she resorted to the same childish behaviour as everyone else in the household and threw soap bubbles in Sofia's face.

"I told you we have a dishwasher. There was no need to run the sink."

There was a distinct twitch of Sofia's lip, where she was trying to suppress a smile and maintain her glare. She'd rolled up the sleeves of her shirt and was wrist deep in suds, with a big blob of them melting down her face. "I'm enjoying myself."

"Oh, well. In that case I'll carry on." Cupping a big mound of bubbles in her palms, V held them up to Sofia's chin, creating a beard. "Ho ho ho! And there was me thinking Christmas was over."

"That is not what I meant, and you know it." She fixed V

with a stare and slowly moved closer until their noses were almost touching. "I'm enjoying being here with you all. It's fun."

"Fun's one word for it. Chaos is probably a better one, but you're more than welcome all the same." It was clear Sofia wanted a kiss, but V was feeling playful now and reached into the bowl again, putting another blob on each of her cheeks. "This is such a good look on you. Have you ever considered growing facial hair?"

"Would you believe I haven't? And you will find yourself in serious trouble if you keep interrupting me. I have almost finished and then I should go home."

Now she was really asking for it because V didn't want her to go home. It was all the incentive she needed to drag this out for as long as possible. She nudged herself between Sofia and the sink, then grabbed a towel from the work surface beside them and dabbed Sofia's face. "Guess now you can't finish the washing up you won't be able to leave." Sucking her teeth, she flicked the buttons of Sofia's shirt one by one until she reached the top and they were facing again. "Sorry."

With a slight smirk, Sofia wrapped her wet forearms low around V's waist and lifted her up, carrying her into the middle of the room. "You were warned."

"Is there something about kitchens which turns you on?" V hooked her hands around Sofia's neck and hung there, her toes barely touching the ground. "Because I think I've had sex in your kitchen more than any other room of the house."

"Mm, no. I don't think so. We just spend a lot of time there, and a lot of time having sex." She dipped her mouth to V's, touching her with the lightest of kisses. It was teasing, and she knew exactly what she was doing because she'd be able to feel the rampant heartbeat next to her own. The corner of her lip hooked up in a brief smile as V sought her mouth again, pulling back and teasing some more. "Have you missed me?"

"Maybe a bit. Have you missed me?"

Sofia let out a grunt of laughter and then pulled tighter until they were pressed completely flush against each other, V's fingers raking through her hair as they kissed. Lost in the embrace, she almost jumped out of her skin when someone coughed loudly behind her.

"Excuse me." Biting her bottom lip, Melissa pointed to the sink. "I left the new bottle of baby soap down here when I unpacked the shopping earlier."

She stepped past and grabbed it from next to the draining board, then punched V's arm playfully as she walked away. All the while the two of them had stood, still wrapped around each other, completely motionless. When they heard footsteps on the stairs, they broke apart laughing and V banged her head on Sofia's chest.

"I think it might be time for me to go," Sofia whispered, still spluttering a little. "Thank you for the food."

"And thank you for my phone. Pick this up next weekend?"

"I'll be waiting."

19

The following weekend, the knock on the door was expected. Grace had already gone to her dad's and V was upstairs packing a bag. She bounded down the stairs to find Sofia stood in the hallway holding Ruby and stopped in her tracks. "Is there something you need to tell me?"

Sofia grinned. "I know, and after we were so careful."

"There was me thinking you were only a comedian when you were drunk." They both wandered into the living room, where Melissa was sitting on the sofa breastfeeding Izzy while eating a previously frozen pizza which looked like it'd since been slung into a volcano. Flicking off some charred bits were her index finger, she then prodded it, and V slid the plate away. Even Hal wasn't interested in eating it, still curled up on the other sofa, which was when she knew the situation was dire. "You can't eat that. Let me make you something else before we leave."

"It's fine, I haven't got the energy."

"Well, where's Jess?" It was gone six, and she was usually home by now. Since the twins were born, she'd been leaving as early as possible.

"Had to work late. She's checking the tenants out of your house, so Mum has time to get some new carpets fitted and—"

"Then I'm definitely helping. No arguments." Taking the plate through to the kitchen, V immediately discarded the pizza into the bin and opened the fridge. There had to be something she could whip up in short order that would be better than a lump of charcoal. Just as she went to grab the eggs for an omelette, though, Sofia's hand landed on her shoulder. "Ah, it's Master Chef."

"Take Ruby. I will do this." She held out the squirming baby and leant in for a kiss.

There didn't seem any point arguing when she looked so happy to have her superpower called on, so V only shrugged and obliged. With Ruby in one arm, she pulled out a pan and showed Sofia the cutlery, then left her to it. As she settled in on the sofa, Melissa was frowning. "Oh, don't worry. I always travel with a cook. She's very good, and she enjoys it."

"Is that so?" Peering through the archway, Melissa nodded. Then she got up and swapped babies, sighing as she started on feed number two. "Are you absolutely sure I can't keep her? Or at least take her on loan for a few hours."

"Not sure how Jess would feel about that."

"No, and she's already pissed because her dad's pressuring her to invite her mum to the wedding."

Letting out another great sigh, Melissa wriggled back into the sofa cushion and spilled what was bothering her. They'd started planning since being prompted and had decided on the end of May bank holiday, with a ceremony late on the Saturday morning and a garden party reception afterwards. It was all low key with only close friends and family invited, and Jess had originally decided not to invite her mum. Given she wanted to have her half-brother there, and he was only fifteen, though, it didn't really seem viable not to have them both without it ending up awkward. Or at least it turned out that was the crux of her dad's argument.

When she'd finished explaining, Melissa let out a puff of air which vibrated her lips. "I really want to help her work it through but I'm just..."

"Exhausted? Preoccupied? Busy enough trying to keep two babies clean, fed and happy?"

"Yeah. Is that really bad?"

"No, I think it's completely understandable, and knowing Jess she'll be trying not to bother you with it. Do you want me to have a chat with her?"

As Melissa agreed, Sofia came in with a steaming mug of tea and set it on the side table. There was a wonderful aroma floating through from the kitchen, and a pan sizzling on the hob behind her. "Here you go."

"Mm, thank you." The sight of her with rolled-up sleeves and the start of her tattoo visible seemed to have cheered Melissa up. She smiled at V while she waited for Sofia to leave again before mouthing "marry her now". Then she laughed and repositioned Ruby, moving her to the other side.

"Hilarious," V mouthed back, her face falling when she realised something which couldn't be any farther from humorous. She sniffed, the smell of Sofia's cooking overpowered by the stench of baby shit, and it had seeped through Izzy's outfit onto her hand. Scrunching her face and carefully standing so as not to squidge it, she started towards the door. "Poo-ston, we have a problem. She needs some clean clothes."

"Are you shitting me? I've only just bathed them."

Through over the top theatrical tears, Melissa mouthed a few expletives.

Spotting the omelette arriving, V continued into the hallway. "Don't worry, I'll get her cleaned up while you eat."

"Thank you!"

This was not how she'd intended to spend her first weekend with Sofia in four weeks, but there was no way she'd leave Melissa with a poo emergency. Bouncing up the stairs and hoping it didn't produce an explosion from the other end, she nudged through the door to Jess and Melissa's bedroom and laid Izzy on the changing table, carefully prizing open the poppers of her baby grow.

"It's a good job babies are so adorable," she muttered, lifting Izzy's legs and whipping out the nappy. "Because this is utterly disgusting." When Sofia appeared in the doorway, V gestured for her to pass a fresh packet of wipes from a bag by the wardrobe. It turned out Jess's preparation for the apocalypse wasn't so daft after all, because at least they never ran out of anything. Mary Poppins needed to hurry the hell up, though. "Actually, can you watch her a second? I need to get her fresh jammies."

Cringing that she'd just said 'jammies', she left Sofia in charge and rooted through the top of the chest of drawers where they kept Izzy and Ruby's clothes, finding a plastic covered book wedged down the side. In it were shoved a load of old photos, and she knew exactly who they belonged to. Leaving them where they were, she pulled out what she needed and turned to find Sofia had already finished wiping Izzy down, and put on a fresh nappy.

"What took you so long?" Sofia bent over and blew a raspberry on Izzy's tummy.

"You should watch out, or Melissa won't let you leave."

Scooping Izzy up so V could put down a fresh baby

grow, Sofia kissed the top of her head. "What makes you think I want to?"

"Oh, fine then. I'll head to your place and you can play house with *her* all night. Don't mind me." She nudged their shoulders together then slotted four podgy limbs into their correct holes. When Sofia batted her out of the way, taking over again, she stood back with her hands on her hips. "Hey, can I ask you something?"

"Me, or her?"

"Ha-ha. You." She was considering the wisdom of approaching this but was still very much interested. "I know you don't want to talk about Anya, but when Angie mentioned little ones, was there something to that?"

When Izzy was all buttoned up, Sofia hoisted her over a shoulder. "Yes, but don't take it the wrong way, okay?"

"How could I take it the wrong way?"

"Well, because I expect what you're gathering is that I would have liked kids and that Anya didn't want them, which is true, but it isn't why we split up." She leant against the changing table, seeming to want to get through this as quickly as possible. "I knew from the start that she didn't. When things began to go wrong, and she wanted us to move away for her new job, she intimated that if I followed, she may reconsider. An incentive, I guess."

"She'd have children to keep you?"

Making a move towards the door, Sofia shrugged. "Who knows, but she *was* very manipulative. It took me a long time to see it, even when others already had. Any insecurity, she found a way to exploit. *That* is why I wouldn't move to Wales with her, and why we aren't together."

"I may be pushing my luck, but is it also what you meant when you said past partners hadn't always been very understanding...?"

"Bingo."

Sensing she'd reached her tolerance for talking about Anya, V followed Sofia downstairs. She was usually quite open and happy to chat, but her demeanour shifted whenever anyone mentioned her ex.

When they reached the lounge, Melissa had propped Ruby on a cushion so she could eat her food, and V gestured to Izzy as if she were a prize on a TV game show. "Et voila, one clean baby. Is there anything else you need before we go?"

After finishing her mouthful, Melissa set her fork on the plate. "You don't need to leave, you know. There's no reason you can't spend the night here. The whole weekend, in fact, if you're going to cook and change nappies."

It was unclear whether she was talking only to Sofia or if she meant both of them, and V shook her head as she settled Izzy into her bouncer. "Um, I'm not sure how to take that. Do you wish to be left alone, or...?" Pointing from Melissa to Sofia, she reached down to lace her fingers through Sofia's and gave them a quick squeeze.

Sofia squeezed back. "There is plenty of me to go around, and I would love to stay some time."

"Ah, that's a shame. See, I have plans which don't really fit with being here changing nappies, so..." Dragging her towards the door, V turned briefly to wave. "Call me if you need anything. I'll be home Sunday."

"Uhuh," Melissa called back. "Thanks for everything, Sofia. Hope to see you soon."

* * *

When Sofia ran upstairs to change, V crouched to open the fridge, almost as desperate for some of Sofia's cooking as anything else. She muttered to the ingredients, which she expected would be turned into cannoli over the course of the weekend. It was rare that she thanked food in person, but after such a long absence the occasion called for it.

Closing the door and heading to the wine rack, she selected a bottle, opened it, and chucked the cork in the bowl. Then, just as she had the first glass poured, she heard Sofia's footsteps thundering on the metal steps. Taking a quick glug of wine, she stared through the window at the red and white lights dancing off the water in the darkness. It was calm, she was calm, and she felt her shoulders drop at least an inch.

Expecting Sofia to have thrown on her usual shorts and a sweatshirt so they could lay out on the sofa and eat, V was surprised to find there was a different agenda entirely. As Sofia pressed into her back, nipping her neck and rubbing her shoulders, she set down her wine glass. Sweeping away the few strands of red hair which fell from a loose bun, Sofia mumbled loudly and whispered against V's ear, "I had a lot of time to think about this while I was away."

"I bet you did. I hope your Nona didn't catch you." When V reached back to run her hand down Sofia's leg, it became obvious that changing had been abandoned part way, because she met only skin until her fingers glanced over the bottom of a pair of boxer shorts. "You should've said you'd introduced a no trouser policy. Hang on, let me catch you up." Unbuttoning her jeans, she quickly wriggled free and kicked them aside. Then she pulled off her jumper, so she stood in only a tank top. The action spilled more hair, and it cascaded over her shoulders. "That's better."

As she curled her arm back and looped a hand behind Sofia's neck to draw her closer, both of Sofia's hands reached under to massage her breasts. It took her a little by surprise and a deep moan escaped, Sofia's obvious need feeding her own and causing a heat to rise between her legs. The tank top was slowly lifted and pulled over her head, then Sofia unhooked the bra underneath and discarded that too.

The cold air caused her to shiver, and her nipples hardened, although that could easily have been from the thumbs now rubbing deep circles in them. Kisses covered her back and then, when the caresses travelled down her sides and Sofia grasped her waist, she braced herself on the work surface.

Sofia pressed their hips together fully now and for the first time, V felt something hard against the top of her arse cheek. Her hand shot back, and she grasped the dildo through a layer of cotton, moaning again when Sofia responded by slipping her own hand in the front of V's underwear.

As her fingertips trailed and teased, she whispered again, "I have *really* missed you. Have you missed me too?"

"You can feel how much I've missed you." It became quickly clear in the desire coating Sofia's fingers and V shuddered, a little overwhelmed at how instantly her body was responding. She'd thought about what their reunion would be like. She'd also worried about it, wondering if things would be the same between them or if Sofia would retreat, clamping up again. So far there were no signs of that. If anything, she'd really found her confidence somewhere in Italy, and it was a massive turn-on.

As Sofia continued, circling V's clit and gently teasing her folds, she pushed down her own boxers with her free hand and the cool silicone nudged between V's cheeks, making her gasp again. "What do you want me to do?"

"I want you to bend me over and take me right here." The rasping desire in Sofia's voice was matched, and V bent further forward. Her palms were once again flat on the counter and she spread her legs slightly.

She was about to respond again but didn't get a chance. Pulling aside the material of V's underwear, Sofia nudged V's legs a little wider with her feet and entered in one smooth motion. After four weeks, each of their resultant gasps was like a sigh of relief. Sofia was slow, purposeful, filling V with the full length before withdrawing and doing it again. And again. And again, until she could feel her legs shaking.

Her nipples glanced over the cool marble as she arched her back and her hands slid forward, Sofia's thrusts pounding her hard and causing her to lose her grip. She inched across the work surface, propped on her forearms and roughly shaking her head as she submitted to the relentless rhythm.

Clawing up V's thighs and then rubbing the heel of her hand between V's legs, Sofia let out a low guttural sound close to a growl. "Oh, I missed you," she mumbled. "Fuck, I missed you."

Using her knee to slide V's legs wider still, she ran her free hand up to massage a breast, and V lost all sense of what was generating the most pleasure. It all combined to send her over the edge, and she closed her eyes as she tightened around the shaft, her nerve endings on fire as it burned down her legs and flushed through her entire body.

Then, in one exquisite long moan which seemed to undo Sofia too, she felt a gush of warmth and her legs gave way. Slumping forward again, but this time to stop from falling, she felt Sofia's arms wrap around her middle and hold her there. After a while, her breathing stilled.

"Suppose I should admit I missed you a bit too." She

grinned and rested her cheek on the marble. "Where did that come from?"

Sofia's voice trembled as she spoke. "Are you complaining?"

"Absolutely not." Straightening up, V turned in Sofia's arms and giggled as she had to stand to one side of the dildo, her legs still wobbly. Raking her fingers up the back of Sofia's neck and finding her head flopped forward, she slid her other hand around to rub Sofia's arse and kissed her neck. "Why haven't we used this before?"

With a quick laugh, Sofia shrugged. "We were just getting to know each other. Was it okay?"

"Are you really asking?" V pushed back the hair from Sofia's ear, tugging on the lobe and then whispering, "It's very sexy when you show me what you enjoy. Don't stop now."

She laughed again and laced their fingers together, pulling V towards the stairs. "Fine, but I really hope you're not hungry tonight because this could take some time."

20

After their reunion, the text activity really ramped up a notch when they weren't together. Three weeks later, with Grace getting ready to go to a birthday party, V was smiling at the latest reply as she wandered into the kitchen to find Jess staring at both baby bouncers. "You haven't got them on your own, have you?"

She peered up through wide eyes. "Yes. It's fine. I sent Melissa on a long dog walk so she could get some fresh air." Glancing at the two bottles of milk on the table in front of her and frowning, Jess scratched at the hair on the back of her neck, not looking as sure as her words implied. "If she can do it when I'm at work, I should be able to manage an hour."

Should and could were two very different things, and V picked up a bottle, giving it a little shake. "Need a hand?" She was supposed to be borrowing Jess's car to pick up some house stuff when Grace went to the party but had a bit of time.

"Yes please."

Tucking the phone back in her pocket, V crouched to lift

out the nearest baby, the bottle wedged between her knees. It was funny how the memories kicked back in and she did it almost without thinking, cradling Izzy in her arm and flicking off the cap before nudging the teat over her lips. "There you go, sweetie. I was about to call you Monster for a second then."

"I don't know how you cope handing over Grace every other weekend. I miss them just going to work."

Kicking out a chair and planting herself in it, V shrugged. "I think it'd be harder if she didn't love going there. Well, usually. I know people whose kids scream about having to go to the other parent, and I have no idea how they manage that. Grace adores her dad, so I try to count myself lucky. Thank god I didn't have a kid with an arsehole." Which neatly brought her on to an important related topic. She hadn't found a moment alone with Jess yet but hadn't forgotten her promise to Melissa. "Have you thought any more about whether you'll invite your mum to the wedding?" There was no point beating about the bush, and she came straight out with it.

Jess squirmed on her seat, almost disturbing Ruby from her bottle. "No. She wants to meet up so she can see her grandkids, too, but I'm not keen." She wriggled again, all the joy wiped from her face until she locked eyes with the baby in her arms and a smile re-emerged. "We're both struggling with similar things right now. Melissa is terrified of turning out like her mum or Rachel talking to our kids the way she does to her. I'm scared my mum will come into their lives and then leave again, and I'm not sure I'm willing to take the risk."

"Just *their* lives?" When Jess looked up, V shot her a warm smile. "Sorry, but you've been in this place of maybe one day wanting to reconnect properly for ages, and you never do. I saw the photos when I was changing a nappy the other week, and I don't think it's only about the twins." It was understandable. She hadn't seen her mum for eighteen years when she reappeared just over four years ago and trusting her again would take a lot of work.

"Yeah, alright," Jess conceded. "Me too, but I want our wedding day to be full of great memories, not tainted by her." She let out a gentle huff and smiled at Ruby again. "I also don't want to deny them the chance to see one of their grandparents, so it feels a bit like a rock and a hard place scenario. Dad suggested I put up some pictures from when I was little, and things were good, but I just can't do it. I know that kid was about to have her heart broken."

"I get that, and you know I'd never tell you what to do, but she seems genuine. She's hung around trying to prove herself for a long time, and I doubt anyone would do that if they weren't."

"Yeah, I guess."

"No pressure, just think about it." V tried to position the bottle in one hand so she could take her phone again, knowing it had flashed up with another message from Sofia. She'd sent a picture of a fresh dessert, and it elicited a wide grin.

"I take it Sofia's the one putting that smile on your face?"

When Jess peered over and tried to look, she held it to her chest. "Might be."

"What do you guys actually get up to, besides sex?"

Returning to her phone and tapping out a reply, she tried to hide an even goofier reaction. "Not much. We hang out at her place, watch films, cook, chat. Sometimes walk her neighbour's dog, too."

"And how long has this been going on?"

V inclined her head as she counted, feeling like she was

taking part in a rapid-fire television quiz show. Jess and Melissa had already grilled her for details when Sofia left the other week, but at the time it'd been more fun not to divulge much as payback for being teased. "Started in September and it's now late January, so almost five months?"

"You've had a girlfriend for five months and not told anyone?" As Jess's eyes widened again, this time she looked a little wounded.

"She's not my girlfriend," V protested, as much to smooth things over as anything else. They usually shared everything, and she could see where the hurt had come from. "And before you say anything, yes, she knows that. We had a conversation when we started spending time together, like adults, where we set out that there are no expectations. We just enjoy each other's company and spend time together... whenever I want."

"Whenever *you* want?'

"Yeah, but it was her idea. She said she understood Grace was my priority and she will take whatever time I have. Kind of like a friends with benefits scenario, although I hate that term."

"Great, then you can call your *friend* this afternoon and get her to drive you to Ikea, so you don't have to borrow my car. I really need to sort some paperwork with Dad, and you're probably right that we should have a chat about the wedding."

It was absolutely typical that trying to help had back-fired. "Come on, you promised. If I don't go this weekend while Grace is out of my hair, I'll have to do it next weekend when I said I'd help Sofia with her neighbour."

"What's the problem with asking Sofia to go with you?"

There wasn't one, strictly speaking, but V couldn't help

feeling it fell out of the realms of their agreement. "I don't want to impose."

"She can say no if that's the case. You want this stuff, I want my car, so call her up."

After a moment of grumbled protests, V angrily jabbed at her phone, her stomach gripped with what was probably an undue amount of nerves. "You're a pain in my arse."

She was doing it. She was stood in the Ikea car park and about to enter alongside a woman with whom she regularly had sex. This had to be the beginning of the end, whatever Jess said, but for now Sofia seemed into it. In fact, she'd been pretty enthusiastic about the idea.

"Don't let me leave without more candles; we've been using a lot." After being distracted by something in the entrance, she grabbed a big yellow bag to hold their stuff. "Are you buying anything big, miele? Do I need two?"

"Hang on, let me pull up the list." V reached into the pocket of her coat and waved her phone. Favouriting everything in advance was about to come in handy, because they didn't have tonnes of time before Grace would be home from the party. "Right, okay. We only need to go to the kitchen section and get bedding. Oh, well then wherever the candles are. There's quite a lot of shit on here, though, so yes to two bags."

"Just those two sections?" Sofia looked appalled by the idea, not to mention a little disappointed. "There is a system. A path you must take through the store."

"Must?" Peering up from her phone as they rode the escalator, V tried to fathom how any shop could insist on dragging you through every section when you only came in for two. Or three.

"Yes, it is part of the experience. We must look at all the wonderful things we don't need, try out every sofa in the lounge showroom, and then finish with the food hall." They followed the little arrows into the first part of the store, and Sofia held up what appeared to be a shoehorn. "Look, utter rubbish that we'll never use. Aren't you feeling joy?"

"Um, no. Put it down." Looping her arm through Sofia's, V ploughed right on through until she reached the kitchenware. This was where they were doing the bulk of their buying because it was the sort of stuff that she didn't want second hand and couldn't do without. "Right. Your mission, since you're clearly well versed in all things Ikea, is to find me this set of glasses." She held up the phone again and scrolled through to the set she'd chosen.

"And what is my prize if I find it?"

This was almost worse than shopping with Grace, but V couldn't help laughing. "Okay. For each returned item, you can have… a kiss?"

"Done." And with that she marched off, returning a few moments later with the exact set and an instrument of torture which may or may not have been something to do with peeling potatoes. "This is for me." She clutched it to her chest and then dropped it into one of the bags, taking a lot more care when she did the same with the glasses. "What's next?"

"Don't you want your kiss?"

Her eyebrows lifted. "I'm saving them up."

"I suppose I'll allow rollovers."

Once they'd retrieved everything from the kitchen department, they went in search of bedding. Grace's bed was being left at Jess's for a while, given V's room was the one being given to the twins, so she could still stay over when she wanted. It was an old second-hand one anyway, and V's parents had offered to buy her a new bed as a sort of house-warming gift. The only trouble was, she needed sheets that'd fit because it was a proper single that she could grow into.

Running her hand over a selection of fabrics, Sofia eventually pointed to a light pink one with Labradors printed on it. "How about this?"

V sucked her teeth. "Ooh, I don't know. She prefers bright pink and spaniels, but..." Laughing and chucking two of them into the bag, she nudged Sofia's shoulder. "It's actually a very good shout. All it's missing are a few pictures of ice cream cones or biscuits and these sheets would sum up my daughter. It's a funny thing because I'm sure I never encouraged her to like pink, it's just what she always gravitated towards."

"You say that as if it's a bad thing."

"No, but..." She shrugged and picked up a couple of pillows, tucking one under her arm and the other in a bag. "I didn't want to pigeonhole her into anything, like dressing a certain way or only playing with dolls or whatever. Not that she's ever shown any interest in them. Her favourite thing used to be her sandpit until Hal came along and then it was anything to do with animals. Perhaps she'll be a vet."

"Or a zookeeper."

"Yeah, well. I expect life at Jess's has prepared her pretty well for that."

They walked on until they reached the kids stuff, and Sofia was immediately bowled over by a giant stuffed dog. She held it up and grabbed hold of a paw, making it dance. "Take me home, take me home." Her voice had shot up at least an octave but then she laughed and cleared it. "We

could call her Sal. She could be a girlfriend for Hal."
Hoisting the dog up over her shoulder, Sofia continued to
rifle through the cuddly toys.

"You don't think it's a problem she's five times his size
and inanimate?"

"Absolutely not, there's nothing at all wrong with *inanimate*, as you already know. I am buying her as a house-
warming gift."

Did they need the gift of a giant stuffed dog? Sofia was
so taken with the idea, though, that V didn't have the heart
to say no. Instead, she went with a "thank you" and tried to
guide her away before Grace needed that veterinary qualifi-
cation. "Stay focussed, or there won't be time for candles."

"You're so strict."

"There was me thinking you liked that." V adjusted the
bag on her shoulder, rattling with all their kitchen items,
and then laced her fingers through Sofia's.

"I do," she whispered, leaning in for a kiss as the dog
joined them in it and his tongue brushed up the side of V's
head. With a quick laugh she pulled away wearing a daft
grin. "This is fun. I'm glad you invited me, even if you did
just want my car."

As Sofia went to walk on, V remained motionless and
their hands slipped apart. She knew it was a throwaway
comment, delivered light heartedly, but there was truth in
every joke. "I didn't *just* want your car." Taking a step
forward, she hooked a finger in Sofia's belt loop and pulled
them closer again. "I also wanted your muscles." Faltering,
she felt a little warmth hit her cheeks. "I sort of enjoy your
company too. You know, from time to time. Not sure if you'd
noticed that."

"I know, miele. I was only teasing. Me and my car are
also available to help you move." Sofia shrugged, now the

one looking a little tentative as she glanced at a set of jumbo crayons. "You have Jess, but... you have me too. And my muscles."

Giving Sofia's bicep a squeeze, V sighed. "I love them so."

"Then, do you want to put me to work? I can lift, drill, screw..." She took V's hand again and led her through a jumble of cots.

"Yes, you're very good at all those things, but perhaps not while Jess is there. We could do with a hand painting, though, if you're serious."

"Why wouldn't I be serious?" She stopped again and offered a shy smile.

"Because—" About to reel off something about it not being what they'd agreed, V shook her head. Perhaps she had been a little rigid in how she viewed that, so long as it was what Sofia wanted. "No reason. I'd love some help."

21

After all the deliberation and planning, on the Friday before half term V left work and collected her keys feeling oddly at peace with everything. She quickly passed the second set back to Jess, then they went to give it a once over. The house was the same as it'd been when they left it four years ago—besides some new grey carpets—which was comforting. All that remained was to fill it with stuff.

They'd sent Grace off to her dad's, with the intention that she'd return to a completely furnished new home. Their first task was painting her bedroom, and V left with Jess as soon as the DIY store opened on Saturday morning to buy it and get started. Meanwhile, Melissa was roped into spending some time with her mum. Rachel was insistent on taking her—and the twins—out for the day so they could all bond while boxes were being moved and they disrupted the house.

"What if we find Rachel's body in a bin liner when we get back?" V joked.

Jess laughed and used a screwdriver to prize the lid from a tin of paint. She didn't have a clue what she was doing, but they'd both decided to wing it. "Then I guess it at least solves one problem." She tipped a glug of pink emulsion into the tray and then stood back to survey it. "Fuck, that's pink. Perhaps it'll be *my* body in a bin bag when Rachel sees it. Never mind, though. I'll be family soon; she'll have to forgive me." Still peering into the tray, she glanced at her watch. "Where's your girlfriend? I thought she was helping us."

After adjusting the black scarf that she was using to tie back her hair, V grabbed a paintbrush, ready to start the edges. "She'll be here." Her stomach gave a loud rumble where she hadn't eaten because Sofia had promised to bring breakfast for them all. Knowing her, it'd be a three-course banquet, and the reason for her current absence.

"Mm, well that's progress," Jess mumbled, sticking out her tongue a little as she worked around the window. "You didn't bite my head off when I called her your girlfriend this time."

"Only because I couldn't be bothered."

At eleven o'clock when they'd finished the first coat, V tried Sofia again. This was definitely pushing the boundaries of breakfast, and help, and the hole in her stomach was now worry as much as hunger. It would be completely out of character for Sofia to not show.

Peering over V's shoulder, Jess whispered, "Still no word?"

She tapped out another message. "No. Not answering any calls and I've sent three texts."

"Perhaps she changed her mind or had something else to do first."

No. Sofia wouldn't do that. She was reliable, and the worry wasn't that she'd changed her mind. It hadn't even entered V's head. She trusted Sofia implicitly and realising that threw her off a bit. She could only say the same about a handful of people. "Sofia would've said, and she'd never ignore me. She usually replies immediately but these haven't even been read. What do you reckon I should do?"

"Radical idea, but you could try going over there."

Tapping the device against her palm, this time V had to admit that Jess was right. "Can I borrow your car?"

After reaching into her pocket and dangling the keys, Jess then did a completely unnecessary sympathetic head tilt. "You know, even if she *has* changed her mind, it doesn't mean anything."

"She hasn't."

V snatched them and started towards the door. Jogging down the front path, she was about to hop into Jess's car when a taxi pulled up behind. Glancing back, she spotted Sofia in the passenger seat and diverted to open the door. She had her arm in a sling, cuts on her face, and a black eye which implied a new heavyweight boxing title, and V's throat burned with sick.

Grunting as she swung her legs around, Sofia reached out a hand for help to get out of the car. "Thank you, miele. I'm sorry I'm late."

"Sorry you're late? Bugger that, what the hell happened?"

She peered down at herself and shrugged. "I got in a minor car accident coming out of school last night. Someone went into the side of me."

A *minor* car accident? She had a full plaster cast to her armpit and was white as a sheet. "You shouldn't be here. In fact, I'm not even sure you should be out of hospital."

"Nonsense, I am fine. It is only a fracture. I have to wear this for at least six weeks, and we may need to go car shopping. By the way, there is a courtesy vehicle coming on

Monday and I want to add you to the insurance. There is no chance that I can drive it, but someone may as well."

It was a struggle to take all this information on board in such short order, and V only nodded absently. She led Sofia up the path, then tried to work through the jumble of questions as they occurred to her. "Why didn't you phone?"

"I couldn't. Mine was smashed in the accident, and I didn't know your number by heart. I went home to change quickly then got the taxi to bring me straight here because I knew you'd wonder where I was." Nodding briefly to Jess, who was now frowning in the middle of the living room with her hands on her hips, Sofia propped herself on the windowsill. "Tell me how I can help."

"By going home to bed. For goodness' sake, did you really think I was going to be more worried about painting than my—" Letting out a shot of laughter, V pressed a hand to her forehead. It was Jess's fault that she'd almost said 'girlfriend'. "Look, I'm driving you home. Don't argue."

* * *

There was a Mini shaped gap next to the house when they pulled up. V clicked off her seatbelt and got out, then opened the door for Sofia. She still didn't have much colour, and even the eye which wasn't black with bruising was dark from exhaustion. Looping her arm through Sofia's good one, V walked to the front door with her and waited to be let in.

A note stuck to the bottom of her shoe as she stepped into the hallway, and she bent to peel it off. "Angie needs shopping, and she says your blanket is ready. Guess you could actually use it now, little one."

"Funny, but how am I supposed to help her like this?"

Jabbing at the cast, Sofia let out a frustrated grunt. "She's relying on me and now I'm useless."

"Are her kids not about?" They wandered into the kitchen and V pulled out a chair for Sofia, then filled the kettle. All she was missing was a packet of Hobnobs to complete the full care package.

"No, she only has one son, and he lives all the way in Canada. It has always struck me how we are sort of in reverse positions. I have no idea what she'll do if I can't help." The thought only deflated her further, and her shoulders slumped as she drummed the fingers of her good hand on the tabletop.

Wrapping her arms carefully around Sofia's neck, V kissed her swollen cheek. "If you were serious about putting me on your car insurance, I could do it."

"Will you have time, miele? I don't want to inconvenience you."

"Inconvenience me? By picking up a few tins from the supermarket when I usually come with you? I'd say doing that and taking you to work every day is the least I can manage if I'm getting free use of a car. Besides, she's important to you which means she's important to me." Pressing her lips to the side of Sofia's head again, she closed her eyes and enjoyed holding her for a moment. There hadn't been time to take it in properly earlier, but Sofia could've been in far worse shape. "I'm glad you're okay. Not sure what I'd have done if..." Clearing her throat, she straightened and kissed the top of Sofia's head. "Let's not think about that."

"I know," Sofia whispered.

Once she'd finished the tea, V shoved Angie's note in her pocket for later and opened the fridge, crouching to look for remnants of food. If Sofia had been at the hospital all night, she was probably hungry. "How about your favourite? I reckon lasagne and chips would go down nicely right now."

"Pah. I am battered and bruised but you will never get *that* past me."

It was a relief to find her spirits lift again, and V pulled out some ham instead. "Sandwich it is. I may have to join you because I'm starving."

"Your breakfast!" Muttering something in Italian, Sofia ran her hand down her face.

"Oh, I know. How could you forget?" V teased, reaching for the big wooden chopping board. "You need to make that up to me immediately." She sucked her teeth as she laid out some bread. "And I saw nothing remotely breakfast-like in your fridge. No smoked salmon, avocado..."

"Then it is for the best because I had only planned to go to the bakery on my way. *Mamma mia*, I am slacking!" She laughed and whistled through a few bars, then stood and wrapped her arm around V's waist. With her broken arm awkwardly wedged to one side, she laid a few kisses on V's neck. "This is me making it up to you, by the way."

"Really? You mean you're not just checking that I'm making your sandwich correctly?"

"What a suggestion... but I *would* quite like some mustard on that." When she was swiped out of the way, she laughed and returned to her seat, finally smiling. As V set the sandwich in front of her, she peered up and bit her bottom lip. "Am I pushing my luck to ask for a kiss to go with that too?"

Gently cupping her cheek, V leant in and delivered, honestly happy to give her whatever she wanted right now. A kiss was the least of it. Her heart thudded as their lips met and she held Sofia there, once again flooded with relief that the accident had been no worse.

A loud knock interrupted them. V squeezed Sofia's arm and jogged through to get it for her, and as she opened the door she was confronted by a stranger in a bright yellow anorak. She had choppy brown hair and bright green eyes, which peered over V's shoulder as she stood on tiptoes.

"Oh, hello. Is Sofia here? I got a call that she'd been hurt, is she okay?"

Just as V went to step aside, the accent registered. The Welsh accent. She faltered, pressing a hand to her forehead as she realised who was standing in front of her. "Yes, sorry. Um, she's in the kitchen. You must be—"

"Anya." She held out her hand and V shook it, unsure what else to do. It wasn't her call to send the woman away. "Sofia's wife. And you are?"

Now completely immobilised, she couldn't find any words. Sofia's *wife*? "V. I'm..." There was a giant gaping pause while she tried to work out what was happening, and who she was, and what to do. "I'm... leaving."

22

"Everything okay?" Jess called from the kitchen.

V stood for a second and inhaled a great gulp of air. It felt like her first breath in the ten minutes since she'd left Anya in the hallway of Sofia's house. Then she took her coat off and hooked it on a peg, trying for a smile as she rounded the door to the living room to be handed a can of drink and a croissant. Jess had obviously given up on breakfast and gone to the shop. "Mhm."

"Are you sure you don't want to go back and stay with her for a while? I could've managed on my own for a bit, we're not *that* pushed for time."

"No, Sofia's fine." She glanced up at Jess and shrugged. "Her wife is here..."

"Her what?"

"Her wife," V clarified. "So yes, she's fine. It's all fine."

She wasn't sure who she was trying to convince, but perhaps if she said the word 'fine' enough times it might be. For now, though, all she could think of was the two of them. Alone. Anya tucking Sofia in on the sofa and making sure she was comfortable. Anya helping her change and putting her to bed. Anya cooking her breakfast in the morning. Anya everywhere, in fact, where V wanted to be. Even if it weren't reality, it was all she could picture now she'd stopped.

"Oh." Tapping the top of her can, Jess was clearly deciding what to say. "You didn't tell me Sofia was married."

"No? Well, that's probably because I didn't know." Stuffing half a French pastry in her mouth, V sighed.

"Okay…"

They both stood and ate, Jess frowning and V trying desperately not to cry. She couldn't think about her own hurt feelings right now, there was too much to do. They only had until two o'clock on Sunday afternoon to finish decorating Grace's room, move all the boxes, put together the furniture, and unpack everything. On top of that, Melissa's brother had offered to pick up a sofa from the charity warehouse for them and was dropping it off soon.

Scrunching the paper bag that'd contained her croissant, V's eyes darted around the room. "Shall we crack on? Haven't got long before the sofa arrives, and the second coat needs to dry before we can move in any of Grace's stuff."

Shuffling from side to side again, Jess shoved her hands in the pockets of her paint smeared old shorts. "Are you sure you don't want to talk about this first?"

The second little head tilt and sympathetic look of the day wasn't helping V hold this together. "Don't do that. I'm fine."

"Yeah, so you keep saying. You look like you're about to burst into tears, though, so come on. Tell me how you really feel."

V's bottom lip trembled, and she rubbed the back of her hand across her brow. "Um, not great." She wiped a tear as it broke, then strode through to the kitchen to find the bin bag they'd left in there, with Jess in hot pursuit. "But I'll get over it, okay? Sofia doesn't owe me anything. I'm just the woman she fucks in her kitchen." She cringed, regretting that the minute it was out of her mouth and knowing it wasn't true.

"Doesn't mean you're not feeling stuff."

She turned, her shoulders dropping as she heaved out another deep breath. Not that it was helping, because her lungs still felt like they were going to explode. Or maybe that was her sad little heart. "I really am okay. Just disappointed. Slightly hurt that she didn't tell me. A bit scared that I might have lost her, when she made me feel supported, and cared for, and—"

"Loved?"

"Yep," V barely got out, her voice thick and catching.

Jess took the screwed-up bag from V's hand, then pulled her into a hug and let her have a cry. "I think you need to speak with Sofia," she whispered, stroking circles in the small of V's back.

"You really *have* mellowed. There was a time when the merest hint of someone dicking me about would've sent you into a protective rage."

"I've matured. Besides, I'm not sure she *has* been dicking you about, has she? Sounds like she's been upfront. Well, about most stuff…"

"You mean besides that fact she's married? I guess it makes some sense why she only wanted this to be casual, anyway." As Jess pulled away, V wiped under her eyes with the sleeves of her sweater. "Do you think I'm overreacting?"

"No, I think you've had a shock and you're upset. It's understandable. First you thought she was seriously hurt, then you found out she has a wife she didn't tell you about. On top of trying to move today. Just don't use this as an excuse to end things, or as proof of your fears, okay?"

"What fears?"

Scratching the back of her neck, Jess let out a huff which implied she knew this might bite her. "You know that chat we had about all the reasons I don't want my mum at the wedding?" When V nodded, she continued. "Perhaps we need a similar one, because you're scared shitless of something and I think I can imagine what it is."

She needn't have worried because V already had a pretty good idea of that, too. She stuck her hands on her hips and tried to act like she wasn't bothered, even though she knew exactly what was coming and was only just prepared to hear it. "Do enlighten me, oh wise one. Come on, all the years of advice I've dished out had better be about to pay off."

"Well." After squirming a bit, Jess stood taller. "You walked away from your last proper relationship with a toddler to take care of, your career prospects in tatters, and nowhere to live. It stands to reason that you'd be nervous about letting someone else in. If you tell yourself it's only sex, even if it's clearly not, you can try to keep some control, or walk away and claim it meant nothing."

V nodded. "Yep. Okay, that was actually pretty good."

"Thank you. I am a parent now, I figured I needed to raise my game." Reaching out a hand to grasp the top of V's arm, Jess did that annoying head tilt thing again. "So, do you think perhaps you should have a chat with her?"

With another sigh, V tried to keep her newfound composure. "Nope. Because you're right. The minute I acknowledge this is about way more than just sex for me, I feel like I'm being completely clobbered. I really don't want to lose her, and it hurts."

"I know it does, but wasn't it also pretty great until about an hour ago?"

"Yeah, it was. But now she has a wife who's in her house,

and I'm torn between being upset and disappointed that she didn't tell me and crushed that I'm not the one looking after her when she's been in a sodding car accident. I already have Grace to worry about today, and now my energy is being taken up by something I probably had no business getting into, when I should focus on what's important—my career and my kid." She'd gradually lost her composure the farther she travelled until the tears were flowing, but then they were halted by a quick sniff and a rough swipe under her eyes.

"Rubbish."

"Excuse me?" Her mouth hung open now, and she frowned at Jess, challenging her to continue.

"It's rubbish. You're all over the place. A minute ago, you were telling me you'd be heartbroken to lose her—which I think is pretty accurate by the way—and now you're trying to say she's not important. Or at least not as important as work. Grace I'll let slide. Are you worried about her ex? Do you think they'll get back together or something?"

"No. God no." The frown deepened, and she shook her head. Despite what she'd imagined earlier, she knew how Sofia felt about their relationship, and had a sense of how damaging it'd been. "Anya was a nightmare and really screwed her around from what I can tell."

Jess reached into her pocket, holding up her car keys. "And you've left her there when she's already hurt and fragile?"

"Shit." Feeling a sudden shot of guilt and panic, V swiped the keys and then her jacket, turning back as she reached the door. "Jess?"

"What?"

She paused for a beat, closing her eyes as she asked, "What if she doesn't want me?"

"There's only one way to find out."

She was back again, pulling up in front of Sofia's house. How had a day of painting been so spectacularly derailed? Popping open the car door, she shoved her hands in her coat pockets and shivered against the cold. This was going to require a hitherto uncalled upon amount of bravery, and she still wasn't sure she could muster it.

As she went to knock, she heard muffled voices. Hitting hard so they could hear her, she found herself in the reverse of her earlier position. Anya pursed her lips and stood aside, folding her arms and then kicking shut the door. "You're back."

"Yep. I shouldn't have left; I need to make sure Sofia is okay."

"Why wouldn't she be?" Anya followed along the hallway.

"Perhaps because she had a car accident?" That part should at least be obvious, even if the implication about being traumatised by an ex she hated wasn't. When V reached the kitchen, Sofia was sitting on a chair, her previously white cheeks now a little flushed. They were also stained with tears, and V placed a hand on her shoulder. "Are you alright? I'm sorry I left like that; it was a bit of a shock."

"I'm sorry I didn't tell you everything," she mumbled by reply, wiping her nose on the back of her sleeve. "It's a little complicated but I'll explain later if you'll let me."

"I'll let you, but for now, do you want her here?"

As Sofia shook her head, Anya rolled her eyes. "Come

on. I only drove all the way down here because the school phoned me, and now I'm the bad guy."

"You're not the bad guy," Sofia whispered. "But it has been a tough day, and it was a surprise to see you. I appreciate you driving all the way here. Really, I do. I can pay for a hotel if you don't want to go straight home."

"Well, can I not just stay here? Hm? At least for a little while. I'll catch up with Angie, maybe make us something to eat, then drive back later this evening. Give us a chance to talk, too."

"We have nothing to talk about."

After a few moments pause, Anya's gaze settling on V's hand as it still rubbed into Sofia's shoulder, she spoke again. "Looks like we do. We *are* still married."

"We're separated. I can see whoever I want, it's none of your business."

"Suit yourself. Okay." Holding up her hands, hopefully in defeat, Anya let out a quick huff. "I'll leave, it's clearly not the time and you've been in a car accident. So long as you're alright on your own."

"She isn't on her own," V cut in.

"No, I can see that." After watching them for a few moments more, Anya nodded her head. "I'll be off then. You'll call me if you need anything?"

With no reply, she grabbed her coat and shoes from the hallway, and the door clicked closed more softly this time. Then it was only the two of them, in stony silence in the middle of the kitchen. Stroking her finger up the side of Sofia's neck, V was wondering how long she could hold her breath again before she passed out, finally letting it go when Sofia spoke.

"I'm glad you came back. We were arguing because I

wanted Anya to drive me to you, and she refused. I needed to explain."

Pulling out a chair and scraping it forward as she sat, V hooked her hands behind Sofia's knee. "Maybe save that for when you feel better."

"No, I don't want to. We really need to talk, miele. All of this. I don't think I can do it anymore."

A lump rose in V's throat, and she sat back in the seat, trying to stop her lip from quivering. "Oh."

"I should've been honest at Christmas, but I knew you didn't want things to change and—" She sniffed again and wiped the tears from under her eyes. "I'm already a mess so I might as well say it now. We promised we would reassess if we needed to, and this is me reassessing."

"You're not happy anymore?"

Shaking her head, Sofia let out a burst of laughter. "I've never been happier."

"Then I don't understand, why are you ending this?"

"This was supposed to stop me from getting my heart broken, but it hasn't. I want you all the time, when you still only want me every other weekend, and if we carry on as we are..." She shrugged and let her good arm drop by her side. "No one is to blame, I knew what I was getting into, but my feelings have gone too far. I can't risk having them hurt any further so it's time to stop. We also need to make sure we don't end up hating each other because we have to work together, so this is for the best."

Taking the limp hand and pressing it tight to her chest as she shuffled forward, V then kissed Sofia's palm. "I could never *ever* hate you, and I don't want to stop. I want to be with you, so much. I'll shout it from the rooftops at work if I have to. Earlier you were putting me on your car insurance, and we were making plans... I know this isn't really what you want."

"You're only saying all of that because you want to keep seeing me, but it will be okay." Now Sofia was tilting her head. What was it with people and doing that today? Another one, and V was going to scream. "We will both get over it."

"I don't *want* to get over it. Aren't you listening?" Her frustration rising, she leant in and placed a hand on Sofia's cheek to stop her looking at the table. If this was all pouring out, on today of all days, then she could bloody well pay attention. "I'm not saying any of this because you're trying to break up with me, I came back because I'm one hundred percent in this relationship. I know we're both scared but we're also so, so good together and we can make it work. I just need you to keep trusting me."

"I do trust you, miele," Sofia whispered as her head rolled slightly and she pressed her lips to the base of V's wrist. "I've always trusted you. Being with you has been... everything. You get me like no one else and accept me for who I am. It has been effortless to fall for you, after I wasn't sure I could open up to anyone again."

"Then keep being with me. We'll work through this— when to tell people at work, introducing you properly to Grace, sorting out the situation with Anya. You don't need to explain why you didn't tell me, because I think I already get it..."

She trailed off, not wanting to dwell on Anya. The effects of that relationship were already plainly evident, and she'd been seeing them for months. It did still hurt a little, not to have known something which was seemingly so big, but she got the sense that Sofia had shown her far more than she'd ever hidden. Those hurt feelings would heal, but the grief she knew she'd feel if she lost Sofia would leave far deeper scars.

Closing her eyes, her chest constricted as she waited.

V's response to Sofia's lips as they moved from her wrist and pressed against her own was instant. She cradled both cheeks this time, hoping that the flood of relief that'd drained away her energy and left her limbs feeling heavy wasn't premature. As she pulled back, she stroked her thumbs along Sofia's jaw.

"Please tell me that's a yes?" she whispered.

"It's a yes." Sofia's eyes glistened as she grinned.

"Good, then shall we get you tucked up on the sofa so I can move? Otherwise Grace is sleeping on that giant cuddly bloody dog tomorrow."

She laughed and leant in for another kiss. "No. I still want to help, and I'm injured so you're not allowed to argue."

23

By five, they'd finished the painting, the sofa was in, most of the boxes had been moved, and V only had to unpack it all. Sofia was made to rest but only lasted a few hours before she turned up in another taxi and set herself to work neatly organising, devising a system in the kitchen, and agonising over the correct position of plates, cups, cutlery, and other utensils. Once the beds had been erected, V joined her to find Rachel had also arrived and was helping. More precisely, she was making suggestions and winding Sofia up.

"I've always thought mugs should go near the kettle." She slid a tree of them across the work surface and Sofia moved them back.

"Perhaps, I hadn't decided yet."

Rachel returned them. "Then they can go here until you do."

"You've met." V interrupted to avoid an escalation. They'd already had enough drama for one day.

"Yes, darling. I was just helping Sofia put away a few things, although I only called in on my way home to check you have everything you need and drop off a few supplies. I doubt you've had time to fill the fridge."

She pulled it open to show off what she'd bought, which was mainly breakfast stuff and milk. It was a good job because she was right, and they hadn't even thought of that yet.

"Thank you, that's very generous."

"Have your parents been yet?"

"Nope, they're coming next weekend when Grace is here. Would you like tea? I came to make us one, we're almost finished with all the heavy stuff."

Seeing Sofia frown, still frustrated with the limitations of her injury, V stepped alongside and gave her a quick cuddle. She'd flatly refused to stay in bed any longer even when they'd tried to send her back there, but in fairness she looked a lot brighter after spending half the afternoon napping, her cheeks full of colour again.

"No, I'm not stopping. Those girls have worn me out." Reaching into her pocket, Rachel beamed as she pulled out her phone and scrolled through all the pictures from her day out.

"It went well then?"

"Very well, yes. We went shopping for the twins, then had a spot of lunch." Rachel's idea of 'well' would be significantly different to Melissa's, but at least she appeared to be making the effort and trying to spend actual quality time with her family rather than telling them what to do.

Once she'd gone, Jess was the next to leave. Gradually their numbers were dwindling, and V's stomach knotted. The prospect of her first night in the new place, not in her familiar old room, was precariously pitched between exciting and terrifying. At least Sofia was staying, but she was being quiet still and not her usual self. Everything felt topsy-turvy and off-balance.

With the beds made and some semblance of order found, V lit one of the candles they'd bought on their shopping trip and tried to chill the fuck out. Lots of people had given her wine as a moving in gift, and she poured them each a glass of red. Then she wandered into the living room and surveyed the place, happy with what they'd achieved in a day, despite all the interruptions. It was still sparse, but she could build it up over time. The important thing was that Grace's room was finished.

Coming down the stairs with a carrier bag in hand and another in her mouth, Sofia's eyebrows shot up, and she dropped them both. "Wine?"

"Uhuh, I think we need it after the day we've had." Cricking her neck, stiff and sore from lugging boxes, V passed over a glass. "I reckon we should call it quits for tonight, the place is pretty much there. Any remaining boxes I've shoved in the cupboard for now and I'll find them in several years when I next move. Why don't you sit with me while I have a bath?" With Sofia nodding firm agreement, V grabbed her lit candle, and they went upstairs. When the bath was run, she switched off the main light and slid in, Sofia settling on the toilet lid. "Are you okay?"

Smiling for what seemed like the first time all afternoon, Sofia let out a great heaving sigh and then took a sip of wine. "Yes, miele."

V twisted for her wine glass from the back of the bath. She settled back in, noting Sofia was fiddling with her fingers. The knot in her stomach giving a little twist, she had the sense that things weren't quite right. Their exchanges were more stilted than usual. Awkward, almost. "Are you sure you want to stay tonight? If you're still not feeling well, or seeing Anya has... I don't know, thrown up some stuff."

"I feel fine." Biting her lip, Sofia peeked up and then her shoulders slumped forward. "It's just... usually when we spend time together, we are very physical. I want to be with you tonight, especially after everything that has happened, but I feel a bit... frustrated? Already, that I have this cast." She rolled her eyes a little. "Six weeks is a long time and I don't want things to change between us. Not like that, anyway."

Sitting straighter, V set down her glass again. "All of this moodiness is because you're worried that we might not be able to have sex? After you could've died?" She stared, her mouth dropping open. "I can't believe I of all people am about to say this, but sex isn't *that* important. I'm just glad you're safe and we're together."

Slipping off the toilet lid and carefully lowering herself to the floor by the bath, Sofia trailed her good hand through the water, and it skimmed over V's knee. "I know that, but I'm feeling a little insecure. Perhaps that is also Anya, but..." With a slight shrug, Sofia leant her chin on the side of the tub, her fingers still trailing over V's skin. "It is important to me because I'm finally in a relationship where I can enjoy these things wholeheartedly. You usually look at me like you're going to eat me alive, and I love that, but today it has only been with pity."

Shuffling forward, V cupped her cheek and offered her a warm smile. "It hasn't been pity, it's been worry. Also, one plastered arm isn't insurmountable, I can absolutely assure you. If you're at all worried, find the box in my bedroom labelled *special friends*."

"Special friends?" Perking up, Sofia raised her eyebrows, her smile considerably lewder. "Where is this box, exactly?"

"I had to shove it in the wardrobe after Jess teased me earlier." She leant in for a kiss but then V laughed and had to pull back. "I'm sorry, I'm only relieved it's all that's been bothering you. I know it's a big deal to you, I'm not poking fun and I *do* understand, but it's... well it could be worse." If they'd come through the day and that was their biggest worry, it wasn't half bad. With another giggle, she gave Sofia a big wet kiss on the cheek. "I'm glad you're here, and I promise to keep looking at you like I want to rip off your clothes. If Anya's made you doubt for one second that you're desirable, or said that you don't measure up in any way, she can fuck herself."

"She never comes straight out and says anything. When we were together, she implied that if I tried a bit harder or was willing to work on stuff... I don't know, being so tidy or not enjoying particular things in the bedroom, I could change and that would be better. For who, I'm not sure. Her, I guess. We haven't seen each other since she moved to Wales last July and I think I'm surprised at how easily it's all been raked up again."

"You know they're not things to *work on*, though, right? If you want your car to be clean and don't want to be touched in a certain way, there's nothing wrong with you. End of story."

Now wearing a daft grin, Sofia splashed a little water. "Yes, I was just having a wobble. I'm glad I'm here too." She laughed and leant in for another kiss. "End. Of. Story."

* * *

They'd flopped out in the end, heavy with wine and exhaustion. Even Sofia's wriggling as she tried to find a comfy position didn't stop V from sleeping, she was too tired to worry much about anything else by the time her head hit the pillow. Waking early, though, she was the only one still in bed. She'd seldom ever found Sofia beside her in the morning and put it down to her being an early riser, but five-thirty was a little excessive.

Padding downstairs and into the living room, she located Sofia on the sofa with a mug of tea in hand, staring at the television set. It had been fine in V's old bedroom but now looked a bit like you were trying to watch an iPad in a cinema. Nudging her over and slipping under her right arm, V gave her a big squeeze.

"Arm giving you trouble?" she whispered.

"I'm a light sleeper." Sofia smiled and made a loud show of kissing V's forehead. At least she was in better spirits. "I will make us breakfast in a moment. Bacon, eggs, the works."

"I'll do it. You rest."

That did not seem to be the response she wanted, because she grumbled, and her smile faded into a frown. "I always make you breakfast. I may be down, but I'm not out yet."

"You're really not going to accept any more help than you have to, are you?"

"Nope. I told you, I don't want this to change anything between us."

"I know, but you're making it sound like I only want you around for sex and to cook me food. I mean, that is partly true, but..."

Sofia's frown buggered off as quickly as it came and they both laughed as she rolled off the sofa, jogging through to the kitchen. She had to accept a little help with the washing up, which was awfully convenient. It also didn't bother her when she needed assistance getting dressed, after she realised her body was going to get a healthy amount of attention.

They'd already agreed she shouldn't be around when Grace got back, but they'd see each other on Monday to sort out the car and get Angie her stuff from the supermarket. With Sofia packed off in a taxi, V spent the rest of the morning unpacking more boxes and buying food, all while nervously fretting. She'd been dreading this part the most and had no idea what the hell she'd do if Grace really hated the place and didn't want to stay. She'd have to; this time there wasn't a choice. That didn't mean it wouldn't be hard, though.

At two-thirty she stood in the window cradling a mug of tea. It was the sort of vigil Grace herself would be proud of. Her eyes fixed on the end of the front path, she sipped and worried, worried and sipped. She desperately wanted for Grace to love this place. When Jess's car finally pulled up, the knot from yesterday was back. Only this time, it'd brought friends.

Setting her mug on the windowsill, she tried some positive affirmations, but repeating "my daughter won't hate me" over and over was only reminding her that Grace may in fact hate her. For a while, at least. She pulled open the door and found a smile, from god knows where, holding out her arms as Grace flew into them.

"Hello, sweetheart. I missed you. Did you have fun with your dad?"

"Yes, Daddy got a new kitten. She's ginger and white, and her nose is all pink, and I got to name her." Wide-eyed with excitement, Grace stepped past. "And Auntie Melissa says Nan and Pops are getting a new puppy which means when we go to Wales this year, I can play with him."

She'd be talking about Melissa's grandparents, who

she'd taken to calling what everyone else did. V took a second to work through the new information that'd been delivered at speed. They hadn't talked yet about whether they'd still all go to Wales, but then she supposed there was no reason.

"*And*," Grace continued, landing on the sofa and pulling off her shoes. "Auntie Jess said that now I have a big room, you might let me have a ger-bil, because Cassie Fairhead has a ger-bil and she let me hold the ger-bil and he was so cute." She finally looked up, flush from the number of times she'd said 'ger-bil'. "She says you have to clean them out lots, but I'd be great at that because I'm used to feeding Hal and helping Auntie Melissa pick up his poop when she's too fat to do it. So, can I have one?"

Shaking her head and trying to work out which way was up, V perched on the arm of the sofa. "Um, I don't see why not. Perhaps we could look at them in the week. You have a bit of birthday money, if that's what you want to spend it on."

"Yes." Grace was definite, but then she frowned, and it seemed perhaps she wasn't. Then she absolutely was again, nodding furiously and jumping off the seat to barge past Jess and put her shoes by the door. "Tomorrow?"

"Well... I suppose so. I actually want to talk to you about tomorrow because we need to help someone, and my friend is going to lend me her car for a little while. Are you up for walking an old dog called Percy?"

"Percy? That's a funny name for a dog."

And Hal wasn't?

"He's a very funny dog. I think you're going to get on just fine."

For the first time, she was sensing that they all were.

24

They took the bus out to Sofia's on Monday morning, and Grace spent the entire trip asking questions—all about rodents. It appeared they had a plethora of people to thank for her coming around to her new living situation, realising that animals were the way to do it. In forty-eight hours, she'd gained access to two dogs, one cat, and apparently a ger-bil. Not to mention the giant fluffy thing Sofia found in Ikea and that now occupied most of her new bed.

There was a shiny silver hatchback in the parking space when they arrived. Sofia had sorted all the paperwork so V could use it while her money came through from the accident, and she leant against the passenger door dangling the keys.

Grace waved cheerily and then pointed at the cast. "What happened to your arm?"

"I had a little accident, but I am fine."

"Fran Woodhouse had her arm in plaster because she fell over her bike. Did *you* fall over your bike?"

Squinting down at Grace as she peered up, her chin

jutting out, Sofia's expression was decidedly quizzical. "Don't you mean she fell *off* her bike?"

"No. She tripped and fell over it." Looking at Sofia as if her question were ridiculous, Grace then declared proudly, "I'm getting a gerbil today."

"I know, your mummy told me. You're going to take the car to pick it up this afternoon. Have you chosen a name yet?"

"No." Shrugging as they led her down the towpath, Grace was lost in thought for a few moments.

When they reached the boat, Sofia knocked on the door before pushing it open. A couple of days had passed since the note was left, so they wanted to check in first and make sure it was still relevant. Picking up Grace and swinging her onboard, V hung back and waited for Angie to respond. The last thing she wanted was to walk in on her in a state of undress.

"Ciao Sofia!" Angie was in another floral creation, a new blanket in progress, but this time V knew to look out for Percy. He was curled up next to her, snoring as he slumbered. Little did he know that wouldn't last for long.

"Is this Percy?" With her elbows tucked in tight, Grace weaved her way through and was beside him in an instant. She knew not to pet him straight away, though, and glanced up at Angie, now with a finger hooked in her mouth and looking a little wary. "Can I please stroke him? Does he like to be stroked?"

"Oh, he loves to be stroked. Fetch down some treats from the side, will you Sofia?" Encouraging Grace up onto the sofa, Angie set aside her blanket and took the box as Sofia handed it to her. "Now, Grace. I understand you like dogs."

"I like *all* animals, but especially dogs. And cats. And gerbils." She was gently stroking Percy's head, but the dog had barely stirred, still curled in a ball with his eyes half-open and his little black nose twitching. He'd probably realised it was safest to play dead.

"We wanted to check there wasn't more you needed from the shop." Sofia stepped back and watched them.

Angie didn't even seem to have registered her arm, or the cuts on her face, she was too busy tipping biscuits into her hand and smiling at Grace. "Oh. That. No, don't worry about that my love. Just make us a cup of tea."

Pushing Sofia towards a chair in the corner, V picked up the kettle before there could be any argument. She grabbed the blue china tea jar from the work surface and pulled off the top, but it was almost empty, so she opened one of the cupboards below and stopped dead. Face to face with dozens upon dozens of neatly stacked tins, she rolled her eyes. "Um, Angie? Can I ask you a question?"

"Anything, unless it's where I've left my glasses because I'll be buggered..." Searching around herself, Angie finally caught sight of Sofia and her eyes widened. "Good grief, what's happened to you?"

"She had a car accident," V continued, not wanting to be taken off track. "But what I'd like to know is why you're storing tins for the apocalypse? Is there something we should know about? Because I've got a hair appointment next week..."

Her eyes now darting around the room, Angie held a hand to her cheek. "Oh."

"Oh?"

"Um."

Hoisting herself back up, V perched on the edge of the sofa and squeezed Angie's shoulder. She had a pretty good idea what the tins were about and wouldn't make her say it. "Why don't you keep Sofia company tonight? We've got a new ger-bil," and with that she rolled her eyes again, "I mean gerbil to settle in and I think you two have a bit to catch up on."

Or a lot, in fact, if Sofia was saying she felt like Angie was the closest thing she had to family in England, but Angie hadn't received that message. For someone who always seemed to have a great deal of emotional intelligence, Sofia had dropped the ball there.

"No, no. I don't want to be a trouble," Angie protested, holding up another treat for Grace to feed Percy.

"You won't be."

"Speaking for her now, are you?" Letting out a chuckle, Angie threw a dog biscuit at Sofia and it clouted her on the knee. "Why don't we *all* have dinner together? Hm? What do you say, young lady?" She nudged Grace's shoulder and then tickled under her arm so she squealed.

"Can we, Mum? Can Percy come for dinner?" She pulled out her cheesiest grin, her eyes pressed tight.

V looked to Sofia. "What do you reckon, Master Chef?"

"You know that is your decision." Glancing at Grace briefly, Sofia bit her lip. "I am happy to cook at your house."

"Dinner at my house it is, then." Now she just needed to figure out why the idea was making her palms sweat. They'd worked out Sofia's discomfort, but she hadn't counted on any of her own.

* * *

Back at home and with Grace upstairs staring at not one but two new gerbils—because they were social animals and absolutely couldn't be lonely—she still hadn't been able to shake that feeling of being ill at ease. Regardless, she got on with some work in the kitchen. Anyone who thought teachers got plenty of holiday were mistaken, because there were piles of textbooks to get through by the end of the week, on top of unpacking the remaining boxes.

Half an hour into it, a knock at the door interrupted her. The invasion of a spaniel, two babies, and Melissa halted all progress. She'd called in after lunch with Jess but was a lot more upfront than Angie about her motivations.

"I can't be in the house any longer, I'm LOSING MY MIND." Hoisting Izzy from the buggy while V took Ruby, all bundled up like two Michelin men with tiny heads popping out the top, Melissa followed into the lounge. Hal had already darted upstairs, hopefully not to dine on any gerbils. "And the worst part is that I mentioned to Mum about going a little stir crazy so now she's calling in almost every day. I don't know what's got into her suddenly, but ever since Christmas she's been... nice. It's creeping me out. I keep catching her smiling at me. She never smiles at me, it usually looks something like this." She scowled and let out a low grumble, before shrugging and perching on the edge of the sofa to free Izzy from her layers. "I'm not knocking it, but I am quietly waiting for her to eat my soul or something."

It didn't seem wise to get into a discussion about Rachel's change of tactic in dealing with her family, so V only laughed and diverted the conversation to safer ground. "How are things besides that? Have you missed us?"

"I won't say it's quiet, because... well, two babies, but it's definitely different. How's the new old place working out? It feels like such a long time ago now, that we were all crammed in here and I was trying to work out how to tell Jess about my *feelings*. She was absolutely oblivious, it was painful."

"You could just have come out with it, you know."

"Get lost." Melissa scoffed and slumped back, cuddling

Izzy and pulling up her trailing socks. "I was terrified. What if I'd got it wrong?"

Still trying to liberate Ruby, with a hand lost in a cloud of fleece lined sleeve, V grunted and cursed the inventor of all-in-one baby outfits. "What, like she wasn't interested?" There was an "ah-ha" as she finally discarded the offending clothing on the floor and adjusted Ruby's little trousers. "Unlikely. She looks at you like Hal looks at steak."

"Um, excuse me," Melissa protested through a gooey smile. It was unclear whether she was talking to V or Izzy, a hand hooked around her lip. "You hadn't realised her feelings either. Had she? No, she hadn't." She was definitely talking to the baby now, her voice shooting up an octave as she cooed and prodded Izzy's podge. "I'm not sure she looks at me that way anymore, though."

"Trouble in paradise?"

"Probably not, it's just I'm ready to get physical with her again and she's not picking up on any of my subtle hints."

"You mean like clubbing her over the head and dragging her back to your cave?"

"Exactly. I got into bed completely naked the other night and she asked if I was too hot. It's February. Of course I wasn't too hot." Taking a deep breath, Mellissa expelled it in a long sigh which brought her closer and closer to Izzy's tummy and resulted in a big raspberry. "We still kiss, but it doesn't go any further."

"I hate to say this twice in one conversation, but have you considered telling her?" Something like 'come here baby and shag me senseless' should do it because Jess had never been great at picking up hints. You needed to spell it out for her.

"I know, but what if she isn't into it yet? My body isn't how it was, and..." Poking her stomach, then outright wobbling it, Melissa wore a frown and tilted her head. "I don't know. I've never struggled with confidence in that department but maybe it's wavering a bit."

"I can't imagine for one second that Jess doesn't find you attractive anymore, I'm almost certain it's only her being ridiculously respectful. You know what she's like. If you're struggling with your own confidence, though, what about getting dressed up or something? Either that or take her out for dinner. Do something special because it can't be easy trying to get romantic with two spewing babies. We could look after the twins for a couple of hours."

"Oh, *we* could look after the twins. Yeah, Jess told me things had progressed. Something about unboxing, but I wasn't sure if that was related to Sofia or the move. Glad you finally took my advice."

Now the one sighing, V stood up because Ruby was grizzling. "I didn't take your advice, we're definitely not getting married, we're just... officially a couple, I suppose." And even that still felt a bit wobbly. "She's coming for dinner tonight. With her neighbour." Wafting her hand, she dismissed what she knew was coming next. "Don't ask."

"You don't sound so sure about this, what's up?"

That was a bloody good question and not the one she'd expected. "I'm not sure, I'm just apprehensive. You know when something isn't sitting right but you can't place what it is? It's been bothering me all day."

"Is it Grace? I know you've never introduced her to anyone before."

Considering for a second as she bobbed around the room, V quickly dismissed it. "Not really. She's met Sofia before, and they get on. We've already agreed to wait so Grace has time to get used to everything and they know each other better before we tell her Sofia is my girlfriend.

Truth is, though, she's settling in fine. She's been up there with those bloody gerbils, happy as Larry."

"So..."

"I'm back to not knowing." Or maybe she knew but didn't really want to admit to what it was because it involved those fears Jess had been so cautious about pointing out. "Well." She stalled, hoping Melissa would be as good at this as Jess, because their conversations were rarely deep and meaningful. They were usually more sex tips and pudding recommendations. "On Saturday, Sofia was trying to break up with me and maybe I'm waiting to make sure she doesn't flip back. She seems a bit... off at the moment, which is probably because of the accident and her ex turning up unannounced. I suppose I want to be sure it's for real, and she won't get scared and try to run away again. Does that make sense?"

"Perfect, so take a leaf out of your own book and tell her."

"I had a horrible feeling you were going to say that."

Stood in the kitchen with Sofia humming as she prepared their meal, V knew what she needed to do—talk. Simple. Easy. They'd done enough of it the other day, so why did this feel like such a big deal? Perhaps because it was no longer in the heat of the moment, with all that emotion running red hot, and she was understanding where both Angie and Melissa were coming from in keeping their mouths shut.

It was the first of what was probably a long line of 'real' conversations they needed to have if this would work, and she wasn't used to doing those. 'Real' conversations in the past had involved the lines "I'm not happy and moving out" or "by the way I'm pregnant". They went nowhere positive, and she suddenly felt horribly vulnerable.

"You're in an excellent mood," she started, sidling up to Sofia and bumping their hips together as she danced along to her own little tune. Grace was happily playing games with Angie in the living room, so they had a bit of time alone. "What's brought this on?"

Sofia slid a chopping board with three carrots and her peeling contraption across the work surface, with the implication that she needed them hacked to bits. That's what she'd get, anyway. "Why shouldn't I be? My arm hurts less, I am cooking for some of my favourite people, and I have an entire week off work." She wrapped her good arm around V's waist, and their hips moved in time as she continued to hum. "Plus, I was worried how your move would go but I can see that Grace is happy and you are coping, and that is a big relief. I'm so proud of you for doing this, miele."

"Thanks, I'm proud of me too." Pausing for a second to gather her confidence, V snatched a quick kiss. "I need to talk to you about something, though."

Lacing their fingers together and then spinning her around, Sofia pulled them back together again. "Anything."

"It's just, I hate to bring this up when you're so happy, but there's something bothering me, and I don't want us to keep any secrets from each other." She squeezed the top of Sofia's arm as they box danced around the kitchen to literally nothing but the sound of mince searing on the hob. "That's not a dig at you for keeping a secret by the way, but... well, I think Saturday shook my trust a bit. I hadn't realised until today when we arranged for you and Angie to come over for this lovely family-type night and it was niggling. Do you understand why?"

"Yes," Sofia whispered, a lilt of sadness in her voice as the dancing suddenly stopped. She pulled back and dabbed a kiss on V's lips. "I'm sorry that I made you doubt me. I'm sorry that I doubted us. However much time it takes for you to trust me completely, you have. Grace too. I will be here as your friend and by the time you tell her, whenever that is, she will know that I am looking out for you and can be trusted. Okay?"

Grasping Sofia's good hand and squeezing it tight, V's face scrunched. "You *want* to be a part of Grace's life, though? Because it's a big deal and I get that. You are *sure*?"

"I do, yes. I am committed to you, and to her, and building a relationship. I will let you set the parameters, but... definitely yes." Another kiss, and then she smiled again. "For now, will you chop my carrots?"

V laughed, grateful for the tension breaker. She nudged her eyebrows as everything unclenched. "Is that a euphemism?"

"No. I am far more straightforward than that."

"Like you were with Angie?" Taking the carrots and peeler, V began slicing them while Sofia grimaced and bit her fingers as she watched. "How on earth didn't you realise that she was sending you for bloody tins because she was lonely?"

"I took her at face value! She asked for tins, I got her tins. I feel bad that I became too engrossed in my own problems and didn't consider hers, but I am rectifying that. We have already spoken, and she will come for dinner once a week." Pausing for a second, Sofia smirked. "She asked if we could play Scrabble next time."

Stopping completely and pushing back the carrots, V stuck her hands on her hips. "Have you been playing Scrabble with other women?"

The smirk turned to a far more earnest expression. "No, I haven't played Scrabble with anyone but you since the day we met." She wrapped her good arm around V's waist and smiled as they kissed.

"I'm glad we had this chat."

"Me too. Never worry about telling me the truth." Stepping back and holding up her pinkie finger, Sofia waited for V to wrap her own around it. "Complete honesty from here on in. I swear. Starting with telling you what Grace is naming the gerbils. I heard them discussing it earlier."

"Dear god, what?" The possibilities were endless where Grace was concerned. She'd probably called them 'Cassie' and 'Fairhead' just to piss off her friend with the single gerbil who'd sparked this sudden fascination.

"Angie was sharing pictures of her husband, Malcolm, so she's called them Angie and Malcolm. Isn't that cute? She said that since Angie was sad and lonely, this way she could come and talk to Malcolm whenever she liked." As her bottom lip jutted out, Sofia wiped a fake tear from her eye.

V only laughed again. "Of course she has. I don't know why I didn't immediately assume we'd have a gerbil called Malcolm rather than something cute like Biscuit or Whiskers."

25

"Are you ready to go?" Sticking her head around the door of Sofia's classroom, V found her sitting at the desk, struggling to write something in black marker on an A3 sheet of paper. It kept moving, and she was contorting herself trying to hold it down. "Leave that for now." V dumped her bag in the corridor and stepped behind, reaching both arms over Sofia's shoulders to take the pen and click the lid in place.

"How will I survive another week like this?" Sofia held up her plastered arm, which was now covered in the signatures of her entire form group. With any luck she was having it taken off following a check-up on Monday—the first day of the Easter holiday. The trouble was, she'd originally thought she'd be out of it by now and was becoming impatient.

"It's not a week, it's three days." Taking the cap back off the marker and crouching to the side, V drew a heart with both their initials in. "Why don't we swing by the pub for a quick drink? I don't need to pick up Grace from the child-minder for over an hour." And neither of them had been in weeks. Sofia usually went every Friday but had been using her arm as an excuse. She was fooling no one. "We can celebrate the end of another term while we catch up with people. Come on, stop moping."

"You are very difficult to say no to."

"Yeah, well. I have the advantage of knowing you find me irresistible." As they collected up their things, V grabbed Sofia's coat and wrapped it over her shoulders. She couldn't get it on properly because of the cast, but even in April it was still chilly. "I'm also your driver so you sort of have to do what you're told."

Sofia had upgraded the courtesy vehicle to another Mini, now the insurance money had come through. She'd opted for a five door instead of three, "just in case", which V had quickly worked out was Sofia's way of saying she was making space to accommodate Grace at some point.

They wandered out to the car park and hopped into it. Five minutes later they were pulling up in town, and Sofia was dutifully following V into the pub. The other teachers would be crowded around the same table they always were, and once V had ordered a glass of red and a Coke, they ambled down to join. Bob was sitting and staring into the bottom of a pint, and this time V couldn't resist asking.

"You look so depressed. Are things still bad?" She pulled out a chair for Sofia and set the wine in front of it, then nudged another seat over and sat as close as she dared. It didn't bother her anymore who saw them, but Sofia was still wary after having everyone gossip about her last relationship. It was, V suspected, the reason she was keeping her distance.

Bob sighed and drummed his fingers on the side of his glass. "I suppose you'll find out soon enough. My wife has left me. I'm staying in a grotty B&B and she won't even let me see the dog which was about the only family member who didn't completely ignore me."

Sofia winced as she sat. "I'm sorry, Bob. Why didn't you tell anyone? I would have offered you a bed had I known you were desperate." She seemed to regret that and caught V's eye, frowning and faltering a few times before speaking again. "Well, if it weren't for my accident, anyway."

"I don't want to be a burden on anyone." He rubbed a hand over his brow and left it there, stroking the deep furrows. "I suppose it's all my own fault. This had been coming for a long time and my mind has been elsewhere."

"Elsewhere?"

"Mm." Bob continued to mumble, a little colour coming to his cheeks, and he set down his glass on the table. "There's someone else. Someone I have feelings for and have for a while. When we came for Christmas drinks, something sort of... happened."

"I'm not surprised she chucked you out, in that case," V blurted. After all that sob story he'd spun about his wife being lovely and not feeling attractive anymore, he had a bit of a nerve. "Is it really what you're down about, though, or is it that you want this other woman? At least I presume it's a woman..." She looked to Sofia again, and they each smirked, but Bob was incredulous.

"Of course it's a woman!" he bellowed, so loud that the entire group turned to stare at him. Once they'd resumed their discussions, he lowered his voice and continued. "She said it was a mistake. Broke my heart, truth be told."

"I'm not sure how I feel sympathising over that, but I'm sorry. Does she know?"

He shrugged, his shoulders slumping forward as his entire body deflated. "No point telling her. My marriage has been in the toilet for years, we both know that, and I don't suppose there's any hope of this other woman changing her mind. I must accept that there are no second chances at love. Not when you get over forty, anyway."

Sofia's eyes grew comically wide. "Thank goodness I am still a few weeks from that, then." She kicked his shoe to rouse him from staring at a splodge of ketchup on the carpet. "There is always a chance for love. Don't give up."

"According to who? All love does is kick you in the privates. You know that just as well as I do." He folded his arms and sank back as if he considered that the last word, but Sofia hadn't finished. She regarded Bob with a warm smile, some of her usual calm energy returning. It was good to see after watching her struggle over the past few weeks. She was becoming more herself again.

"Do I?" She slipped her arm from the sling and pointed to the heart V had drawn before they left school. "Perhaps those knocks can make you wary, but they should never stop you from hoping. Trust me that it will be worth taking a chance on love when it comes."

This perked him up, but perhaps not for the intended reasons. "You dark horse." He leant forward with his hands on his knees, grinning at Sofia. "Does this mean you're seeing someone? You kept that quiet, who is she?"

Sofia caught V's eye again, which was still on the plaster cast. She could see where this was going and felt suddenly apprehensive, but not because she'd changed her mind about wanting people to know, it was more that she knew Sofia really didn't. "Yes, I am seeing someone."

"For how long?"

"Since September."

"September?" He looked down at his watch. "Bloody hell, that's seven months."

"I am aware. Anya and I are getting a divorce—finally—

and I couldn't be happier. So, you see, you cannot give up hope. If you care for this woman, tell her. Better still, show her." Sofia balled her fist and shook it. When she caught the shocked expression it'd elicited from V, though, she backpedalled. "I only just found out." Her eyes were pleading, but they needn't be. "Your friend Rachel put me in contact with someone the other week and Anya has agreed to proceed."

"Well, at least you didn't start shagging someone from school this time. You've learnt your lesson there." Then Bob muttered, "Wish I had, too."

All the colour drained from Sofia's face, and she took a big gulp of her wine. She didn't make eye contact this time, letting out a small sigh as if resigned to what was about to happen. "Yes, I suppose." Still struggling to find her confidence, she cleared her throat. "Well, actually, there is something I need to tell you—"

"We need to go," V interjected, suddenly filled with panic. She didn't want Sofia doing this for the wrong reasons. The rush to get a divorce and to tell people at work felt like it was some way of repenting, and it wasn't necessary. It was none of anyone else's bloody business. "Sorry, but I just realised Grace has to be picked up early tonight. Won't have time to drop you at home if we don't go now." She stood and grabbed her jacket from the back of the seat, ushering Sofia out of hers. "Come on."

"But—"

"No buts, shift." Now pushing Sofia away from the table, V turned back to wave at Bob. "Sorry, see you after Easter!"

Once they were outside, Sofia turned to halt them, her face written with an understandable amount of confusion. "What on earth? I was going to tell him about us."

"I know you were. Don't."

"But—"

"You're trying to prove you're committed, and I get it, but you don't have to do this for me. I never needed you to blab to the whole school, and I didn't need you to fast track your divorce. Okay? Do it when you're ready, or don't, but... no one else matters. Apart from Grace. She matters a lot, so how about we pick her up and go for a burger?"

Even the thought of a greasy burger didn't seem to discourage Sofia, who let out a deep sigh. "I'm sorry, I just wanted you to see..." She trailed off and her face broke into a big soft grin. "No. You're right. Let's eat."

* * *

"Cassie Fairhead says when she comes over next week, she's going to hold my gerbils, but I told her she couldn't because she won't be careful enough and Mum, does she *have* to hold the gerbils? Because they're my gerbils and if I don't want her to, I don't think she should, even though she let me hold her gerbil. But she doesn't know as much as me about gerbils, or dogs, and when I told her I walk Percy now too, she said it was silly because they weren't even my dogs but that doesn't matter because all dogs need to be walked even if they aren't yours really and Cassie Fairhead is dumb."

"Um," V stalled, trying to unpick the jumble of words that'd fallen out of her daughter at speed. "What?"

"Cassie Fairhead," Grace continued, becoming further exasperated as she folded her arms, peering into the rear-view mirror from the back seat.

"If you don't want her to hold your gerbils then that's your decision. And as for walking Percy, it's a lovely thing to do and you're quite right. Perhaps don't call Cassie dumb, though. That's less lovely."

They pulled into the supermarket car park again having heard every detail of Grace's day, including her various arguments with Cassie Fairhead. Sofia had sat through the entire journey with an amused smile on her face and now turned, hooking her good arm over the back of the seat.

"Your mum is right. When I had dinner with Angie on Monday evening, Percy told me how much he appreciates your walks."

Letting out a derisive laugh, Grace tilted her head. "Don't be *silly*, Sofia. Dogs can't talk."

"Yes, they can! He said ruff ruff! I ruv my walks with Grrrrrace."

Belly laughing this time and clipping off her seat belt, Grace waited for the door to open for her and then slid out, adjusting her school dress. "I'm not *dumb* like Cassie Fairhead."

"I know you're not. You're just about the cleverest kid I've ever met."

"It's true, I am very clever." She nodded and rounded the car, taking hold of Sofia's hand.

The burger place was styled like an American diner, with red booths and an old-style jukebox in the corner. Grace was given a balloon on entry and climbed up onto the seat, sliding over so V could sit next to her and then shuffling back so they pressed against each other.

Wrapping an arm around her shoulder, V grabbed a menu and held it open between them. "What would you like?"

"A burger and a pink milkshake please."

"No fries?"

"No, I'll eat Sofia's." Sticking out her tongue, she found one shoot back and hid behind the menu, giggling to herself.

"Just like you stole my biscuit at Angie's the other day? You told me it was Percy, but I knew it wasn't." Laughing as she reached to pull the menu away, Sofia sent Grace wriggling into V's side to hide her guilty little eyes.

"I don't know *what* you're talking about, Sofia," she protested, wiping the hair from her face and recomposing herself. Sticking her nose high, she was indignant.

Once the waiter had been to take their order, V climbed back down from the booth and held out her hand to Grace. "Come on. We need to wash our hands."

"Doesn't Sofia need to?"

"Yep, but she can go after us. She's looking after the table."

With a great huff, Grace jumped down from the seat, tugging V's hand and leading her towards the toilets. Inside, she stood on the little step that was left under the basins so that kids could reach and held out her hands, waiting for the water to be turned on for her.

The minute Grace said the words "Cassie Fairhead" again, V laughed and flicked the tap. She'd returned to the importance of dogs being walked, regardless of their age and the age of their owners, and it was once again spilling out at speed. When she finally ran out of steam, hopping off the stool with clean hands and wiping them on her dress, she closed with "and so, we need to take her to meet Percy when she visits next week so she *understands*."

"I'm not sure Angie's boat will fit everyone, sweetheart." Or that Percy would cope with the attention of a second rambunctious six-year-old.

"Cassie Fairhead is only small."

"I know she is, but..." There wasn't really an answer to that. Instead, V held the door open and Grace ambled back, casually taking the seat next to Sofia this time.

"Sofia, do *you* think Cassie Fairhead will fit on Angie's boat?"

"Excuse me?"

"I want to take Cassie Fairhead to see Percy so she can see I'm not weird."

That was very different to what she'd said earlier, and V's look of worry matched Sofia's. "Why did she say you were weird, sweetheart?"

With a little shrug, Grace pulled herself onto her knees and leant across the table, fiddling with the salt and pepper pots. "*Because*... she says Auntie Jess isn't really my auntie, and Auntie Melissa isn't really my auntie, and it's strange that I spend so much time with Angie because she isn't my real granny, not like her granny who's boring and smells funny, and that I shouldn't say auntie if they're not my real family because it confuses people."

Exchanging more glances with Sofia, V's frown deepened. There was always a chance something like this would come up, but that didn't mean she was any more prepared to deal with it or had a bloody clue what to say. "Well, Cassie Fairhead may not be dumb but that doesn't mean she knows everything." That seemed a decent enough place to start, but the rest was... complicated. How did you explain the concept of family to a six-year-old when they were having their little world challenged for the first time? "There are some people who are your family because you're related to them, like Granny, and then there are other people who choose to have you in their family because they love you and want you there, like Auntie Jess. Perhaps Cassie Fairhead finds that a little weird because she only has the first kind of family, and that's why she's confused."

Considering for a second, salt pouring into her hand, Grace then glanced up. "I think *she's* the weird one because she only has *one* gerbil when they get lonely. If she knew anything, she'd have at least two."

"Well... quite." It wasn't entirely the point, but if it helped, all the better. "I expect what she really means is *different*, and weird is the word she's chosen, but different isn't bad. Different is just... different."

Sofia smiled and took the salt pot, sliding it out of reach while there was still some left in there. "I think difference is a wonderful thing. Wouldn't life be boring if we were all the same? You can tell Cassie Fairhead all about your family, and you can learn about hers."

Dumping the salt from her palm and bashing her hands together, Grace twisted, so she was almost peering at Sofia upside down. "Where are *your* family, Sofia?"

"In Italy. I only get to see them twice a year. They still know I love them very much, though."

"But don't you get lonely?"

"Sometimes. I am a bit like you, though, because I have people who I consider my family but am not related to. They are there for me when I feel lonely, and I am there for them."

"You have an Auntie Jess, too?"

Sofia laughed and began wriggling out of the other side of the booth. "Something like that. I am going to wash my hands now, because our food will be here in a second."

Once she'd gone and they were on their own, V continued the conversation. She had no idea how to approach this either and was very much winging it while waiting for her parenting manual to come through. Some days she just had to close her eyes, pray a bit, and hope she wasn't getting it all entirely wrong. "How are you getting on with Sofia, sweetheart?"

"She's funny. Did you hear when she pretended to talk

like Percy?" Giggling and finally righting herself, she sat straight in the seat as the waitress delivered their food on a big silver tray. Her eyes widened, and she tried to still her hands in her lap.

With the woman gone, V continued. "Yes, I heard." She laughed a little as Grace side-eyed the fries she'd openly admitted an intention to steal. "How would you feel if Sofia was my girlfriend?"

"What, like Daddy has a girlfriend?"

"Yes, and like Auntie Jess and Auntie Melissa are girl-friends." Although on second thoughts, perhaps not quite like them, because they were too disgustingly mushy with one another. "I'd like her to stay sometimes, and for you to get to know her better. Would that be okay?"

It felt a bit odd, asking for permission from a six-year-old, but it wasn't really permission. She just couldn't think of any other way to word a question that'd confirm whether the idea would cause Grace any psychological damage.

"Like a sleepover?"

"Yes, a bit." Not the type she had with Cassie Fairhead, but that comparison would do. "And I might want to hold her hand or kiss her. I know you're not used to me doing that with anyone, but it wouldn't change anything between us, I still love you more than anything in the world. The way I love Sofia is very different."

Grace shrugged. "Okay."

"Okay?" What did okay mean? She'd happily sat down and started slurping on her pink milkshake, nicking one of Sofia's chips before she'd even come back from the bath-room. That had to be a good sign, didn't it? "I was thinking we could all have a day out this week, what do you reckon?"

Her eyes lit up, and the straw dropped from her mouth. "Zoo?"

Rolling her own eyes, V laughed. "Yes, okay. If you want to go back to the zoo that badly, we can."

The level of emotional scarring did, on first inspection, seem minimal. The bigger worry now was whether the grown-ups would feel the same after being dragged around the zoo and lectured on the importance of suitably large enclosures.

26

Sofia held up both arms, free of plaster, and did a spin on the doorstep. She'd been out of it for four days and had to do exercises to restore proper movement but was delighted and hadn't shut up about it since they left the hospital. "Are you ready?" She stepped inside and planted a quick kiss on V's lips.

As V shut the door, she called up to Grace, who'd been picking something to wear for almost an hour. God only knew how long she'd take to prepare for the wedding in a few weeks, if this was the effort that went into a simple day out. "I am, but my daughter is turning into a bit of a diva. I hope you're ready for this."

Sofia leant forward with another big grin and kissed her more delicately this time. "I am very excited," she whispered. "I hope it goes well."

"Don't worry. If it doesn't, we'll feed her to the lions or something."

"Does London Zoo have lions?"

"I don't know. There'll be something carnivorous and hungry." V laughed and cupped Sofia's cheek, unable to resist another kiss. It was cute that she was so into this. Then she turned to yell up at Grace again. "Come on, sweetheart. We'll miss the train if you take any longer." When Grace appeared at the top of the stairs in a tutu, pink tights, her pink Converse, and a mismatched sweater, she didn't have the heart to argue. "Beautiful. Shall we go?"

"Wait, I need my bag." Grace ran back into her room, her feet thumping on the flimsy landing. Then she re-emerged with her unicorn backpack, which in fairness did really set off the look. She hopped down the stairs, grasping for the handrail, and then peered up with a cheesy grin to rival Sofia's. "Now I'm ready."

"Good. Are you going to say hello to Sofia or are we dispensing with the niceties now?"

She turned her head. "Hello Sofia. What's your favourite animal?"

As Sofia thought for a second, she let out a loud "umm". Then she opened the door so everyone could filter through. "I was going to say penguins, but they are technically birds. I think I will go for monkeys."

"Oh, I *love* the monkeys."

Grace trotted off in front of them, still chattering away, and once V had locked the door, she slid her hand into Sofia's. "Okay?" she whispered.

"Mhm, I'm taking your lead."

"As ever."

Twenty minutes later they'd boarded their train and sandwiched Grace between them. She pulled a book from her backpack, along with three juice boxes and three cereal bars. "Would you like one, Mummy?"

"When did you pack all of this?"

"Last night." She dropped a juice box in Sofia's lap, then re-zipped her bag and put it under the seat. Piercing her drink with the straw, she opened her book and sucked hard as she read. Then, when Sofia stood and moved to the opposite seat, Grace looked up momentarily before following her.

Once she'd resettled, resting back against the seat, Sofia leant forward to mouth at V, "What does that mean? She wants to sit with me."

It was hard not to laugh at Sofia's desperation to analyse. "I don't know," she mouthed back. "Just go with it."

Sofia relaxed and peered over Grace's shoulder, sipping from her carton, and smiled when she shuffled closer. The book was half rested on her knee so she could see properly, and Grace kept glancing up to make sure she'd finished with the page before turning it.

Once they'd both reached the end, Grace closed the book and tucked it back in her bag, then pushed past their legs to stare out of the window. "When Auntie Jess took me to the zoo, we had ice cream." She turned and put her hands on Sofia's knees. "Will we have ice cream today?"

Sofia shrugged. "I expect so, if your mum lets us."

"You have to ask Mummy for permission too?" As Grace frowned, one of her little pouts emerged.

"Yes, I do. Neither of us is having ice cream without her say so, which means we both need to be very good."

"Huh." She gave up on Sofia for now and climbed into V's lap, resuming her stare out of the window with her feet swinging.

As V dabbed a kiss to the top of Grace's head, she stroked away some errant strands of hair. "Are you okay, sweetheart?"

"Yes," she mumbled. "I just wanted a cuddle."

"Because you want ice cream later?" Her face broke into a cheeky grin and she shot Sofia a knowing look which said it all. "I thought so, but I'll take it." V hugged her close and rocked her, nudging Sofia with a foot when she regarded them with a warm smile.

* * *

Two hours later Grace was enjoying her ice cream in front of the lion enclosure, tilting her head while she licked and splattered Mr Whippy all up her nose. "How do they get the lions into the zoo without being eaten?"

"Carefully." Sofia stood behind her, sucking an orange ice lolly with her other hand shoved in her pocket. It must have been a relief to do that again, after over six weeks.

"One day I'm going on safari."

"Is that so? Where are you planning to go on safari?"

Imagining South Africa, or Kenya, V laughed when her reply came back. "Longleat."

"Sweetheart, that's a safari *park*." A very nice one, probably, but very definitely in the south of England where there were still big electric fences keeping everyone where they needed to be. "It isn't quite the same thing as an actual safari, where the animals are in the wild."

They walked on, having planned to get to the penguin beach for the next show. Grace had been insistent that Sofia shouldn't miss it and kept asking for the time. They passed through the butterfly house with her tugging on V's sleeve, not at all interested in anything that only ate leaves and wasn't either terrifying or cute.

Finding them a seat, she wedged herself in between with a hand firmly planted on each of their knees as if to hold them there. "Mummy, are we having burgers again tonight?"

"No, we're going home for food. Sofia has offered to cook for us. That was nice of her, wasn't it?"

"But I don't want Sofia's cooking, I want burgers." She pouted again and fell against V's side, head-butting a boob.

"Steady on, that hurt." Nudging her back up, V wrapped an arm around her back. "We ate out the other night and the zoo is expensive. We're not paying for burgers again." Spotting Sofia's mouth open and knowing she was about to offer to pay, V tugged on the bottom of her top and shook her head. She wasn't here to fund Grace's burger addiction. "No more about it, please. Sofia is a great cook, it was very generous of her to offer, and we're having that. Now stop sulking because the penguin keeper is coming out and the show's going to start."

She was easily distracted, jumping up and standing with her nose pressed to the glass. It was quiet today, so they'd bagged seats at the front.

As Sofia shuffled over to close the gap, she leant in and whispered, "I can buy us a meal."

"I know you can, and I appreciate the offer, but if I'd wanted a sugar daddy, I'd have taken up one of those many offers over the years. Besides, Grace needs to learn she can't click her fingers and get what she wants."

She didn't include herself in that, though, and took the kiss she wanted before wrapping Sofia's arm around her own shoulder for a cuddle. The sun was shining, and she moved the sunglasses which had been propped on top of her head down to cover her eyes, laughing as Grace jumped and spun around with excitement. The penguin keeper was throwing fish into the pool and it didn't seem to matter that she'd seen the same show before, she watched with the same pure joy.

"To be six again." Sofia let out a sigh. "All that innocence."

"Innocence? Do me a favour, she knew exactly what she

was playing at earlier trying to manipulate you into buying her ice cream. Don't be fooled by the gap teeth and the tutu."

"So cynical, miele!"

V peered over the top of her shades and wore a devilish smile. "Oh, really? Just you wait…"

Once the show was over and they'd taken pictures, they did another loop so Grace could see the monkeys again, but she was flagging. Her arms had gone all droopy, and she looked like one of the primates, so they decided to call it a day.

"Can we go to the gift shop, Mum?" She tugged on V's sleeve again, trying to pull her over.

"We can look, but you spent your birthday money on the gerbils." And a bit more besides.

"It doesn't cost to look." She did that exasperated head shake she always pulled out when she felt her statement should be obvious and then slumped towards the door.

"Fine, if you really want to look, be my guest."

Following her in, V hung back and fiddled with some over-priced pens while Grace dragged Sofia towards the cuddly toys. She knew exactly what was going to happen, but Sofia had been warned. If Grace liberated her of twenty quid for a stuffed penguin, it was her own doing for being so cocky.

"So, er, how did that go?" As they walked out ten minutes later, V peered around, trying to get a glimpse at what was hidden under Sofia's arm.

"Nothing, miele. A memento for myself. To remember the day."

"Uhuh."

They had to walk through the park to get back, and

Grace had run off ahead, chasing pigeons. She may not have that penguin yet, but she would.

Back at home, Grace had a second wind and insisted on helping cook dinner. Stood on a chair that butted up against the work surface, she'd ordered Sofia around the kitchen and asked innumerable questions about what she was doing, expecting a blow by blow explanation. Then, with food out the way, she'd gone off to play with her gerbils for a while, far less interested in the washing up.

Thinking they may get a little time alone, V snapped the tea towel against Sofia's arse and then dumped it on the draining board, before stepping behind and cuddling her while she did that last couple of dishes. "I have good news for you, because when Jess lived here, she put a lock on the master bedroom door, and it's still there. So, when Grace goes to bed, we can have some adult fu—"

That thought was interrupted by Grace, who had appeared in the kitchen doorway wearing her pyjamas and an excited grin. She had her teddy in one hand and a blanket in the other, trailing across the linoleum. "You need to get undressed."

"Excuse me?" V's eyes widened, and she pressed her hand to a scorching cheek as she jumped back. How much of that had her six-year-old daughter heard?

"For our sleepover, Mummy. Can we have popcorn?"

"Sleepover?"

"Yes, you said we were having a sleepover with Sofia tonight. I've fed Malcolm and Angie, picked a film, and I'm ready."

We? There had been no 'we' mentioned, but she looked

so excited that it was hard to say no. "Well, okay sweetheart. Sure, I guess we can have popcorn." With any luck she'd crash out anyway, after such a big day. "Why don't you set up the film while we finish this and make it?"

She raised both arms in the air and shouted "okay" before running off again, the blanket and teddy dragged along behind her.

Resuming her cuddle, V kissed Sofia's back while she dried her hands. "Still want to be with me?"

Sofia laughed. "Well, I don't know..." Dumping the towel, she spun around and tucked her hands in the back pockets of V's jeans, giving her arse a little squeeze. "Relax. I am a teacher, an aunt, and in a few weeks, I will be forty. As a grown-up, and someone who is around a lot of children, I can promise you I had some idea what I was getting into when I fell for a single mother. Not for one minute did I imagine we would neatly package her off to bed at the end of the day..."

"You didn't? Because I'd always hoped I'd be able to do that at some point." Raking her fingers up the back of Sofia's neck, V laughed when she purred like a kitten. "Thank you for dinner. And for today."

"I've enjoyed myself. I know it won't all be fun trips to the zoo and popcorn in front of the television, but it's been... fun. In fact, there's something I want to run by you."

"Beach holiday in the Seychelles?" Or a beach holiday anywhere, for that matter.

"Close. I've been thinking about what I'd like to do for my birthday, and I don't want to make a big deal, but do you think Jess and Melissa would like to come over for cake? I'd like to get to know them better, too, and perhaps by then you two could... stay over?"

With a big grin, V leant in for a kiss. "You had me at cake."

She put Sofia down to make popcorn, hearing the first strains of the title music drifting in from the living room, and then they both ran upstairs to change quickly. Settling in on the sofa with Grace wedged between them, they pulled up a blanket and got about twenty minutes in before she flaked out, her head lolling into the popcorn.

"Welp, that lasted about as long as expected." Stroking a hand through Grace's hair, V carefully extricated the bowl and watched her slump against Sofia.

"Would you like me to carry her up?"

Going to do it herself, V stopped. "Can you manage with your arm?"

"Should be able to."

Sofia wriggled to free her good arm and wrapped it around Grace. Haphazardly gathering her up, she grunted as she stood. They all wandered upstairs, and V pulled back the cover. Holding out her hand to stop Sofia for a second, she pointed to the middle of the bed.

"What is this?" she whispered.

Sofia shrugged, moving the cuddly toy out of the way as she carefully lowered Grace's head onto the pillow. "Oh, has she not always had a penguin? Funny, isn't it? Because I've got one that looks identical."

"Yes, isn't that a funny coincidence..."

27

Back in Sofia's kitchen for what felt like the first time in weeks, V strained to pin up a 'happy birthday' banner over the window. "Don't you want to see *your* friends for your birthday?"

"I *will* see my friends, but I am forty." Sofia grunted as she tried to keep from toppling with the weight on her shoulders. She'd never had a problem with a pair of legs wrapped around her head before, but usually she wasn't upright. "I can have as many celebrations as I desire."

"Okay, but they're going to make a mess. You know that don't you?"

"Relax, miele."

She was trying to, but the idea of having three kids and a dog in Sofia's nice house was giving her palpitations. Since their trip to the zoo they were spending a lot more time at V's house, where sticky marks didn't matter. Here, it was likely to be a different story.

"I am relaxed," she lied, slipping off Sofia's shoulders. "This is lovely, and I am very grateful that you're making such an effort, I just don't want you to regret it."

"Am I really so set in my ways?" She reached for a jar of rice at the back of the work surface and popped off the lid, sprinkling a handful of grains over the marble. "There you go. See? I can make a mess."

"You don't have to do that." V wiped the rice into her palm and stepped on the pedal bin to discard it. "I wasn't criticising you at all. I love your ways, and how neat everything is here. Perhaps it's my issue." She wrapped her arms around Sofia's waist and kissed her chin. "I'm used to coming here and relaxing, only the two of us. Maybe I'm struggling a little to let that go and share you."

Sofia dipped her head to kiss V's nose. "There is plenty of me to go around, but we can cancel if you don't want to do this."

The look of disappointment on her face showed they couldn't simply cancel without repercussions, but V wouldn't in any case. She wanted Sofia to be part of their lives—properly so—and that meant submitting to a space invasion. "I want this, it's just a change. Grace is sat upstairs on the sofa where we're usually having rampant sex. It's like two worlds colliding." As V laughed she squeezed Sofia tighter. "I'm not sure whether it's fear of losing a sanctuary, or of being hurt, or—" She shook her head. "I don't know, but I do know I want to be with you. I trust you, with my heart and Grace's."

"And I will be very gentle with them," Sofia whispered as she brushed V's lips with the lightest of kisses. "Well, if you discount the amount of butter and sugar I put in the cake."

She glanced behind herself at the decadent creation, topped with royal icing and then utterly destroyed with glitter and sparkles where she'd put Grace in charge of decoration. They'd spent all morning together in the kitchen, and Sofia had even bought Grace a little pink apron. It now hung over the back of a chair covered in smears of batter.

"You are very cute with Grace. It's almost making me wonder who you're more interested in, me or her." V laughed again, having entirely meant it as a joke, but Sofia grew flustered and shook her head as she tried to justify herself.

"N-no. I adore Grace but—"

She was halted by a kiss which occupied her mouth, and then her hands as they curled into V's hips. Hooking her arms around Sofia's shoulders, V planned to keep her there for as long as possible before everyone else descended and they had to cool it. She didn't get very far, before a loud "muuuum" caused them to jump apart. When she turned, Grace was standing on the stairs, staring at them.

"Yes, sweetheart." She straightened out her T-shirt and flicked the hair off her face as she stepped over to place a hand on the metal balustrade. "Are you okay?"

Grace tilted her head and yawned. She'd clearly been asleep, if the imprint of a remote control on her cheek was anything to go by. "You're always kissing."

V cleared her throat and tried to keep from smiling. "We kiss sometimes, yes. Is that a problem?"

"No, just saying. Can I please have a drink?"

Sofia sprang into action, opening the cupboard next to the sink and pulling out a pack of juice boxes. She tore away the plastic holding them all together and held one out. "I got the apple ones you brought on the train."

Was there anything she hadn't been out to buy? There was a new colouring book, pencils, snacks, a pink fleece blanket for Grace to use on the sofa, and that was for starters. V took the juice and passed it over. "Only one of these, then water. You'll have enough sugar today." Grace slid it into her pocket and clutched the railing as she made her way down. "What do you say to Sofia?"

"Thank you, Sofia. Can I have a biscuit, too?"

As Sofia went to speak, V cut her off. "No. You're having cake later, that's enough. And don't go asking Sofia again, when you think I can't hear." She caught Grace as she reached the bottom step and looked her in the eye. "Okay? I know you think she's wrapped around your little finger."

Grace smirked and then giggled. She pulled out a chair at the table and climbed up, her legs swinging as she pierced the top of her juice and sucked on the straw. "Is Sofia allowed to colour with me?"

"Of course she's allowed to colour with you. I'll get your pencils from upstairs." She ran up the steps and into the living room with Sofia in hot pursuit. Grabbing the new book and supplies from the coffee table, she turned and banged into Sofia's chest. Usually that would be an advantageous position, but it startled her. "Are you alright?"

"Yes. I'm sorry about the juice, I didn't know she shouldn't have it."

Gripping gently around the top of Sofia's arm with her free hand, V leant in to give her a quick kiss. "She can have it, don't panic. It was very sweet that you remembered they're her favourite."

Sofia's shoulders dropped and she let out a brief sigh. "Okay. Sorry, I know I deal with kids all day, but this is different." She leant in and her eyes glinted. "I care."

"Oh, I see." V laughed and slapped her playfully this time. "Sometimes you will have to put your foot down and she might sulk, but it's like at school. It'll earn you respect and you can't let a six-year-old think she's in charge. If she's out of line or pushing her luck, tell her."

"But she's your daughter, I don't want to overstep the mark."

"And I'm not asking you to do my parenting for me, I'm just saying don't let her push you around. Especially if it's for fear of her not liking you, or you're concerned I'll be upset." Sensing Sofia was still worried, V took her hand and gave it a squeeze. "How about we make a pact? If I ever feel remotely aggrieved about something you've said to Grace, I'll tell you and we'll talk it out. If you ever feel confused as to how to deal with something, you'll tell me and we'll also talk it out. Okay?"

"Okay. That sounds good." Sofia smiled and took the colouring pencils, then tucked the book under her arm. "Thank you."

As Sofia bounded back down the stairs, V dropped a quick text to Jess, making sure they were on their way. When she made her way back into the kitchen, the two of them were sitting at the table colouring the same picture of a lion, Grace's feet still swinging as she hummed to herself.

Pulling out a chair opposite, V surveyed them for a while. All that time worrying how Grace would cope with the move, the babies, and then having her mum in a relationship for the first time seemed to have been for nothing.

* * *

Fifteen minutes later they were still silently colouring. When there was a knock at the door V jumped, so engrossed in watching the pencil drag over the page that she'd zoned out. Jogging down the hall expecting to find a spaniel and two babies on the other side, her face fell to find Anya. It was the second time that woman had caught her out.

"Oh. It's you." Anya's delivery was curt even in that lilting Welsh accent, but she managed a tight smile. In her arms was a navy blue shoebox, which she was holding like it contained the Crown Jewels.

"Yep, me again. I take it you want Sofia. Hang on." As V backtracked into the kitchen and stuck her head around the door, she tried to resist the urge to tell her to fuck off. It wasn't her call. "Anya's here." And apparently, she'd decided to walk straight through.

As Sofia stood, she placed a protective hand on Grace's shoulder, her knee resting on the seat. "This is a surprise, what are you doing here?"

Setting the box on the table, Anya looked around the place, her gaze settling on an oblivious Grace. "This looks like good fun. Are you letting her colour outside of the lines?" She found her own comment amusing, but Sofia hadn't, squirming with discomfort and frowning. "Yours I presume?" She turned briefly to direct her question at V, as if she were talking about some new piece of furniture, and then placed the jacket over the back of a chair before she pulled it out to sit.

When Anya had been here before she'd been relatively relaxed and friendly, but there was an atmosphere now, and it had set V on edge. She lingered in the doorway, resting against the frame and digging her hands into the pockets of her jeans. "Yes. This is my daughter, Grace."

"Who are you?" Grace finally looked at Anya, her delivery decidedly cold. She would usually have been pulled up for being so rude if V weren't preoccupied wondering what the hell Anya wanted on Sofia's birthday and sharing her daughter's sentiment.

"I'm Sofia's wife."

"Ex-wife," Sofia corrected. There was another knock at

the door, and she shot V an apologetic look before addressing Anya again. "I have some guests arriving, so this isn't a very good time. If we need to discuss something about the divorce, perhaps you could call me."

V went back to the door and inched it open, expecting Hal to run straight through, but they'd had the sense to put him on a lead. Jess had it in one hand and held Izzy in her other arm, grasping a wedge of hair and yanking it so she grimaced.

"Could you give me a hand?" She leant sideways in the direction of the hair pull and passed over the lead, just as Grace came barrelling in from behind and wrapped her arms around Hal's neck. She ran back through with him following behind, his collar jangling and his claws clipping on the wood, but V still hadn't stepped aside to let anyone else pass and Jess was gesturing for her to move. "Can we come in, then? Or did you only want our dog?"

Still straining to hear what was going on in the kitchen, V smiled briefly and wandered back through, leaving them to shut the door. Anya remained in her seat, looking over Grace's colouring, and her eyes lit up when Melissa and Jess came in.

"Oh, they are gorgeous. How old?"

"Six months." Jess beamed, seemingly uninterested in the stranger's identity as she made Izzy wave and then kissed her hand. She crouched down so Anya could get a closer look. Grace joined them, having let Hal off his lead so he could sniff around the kitchen like a drug dog with the scent of class A's in his nostrils, and was stroking Izzy's head.

"Can I have a quick hold?"

Before anyone could stop her. Jess had passed Izzy over. She bounced on Anya's lap while everyone stood and watched. They were stuck with her for now, although what she wanted was anyone's guess. As were the contents of the shoe box.

"I expect you're in your element," Anya continued, smiling up at Sofia.

She only shook her head, almost incredulous as if she also couldn't work out what the hell was happening, and then looked up at V again wearing a tight smile. "Why don't you give Jess and Melissa a tour of the house. I think we need to have a quick chat."

Now, when Jess took Izzy back, she frowned at Anya. As they reached the top of the stairs, she tried to peer back down, but the angle was too tight. "Who is that woman?"

"That's Sofia's ex," V whispered. "She turned up about five minutes before you arrived, and I have no idea why but I'm guessing she didn't drive all the way from Wales without a good reason." And she could guess at what that good reason was, but at least Sofia seemed more in control today. The last time she'd fallen apart, but then she'd just been in a car accident. V had to trust that if she'd sent them all away, she could handle this. "We should give them some peace. C'mon, I'll show you upstairs."

Leaving Grace to sit on the sofa and stroke Hal, spreading a suitable amount of hair all over Sofia's soft furnishings, she led Jess and Melissa around the rest of the house. It was more to give them something to do than anything else and seeing as there wasn't much to explore, they were back in the living room within minutes.

"Where's Grace gone?" V pointed to the sofa where Hal was now sitting on his own. She pressed a hand to her forehead, feeling a sudden swell of panic. "Shit."

As Melissa sat and stroked the dog, Ruby bouncing on her lap, she casually shrugged. "Relax, it's not like she can have gone far."

She knew she wouldn't have gone far or left the building —that wasn't her worry—and V made a quick bolt for the stairs. Skipping down them and into the kitchen, she found Grace pulling at Sofia's sweater.

"Can I have another drink please Sofia?"

She got halfway across the room and gestured her over. "Come here, sweetheart. Sofia needs to discuss something with Anya."

"They weren't discussing, they were arguing." Grace was matter of fact in her assessment and didn't move.

Sofia turned to grab a plastic beaker from the draining board. "Of course you can have a drink." She smiled and held it out, wiping a few drips from the bottom. "I'm sorry if we upset you."

"You didn't upset me, but I don't like *her*."

She delivered it with a venom V had never heard from her daughter before, and it stunned her into silence and inaction for a few moments. The colour drained from her face and she looked to Sofia, mouthing a sincere "sorry" before addressing Grace again. "Apologise to Anya, please. That was rude."

"No." She'd never been this defiant before, sipping from her water and glaring at Anya over the top of it. "*She* was being rude to Sofia and telling lies. I won't apologise because it's true. I don't like her one bit, Mummy."

Faltering and unsure where to go next, V was interrupted by Anya. "It's okay. She doesn't need to apologise to me for being honest. Now I'm going to be. I love you, Sofia. I think you still love me too, and you don't really want to go ahead with this divorce." She patted the box on the table. "A few memories here; I thought you'd want them. I'll go, but think about it. Okay?"

As she turned to leave, V remained in stunned silence,

her stomach containing the full US Olympic gymnastics squad. She could slap Anya for saying all that in front of Grace but knew it wouldn't help. With trembling hands and her eyes prickling, she was alarmed to find it was Grace who spoke again.

She peered up at Sofia as she delivered her question. "That's not true, is it? You love us, not her."

The gymnasts were doing cartwheels now, as part of a full floor routine. Willing Sofia to keep her promise, V could barely breathe. If she wavered now, in front of Grace, she'd be hurting them all.

"No, it's not true." Sofia stroked a hand through Grace's hair as she crouched and smiled. "Don't worry, cucciolo. Anya is a little upset and you shouldn't have heard all of that, but she is mistaken. She is going home, then we will carry on our party and cut the cake we made. Okay?"

"Okay." As Grace took Sofia's hand and tried to drag her towards the stairs, V finally sucked in a deep breath. "Come on, we need to get Izzy and Ruby."

Sofia laughed and hauled Grace over her shoulder in a fireman's lift, tickling her sides so she squealed with glee. While this was happening, Anya had slunk off into the hallway, leaving her box on the table, and V had followed. She closed the internal door behind herself and crossed her arms, wanting to make sure Anya left.

She slipped her feet back into her shoes and grabbed her coat from the peg. "Sofia wants a family, you know, and I've told her we can have that. She'll change her mind once she thinks this through, I'm just warning you."

"And I'm so grateful, Anya." The sarcasm was coming in handy right now. Thank god she'd had Grace to practise on all these years. "But if you really imagine you're going to win Sofia around by saying all of that in front of a six-year-old who she thinks the world of, you don't know her as well as you presume."

"Maybe not, but I know her a damn sight better than you do. I can promise the sole reason she's with you is because you've already got a kid. Sure bet, bound to be up for another."

V shrugged. "I don't believe you."

Anya leant in. "Really? Because from what I can see, she's more interested in your daughter than in you. Look at her, she's smitten."

"So?" Anya was right, Sofia adored Grace and vice versa. That was a good thing. She could never be with someone who didn't want a child hanging around, saw her as an inconvenience, and was phoning it in for the sake of the relationship. It didn't mean it was the only reason Sofia was in this. In fact, V was sure of herself. Anya wouldn't succeed however hard she tried.

What she *would* get was a kick out the door.

28

With Anya gone, V had pulled out the cake, lit the candles, and tried to wipe that little interlude from memory. More than anything, she didn't want Anya to have the satisfaction of ruining Sofia's birthday. As the afternoon wore on, though, she relaxed for real. They chatted through last minute wedding arrangements, she joked with Sofia about how she hadn't yet had a formal invite, and by two o'clock they were all smiling again.

"That was delicious," Jess muttered through her second piece of cake. She had icing all over her fingers and Izzy was sitting in her lap trying to suck it off, rather than the strained something or other that Sofia was attempting to feed her to free up Jess's hands. "Thank you." She licked them clean and set the plate on the edge of the sofa next to her. Then she took the spoon from Sofia and tried to return her daughter to the intended meal, but she wasn't having any of it. The end of the spoon was grabbed, and the contents splattered onto the carpet. "Oops."

"Don't worry." Sofia smiled and reached into her pocket for a tissue, wiping up the worst of it. Ordinarily Hal would've come along and cleaned it up for her, but he'd gone out for a walk along the towpath with Grace and Melissa, so he could have a wee. They'd been a while, which probably meant that'd stopped to see Angie and Percy.

V sat on the floor with her head resting back between Sofia's knees, her legs outstretched as she tried to feed Ruby, who was far more into her food. She was gulping it down without hesitation and would probably have eaten the spoon too given the opportunity. "I got the good baby, didn't I Rubes?"

"Hey." As Jess protested and covered Izzy's ears with her hands, she put another streak of goop in her hair. "Don't listen to her. We all love you both equally."

With the jar now empty, V turned it to show Ruby. "All gone, see. No more." She set it down and dropped in the spoon, then reached for the pack of wipes from the coffee table and cleaned her up. "Mission accomplished, how are you two getting on?" As she craned around, she saw that Izzy was smeared with orange, from her blonde curls to her little pink socks, and both Sofia and Jess were looking rather sheepish.

"Well excuse us if we're not seasoned pros yet." Jess also had icing on her chin and was trying to lick it off. "I'm still getting to grips with weaning."

"Yourself, or the twins?"

"Oh ha-ha. I don't think she wants this so I'm giving up and taking her to the sink. Is that okay?"

As Sofia gestured upstairs, she took the jar back with her other hand, reaching over V's head to put it on the table. "Of course. You can use the bathroom, and there are some fresh towels in the cupboard on the landing if you need them."

Holding Ruby straight up in the air, V had an instinctive

sniff to make sure Jess shouldn't be taking them both. "Go to Auntie Sofia. I think she'd like a cuddle."

"I would love a cuddle."

With the baby out of her hands, V hoisted herself up and sat beside them on the sofa, smiling at Sofia as she whooshed Ruby above her head and then kissed her stomach. "I wouldn't do that if I were you."

"Why not?"

"Think about it, genius." She waited a few moments for the penny to drop and then laughed as Sofia sat Ruby in her lap, gently covering her mouth as if she expected it to erupt with sick.

"Now we are alone, are you okay?" Her attention was still on Ruby as she strained to stand with Sofia's support, her little legs desperately running along Sofia's lap.

"Mhm, don't worry." V relayed the contents of her brief exchange with Anya, her head resting against Sofia's shoulder. "I was right to trust you, wasn't I?" She twisted and hitched up her knee so she could see Sofia's reaction.

"One hundred percent." She stressed every word and looked V in the eye, before almost having one of them poked out by a little finger. "I am sorry we dragged you into that earlier, I had absolutely no idea she was coming here today or that she felt that way, and she has twisted everything."

"So, you're not desperate for kids and only with me because you think I've got a factory somewhere that produces them?"

Sofia laughed. "No. I told you I have always been open to the possibility of having them, but only if I were in the right relationship and we took the decision together. I'm certainly not *desperate*. Anya came out and said point blank that if I go back to her and move to Wales, we can have a baby. She has entirely missed the point, though."

"Because it isn't the right relationship?"

As she touched noses with Ruby, Sofia smiled and scrunched her face. "Exactly, miele. Children are not a bargaining chip or a toy to play with. I see too many with chaotic homes and people coming in and out of their lives. I would never do that."

It felt like that was more than a general comment. It was a good job, because if her earlier performance was anything to go by, Grace was as deep in this as they were. V just had to trust that Sofia really would be true to her promise of being gentle with her heart, because it was too late now. It was getting late generally, and when Jess came back down, she wanted to get the girls into the car ready to go home.

As Grace got back, running along the towpath with Melissa lagging somewhere behind, Jess and Sofia were loading the twins into their car seats. "Are you going?" She pouted and peered across the back seat.

"Yes, Monster. Izzy and Ruby need a nap, but we'll see you soon. Your flower girl dress arrived the other day, ready for the wedding. Mummy's bringing you over to try it on."

Grace gasped and jumped up and down, jingling Hal's collar where she was holding his lead. Flower girl had in fact turned into ring bearer, but she didn't really care about that. She was only bothered that she had a role and a new dress. "Is it pink?"

"You know it's pink, we showed you the picture online."

As Melissa finished packing up the car, V pulled Jess into a hug and whispered, "Hen do?"

"I already said no."

She had, although it seemed like a missed opportunity

for some much-needed fun and a rare evening out. Jess and Melissa hadn't spent a single night away from the twins since they were born, and V couldn't help wondering if they'd resolved their little sex communication issue. "You're not even having a honeymoon, though. What gives with that?"

"We don't want to go on holiday and leave the girls. We'll have a family trip instead."

Still talking in hushed tones, she dragged Jess towards the front door and probed further. "Don't you want to... you know? Or is that it now? Dead from the waist down." Never one for subtlety when talking about sex, she was struggling not to shake Jess's shoulders and scream in her face.

"Why are you so bothered about my sex life?"

"I'm not." But Melissa was, and V glanced at her chatting with Sofia to make sure she wasn't listening. "Let us look after the girls for a night. A sort of wedding gift. You know you can trust us, and you can go off and do that thing... you remember, the one that makes Melissa—" and with that, she breathed heavily in Jess's ear and let out a series of groans.

Jess recoiled. "Ew, never do that in my ear again. Has she said something to you?"

"Whatever do you mean? I'm sure if there was a problem she'd talk to you about it. But, you know, if she *had*..."

"Not that it's any of your business, but now we have *our own* bedroom back and don't have two babies in there with us, things are perfectly fine. I wonder what might have been hindering us before? Perhaps being on top of each other because our house was full."

"Alright. Touch-y..." V stepped back and shoved her shoulder, wearing a little smirk. "Although I would've thought being on top of each other was a good thing." She held up her hands and backed away further when Jess swiped for her.

Laughing as she jumped into the driver seat and shut the door, Jess whirred down the window. With Melissa and Hal now also inside, she waved through it, and they both yelled goodbye.

As they watched the car pull off down the drive, Sofia wrapped her arm around V's shoulder. "Are they really not having a honeymoon? We should book them a night in a hotel or something, as a wedding gift. We could even offer to look after the twins for them, so they can be alone."

"Joint wedding gifts, huh?" She tickled Sofia's side, deciding not to tell her she'd already had the same idea. "This is getting serious now."

"Deadly."

She laughed and scooped V up, carrying her back through to the kitchen and kicking the door shut. Grace was already at the table sticking her finger in the cake but stopped abruptly when they caught her out. She bolted towards the stairs but didn't get very far before V was dropped to the ground and then stopped her.

"Not so fast. Come back here, we need to talk about what happened earlier."

She turned, looking a little sheepish, and then inched back. "I only did it once, and I washed my hands first."

"Not the cake, with Anya." Pulling out two chairs, V patted one of them and sat on the other, Sofia taking her own on the opposite side. She'd been considering how to play this. "I know you were only telling the truth, sweetheart, and that she made you angry. I don't ordinarily want to hear you speaking to people like that, but I understand where it came from." Instead of taking the offered seat, Grace climbed up onto V's lap. "Are you alright?"

Resting the side of her head on V's chest, she nodded. "Yes. Can we still stay here tonight or am I in trouble?"

"Yes, we can still stay here."

"And can I give Sofia her birthday present now?" She didn't wait for a response, slipping back off and running through the hallway where she'd hung up her backpack. Returning with it, she pulled out a round parcel with shoddy pink wrapping paper and far too much sticky tape. Sofia might need a pneumatic drill to get through it, but she was beaming as Grace handed it over. "I know penguins are your favourite."

After what felt like an eternity of unpicking strips of plastic and paper, Sofia got into it and held up a round clock, the same as V's from Christmas. Where on earth she was getting all these clocks from remained a mystery. On the face was another image, but this time it was from their trip to the zoo. They were all crouched next to the edge of the glass enclosure with a penguin standing in shot.

When both V and Sofia burst out laughing, Grace pouted. "You don't like it." She jumped up and down, her eyes welling with tears, and Sofia pulled her into a hug.

"No, no, cucciolo. I *love* it. This is the best present anyone has ever given me. Thank you so much." She stood up and slung Grace over her shoulder, taking the clock in her other hand. "Now, help me choose where to hang it. Somewhere everyone will see."

Grace's hair fell over her face but she was giggling through it and trying to wipe it away so she could see. When Sofia set her down on the work surface, she pointed to a space next to the window. "If you put it there, you can see it when you cook."

"An excellent idea. I spend a lot of time cooking, so I will see it often."

* * *

With Grace tucked up asleep in the spare bedroom, V wandered back downstairs. The evenings were becoming lighter and Sofia had opened the balcony doors for the first time, resting forward on the railing and looking out over the canal. She'd been speaking to her parents, who'd phoned to wish her happy birthday, but now had a glass of red wine in hand. There was another on the coffee table, but V left it, sliding her arms around Sofia and resting her head on her back.

"Whatcha thinking about?" she whispered.

"Honestly? I was still thinking about that clock."

V laughed. "Yeah, she must get someone to order them for her. I'd presumed her dad, but it could just as easily be Jess or Melissa." She let out a sigh and another grunt of laughter. "Pretty cute, though. Moments like those I'm very proud of that kid. She's turned out okay."

As Sofia rotated, leaning back and crossing her feet over, she wore a bemused smile. "You know that isn't what I meant, but yes, she has turned out very well. You are an excellent mother."

"And you—" V pointed in the centre of Sofia's chest. "Are great with her. She's never been this bothered about Matty's girlfriend. I think you may already be her favourite step-parent type thing. She has so many adults in her life by now that I'm sort of losing track. I suppose it's six, discounting any blood relatives on either side, like her grandparents. Oh, and it's seven if you include Rachel, because they are also pretty close. Eight with Angie, who she's growing increasingly attached to. But you're definitely up there."

"It's a good job that I'm not competitive." Sofia laughed, pulling V forward by the bottom of her T-shirt. "Although no one is ever going to trump you, *miele*. I think that's why she was so protective of me earlier. She has seen that I make you happy and she will do anything for you. *Anything*." Her eyes rolled skywards, and she smiled again. "You're her absolute hero."

"If you keep flattering me like this, you might see your way towards another surprise birthday present." V nudged her eyebrows suggestively and slipped her hand around Sofia's waist, then down the waistband of her boxers, giving them a quick ping. After the day they'd had, all she wanted to do was climb under the covers and let it all out.

"When you snap my underwear like that, how can I resist?"

"Well, quite." Lacing their fingers together, V led her through the living room. She picked up the other glass of wine on the way and didn't stop until they were in the bedroom with the door closed. After setting her wine glass down, she grabbed her overnight bag from the floor and pulled out a bottle of almond oil, holding it up. "Strip," she deadpanned. "All clothes gone—now."

"Mm, stern." Sofia was already wriggling out of her jeans at speed and a few moments later had landed face down on the bed, not wearing a stitch. She shuffled to get comfy, resting her face on her arms. "I enjoy it hard, a bit like you."

"Steady. Now, would you prefer me clothed or unclothed for your massage? This is your present—given you forbade me from buying anything—and you are forty today, so it only seems fair."

Sofia raised her face, her voice still muffled by the sheets. "Are you really asking?"

"True, although you haven't seen the clothing options yet..." Digging into her bag, V pulled out a black silk night-dress and it hung off her index finger. "There's still time to reconsider." Seeing Sofia's eyes widen, she knew the answer and stepped into the recess to change. When she emerged,

Sofia had turned herself over and propped herself on some pillows, a hunger in her eyes which suggested she had cancelled the massage. "What is happening here?"

"Get in my lap," she pleaded.

"Nope. Roll back over. It's only a massage, and you can have that after."

"But miele..." She pouted, holding out her hand and trying to pull V over. "It's my birthday."

"It is, and I will not touch you in any way that you are not entirely comfortable with but have some patience."

She huffed and did as she was told, stropping as she wriggled down the bed. "Fine."

"Oh, stop moaning. I've never known anyone complain so much to get a nice relaxing massage."

"I wanted a nice relaxing something else."

She finally shut up after that, resting her head on her arms. Grabbing the bottle again, V climbed onto the bed and sat in the curve of Sofia's back, laughing when she let out a longing moan. "Oh yes, sorry. I'm not wearing anything but this..." She tipped some oil onto her hands and rubbed them together to get a little warmth, then stroked up Sofia's back to spread it. "See, not so bad."

Ten minutes in, the moans, groans, and gripes had stopped, and V was feeling pleased with herself. Perhaps she'd relax Sofia enough that she even got a full, interrupted night of sleep for once. The only trouble was, she got the horrible sense that it may have happened too early, as the sound of gentle snoring filled the room. Leaning over with her hands either side of Sofia's head, there was no response.

"Hello," she whispered, but it was no good because Sofia was sparko. Laughing quietly and kissing her cheek, V carefully climbed off. She opened the wardrobe and pulled out a spare blanket, wrapping it over Sofia's back, then slid underneath it and cuddled up next to her. It wasn't even eight o'clock yet, but she was content. With their noses only inches apart, she stroked the hair out of Sofia's eyes. "Happy birthday," she whispered again. "I love you and I hope this year will be a better one."

29

"Are you ready for this?" V placed a hand on each of Jess's shoulders and looked her straight in the eye. "Because it's not too late to back out. I can go in there and tell them you've changed your mind."

Jess frowned, adjusting the cuffs of a white dress shirt as they waited in the registry office lobby. "You've been watching too much television. Of course I want to go through with it. I'm about to marry the woman of my dreams, who I already have two bloody kids with."

"Thought you might say that. Good."

One last glance over her outfit and they were ready to go. She'd kept this a secret for weeks, which was an impressive feat for someone who was usually honest to a fault. V had taken her down to London for the day and sat for hours as she tried on tux after tux until they found the perfect one. All the while Grace had dragged Sofia around the aquarium after she insisted that she could watch her, and returned to them with a new colouring book, a backpack in the shape of a clown fish, a cuddly sea turtle, and an extendible snapping shark.

The plan was for Jess and Melissa to enter separately, although there wasn't space for much pomp and circumstance given the registry office only held about thirty people. It was a small room on the back of the town hall, with heavy old mahogany furniture and a worn carpet. Rachel had already pointed that out more than once but would hopefully mellow later with the aid of Champagne.

Jess took a deep breath and exhaled it slowly as she tugged the ends of her tie, which hung loose around the open collar of her shirt. "You should sit down. I think we're almost ready to start."

After pressing a kiss to Jess's cheek and wishing her luck, V pushed open the door and made her way to the seat Sofia was saving. Grace was tucked in next to Rachel holding the box of rings and trying to stuff Izzy's fist in her mouth, her legs swinging as they hung off the chair, and didn't seem at all fazed by her duties. V, on the other hand, felt a swell of nerves for all of them.

"Everything okay?" As V sat, Sofia beamed and leant in to kiss her. "I love weddings."

"Really? You weren't put off by... you know?"

"No. I don't know if marriage is something I'll ever do again, but I enjoy seeing two people happy and in love. All the excitement and possibility. Even if it doesn't work out, it is worth the risk. I am very honoured that they have allowed me to be here."

They hadn't received a great deal of choice, not that either would have objected.

Sofia was in a pair of tailored trousers and a shirt, the matching cream coloured jacket draped over the back of her chair. Even sitting she cut a striking figure, and V took a moment to admire her. "You look... exceptional." It was hard to put a word to her thoughts, but that one would do. "I'm struggling to take my eyes off you."

A slight blush warmed Sofia's cheeks. "Then don't. I am all yours, and the feeling is quite mutual." Her thumb stroked into the top of V's knee and grazed the green satin of her dress. "Although perhaps we should both pay a little attention to the ceremony."

"What a drag. I've been enjoying this opportunity to see you dressed up. It's odd, I thought I only liked you with your clothes off."

"Is that so?"

Lacing their fingers together, V stroked her thumb into Sofia's palm and her heart did a little leap as the music started. Everyone turned around as Melissa entered on her dad's arm, not wearing the cream lace dress but having opted for the bright pink one from their first ever date—after they let it out a little. She'd reasoned that they were doing things their way, and tradition could be completely buggered.

There was a gasp over the music and V stifled a laugh, knowing where it'd come from. She peered forward, seeing Grace's mouth was hanging open, and she was tugging at Rachel to look at the dress because it was the same colour as her own. Melissa's nan was next to her with Ruby on her knee but having far less success covering up her amusement.

When Melissa got to the front, it was time for Jess's big moment and V squeezed Sofia's hand, willing this to go well. She was fairly certain it would do, and Melissa was about to melt into the carpet. She bit her bottom lip, watching the entire reaction unfold as Jess entered, absolutely working that tux. They'd slicked her hair back, applied a hint of make-up, and added her best perfume to knock Melissa out at the end.

If she got that far, anyway, because three paces down the middle of the room, Melissa had already lost it. She had tears running down her face, first with laughter as she bent over double, then they turned to something else. When Jess reached her, casually shoving both hands in her pockets, Melissa ran her hands over the lapels of the jacket but then faltered. She'd be looking for something funny to say but seemed to come up blank, her bottom lip still quivering.

"What do you think?" Jess smiled and slipped one of her hands back out of her pocket, wiping away Melissa's tears with her thumb. "I know it wasn't me you wanted to see in a tux, but do I measure up?"

"You'll do," Melissa finally whispered, her voice cracking. "I suppose."

"Then shall we get married?"

Right on cue, Izzy let out a giant wail and everyone laughed. Melissa waved at the twins and smiled, then turned to face Jess again. "Oh yeah, let's do it."

She composed herself through most of the vows and ceremony, but as the registrar said the word 'kiss' she jumped on Jess like Grace on a chocolate pudding. Wrapping her arms around Jess's neck and kissing her with more passion that V had ever seen—or wanted to see—Melissa was only a step away from stripping her naked in the middle of the registry office.

"Wow." Sniggering and burying her face in Sofia's shoulder, V tried not to laugh too hard.

"Yes, wow. Perhaps that wedding gift was a good shout. They might want to use it *now*."

* * *

With the ceremony out of the way, Sofia drove them to Rachel's house for the reception. This part was almost more nerve-wracking than the actual wedding, and V was scanning for Jess's mum and brother. They were turning up at some point, but no one seemed to know exactly when.

"Will you calm down, miele? I've never seen you like this." With Grace atop her knee on a chair in the garden, Sofia was struggling to speak as she had chocolate fingers wedged in her mouth.

"I can't because I feel partly responsible if this goes wrong. I encouraged her to invite her mum and now I'm not sure I should have."

"You didn't force her, though, did you? I'm sure Jess listens to your advice, but she has her own mind."

"No, she doesn't. Shush." Taking another sip of Champagne, V caught hold of Rachel bossing around the caterers. They were still setting up the buffet while people were arriving, and she wasn't happy. "Do you know what's going on with the whole Jess parent situation?"

"Yes, darling. They're in the living room. I'm staying away, trying to give them some space. My sister is here, though, I'll grab her for you."

"No, don't do that. I'll catch her later." Or not.

"You haven't changed your mind, then?" Glancing over at Sofia as she giggled with Grace, Rachel tilted her head. "No." She sighed. "I won't argue. This is me... not interfering."

"Are you ill?" Regretting that in an instant and cringing, V shrugged and tried to backtrack. "Sorry, too much Champagne. I appreciate it, but no, I haven't changed my mind. I don't know what'll happen in the future but for now work is actually going well, I'm about to start the last term of the year, I have a great relationship, and Grace is thriving so—"

She took a deep breath, having blurted that with residual nerves. "I'm happy."

"Well, you seem it, and Grace has taken well to Sofia. I only hope it's a similar story inside."

"Me too. I can't say this to Jess, but I sort of sympathise with her mum. Well, maybe not the right word, but to not have Grace in my life... I know I never left her but to have done that, things must have been pretty bleak. You know?"

"I think I do, yes. Not the same thing, but when I was sitting with you on the day the twins were born, I remember thinking *I might lose them*, and it terrified me beyond all belief." Rachel was welling up just talking about it, although that could also have been booze related because she'd recently drained the rest of her glass "Would you ever have any more, darling?"

Starting to say no through instinct, V stopped herself and reconsidered. "You know what? I honestly don't know. If you'd asked me a year ago, I'd have said no, but I'm not sure how much of that was fear and a trauma response." She loved Grace to bits and always wanted kids, but never imagined it happening the way it did. "I swore I'd never go through it again. It wouldn't be the same, though, not if I made a choice to have another child with someone I loved."

"Someone like..." Quickly pointing at Sofia as she tried to wipe the chocolate smears from her face, Rachel wore a warm smile.

"Yeah." V laughed and cocked her head.

"I take it you'd be the one to...? You know."

"Well, Sofia's already forty and I'm not sure she'd want to anyway... so yeah. I guess." Was she really talking about this like a thing that was going to happen?

"Forty? My, you do have a thing for older women, don't

you?" Raising her eyebrows, Rachel took another glass of Champagne from a passing waiter.

"Excuse me?"

"Oh, nothing darling."

As Rachel gave the top of her arm a quick squeeze, she was sure she saw a wink. Either that or she had something in her eye. Whatever it was, it made V blush and she needed to get away. There were more guests filtering in, and she made an excuse, heading towards someone she knew.

An hour later there were still only perhaps forty people, but enough to fill the garden with chatter and the sound of clinking glasses. When Jess emerged with Melissa, each carrying a baby, everyone cheered. They'd been in the living room having their reunion for ages, but the fact Jess had a smile still was enough to relieve a little of V's tension.

She made a beeline for them and pulled Jess to one side by the patio doors. "Hey, are you okay? How did it go?"

"Weird as hell, but we had a good chat. She absolutely melted over the twins, and Dad got all protective of her." As she glanced at her parents, embracing by the buffet table, Jess let out a quick sigh. "I think he's being very careful, but..."

"There are feelings?"

"Yep."

Pausing for a few moments, the wisdom in asking this question was deliberated. It was a whole can of worms Jess probably didn't want opened on her wedding day. "And if they got back together...?"

"I don't know." Her lips vibrated as she let out a puff of air, and it dissolved her smile. "I want Dad to be happy but I'm worried. You know what about, and why, but I don't suppose I can do anything about it. You love who you love, and I don't think he ever stopped loving her."

There wasn't much to argue with there, so V only nodded and took a sip of Champagne. "For the second time today, I find myself saying that you will just have to see what happens."

"Second?"

"Oh, yeah." She waved dismissively and then caught hold of Izzy's hand. "I may have entered into a conversation with your mother-in-law about having more kids..."

"You?" Jess exclaimed rather more loudly than the suggestion warranted. It won her a clip around the ear.

"Don't sound so shocked."

"I'm actually not, I knew this was going to happen." Shrugging, Jess adjusted the baby on her hip. "I tried to make a bet with my wife, but she wouldn't take it because she knew she would lose."

"True story," Melissa interjected as she held out Ruby. "Here. Take."

"No, I can't. The mood I'm in and after all the Champagne I've consumed, my ovaries will cry." Relenting and taking the baby into her arms, V sniffed the top of her head and her eyes rolled back. "Why do babies smell like that? It's a conspiracy. Tell me when you're having another." She'd intended that as a joke, but they were looking at each other and grinning. "Oh, dear god, you can't be serious? At least my daughter is six and becoming relatively self-sufficient. You have seven-month-old twins. *Twins*. Can you imagine adding another child to that? Not to mention the physical toll."

"Well, that's no problem, because..." As Melissa pointed to Jess, she gingerly raised her hand.

"You?"

"Hey!" Jess protested.

"Yeah, now you know how it feels." Shoving her playfully on the shoulder, V's eyes widened. "Well, this really is a day for revelations. How soon are you planning to do it?"

"Not yet. We're not idiots, and we would like to sleep at some point, but in the future. I never thought I'd want to, but the last year has changed things. I want what you and Melissa have."

V laughed and pressed her legs tight together. "What's that? The worst pain of your life?"

"No, the bond. I couldn't love the girls any more than I do, but I want to do the whole thing. We haven't told anyone else, though, so—"

"Mum's the word?"

As the afternoon wore on, everyone pillaged the buffet, then they set up a small dance floor. It was only the patio at the end of the garden with a few disco lights and a phone plugged into a speaker, but after five glasses of Champagne, the effect was the same. With her shoes off and Grace stood on her feet, V swayed to late nineties pop ballads and tried not to fall over.

All weddings should be like this—budget and fun. There were no stuffy speeches, tiny sit-down meals, and everyone was enjoying themselves. Even Rachel was mellow, giving up on trying to direct the buffet in favour of getting drunk. She'd joined them in a dance for a while, but then disappeared to find her grandkids.

When the track changed, Grace ran off to play with the dogs again, having spent most of the late afternoon entertaining herself with not only Hal but his brother and father. It was a spaniel family reunion too, which was quite apt. Swerving down the lawn, V followed her, finding Sofia laid out on a picnic blanket in the middle of the grass with a baby attempting to crawl over her stomach.

Flopping out next to her, a hand pressed into V's boob and she winced. "Blimey, Rubes. Less of that, I might want those later." Repositioning Ruby on her belly between them, she rolled over onto her side. "I might have known you'd have been distracted by something small and cute. You're just like my daughter, only her distractions are a lot hairier."

"I was being helpful, miele. Purely selfless."

"Mhm. Lucky for you, I think it's adorable. In fact, I'm finding myself going decidedly squishy today."

"Squishy?"

"Yep. Over babies, and you, and... the whole thing, really." She sighed, but then laughed. It was at herself, more than anything. "You should not take this as a statement of definite intent, but I keep thinking what it might be like if we had a baby. In the very, very, *very* distant future."

Propping herself on an elbow, Sofia stroked the wisps of blonde hair on the back of Ruby's head. "And what do you picture?"

"Let's see. You would of course wait on me hand and foot throughout the entire pregnancy." Sucking her teeth for a second, V rolled onto her front and rested her head on her arms. "Then you would do at least half of the nappy changing, burping, washing, and general caretaking..."

"That is a given. I meant how does it feel?"

"To share all those things with someone who's in it as much as I am? Yeah, pretty good." She found her cheeks were burning and they hurt from smiling so much. That squishy feeling had taken root, with the help of a vat of booze. "Better than that, actually. And sort of liberating." Reaching forward, she picked a daisy from the grass and twirled it between her thumb and forefinger. "How do you feel about it?"

"Happy to hear that you feel liberated. Excited that it might be a possibility..." Sofia laughed and her face screwed into a big daft smile. "Completely in love with you either way."

Tucking the daisy in Ruby's hair, V glanced up at Sofia and bit her lip. "You've never actually said that before." She returned her attention to the baby and tried to stop her eating the flower. It was discarded into the grass and then V sat up, encouraging Ruby to use Sofia as a climbing frame. "I'm pretty sure you've told Grace you love me, and Anya, and Bob, but never actually me."

"Then let me correct that." Sofia tried to lean in with Ruby's hands grabbing at her shirt, and whispered, "I love you." She fell back and laughed as two podgy fists pounded her side and Ruby squealed. "I'd like to kiss you now but there is a baby crushing my sternum."

V only shrugged and left her to deal with it. "Better get used to that, if you're serious." She went to get up but then rolled over and made a loud show of kissing Sofia's forehead while she continued to take a tiny beating. "Oh, I love you too by the way. In case that wasn't clear."

30

Pushing the classroom door shut with a flourish, V threw her hands in the air and would've sunk to her knees if she didn't know it would hurt to thwack them on tile. Ten long months and she'd just finished her last lesson of her last day of the last week of her first year. She'd met every one of her standards, Bob looked vaguely happy, and she was staring down the barrel of six weeks off.

As her phone vibrated in her pocket, she fumbled to pull it out. "I'm free!"

It was Jess, and she laughed. "Yeah, me too. Two weeks off start now. Where are you, can I come in?"

"Where am I? Where are you?" Looking around herself as if she might find Jess in a drawer or on a shelf, V twisted awkwardly.

"I'm in the car park. Thought I'd come and see your classroom, and I got you a present."

"In that case, you can definitely come in. Technically you should sign in at reception, but I'll meet you out there and sneak you in. The kids are all fleeing pretty quickly."

Five minutes later Jess had arrived and was prodding

around the displays, nodding and mumbling to herself. She had her work bag over her shoulder, and V was sneaking her hand under the flap because there was clearly a present in there.

"Um, excuse me?" Twisting, Jess slapped a hand down on it. "Rude, hang on." She set it on the desk and pulled out a small square parcel wrapped in shiny silver paper.

Ripping into it and lobbing the gift wrap in the bin, V held up a 'World's Greatest Teacher' mug. "How did you know?" She let out a few false sobs, clutching her chest. Then she set it on the desk and perched on the edge. "Have you recovered from your night away? You know... *sexually*."

Rolling her eyes, Jess wandered over to the board and grabbed a marker. "I don't know what you think we got up to. It was one night in a hotel."

"It was your first time spending an entire night alone, with no babies crying and pureed food matted into your hair, for nine months. Given we were the ones enduring that on your behalf, I should bloody well hope you did everything in the book." With her hands on her hips, V squinted over Jess's shoulder. "What in the world is that?"

"It's you." She turned, wearing that same wounded expression Grace did when you hadn't understood a word that'd just fallen from her mouth. "I'm drawing us all at the beach next week." Pointing at something which looked like a cloud with problems, she continued. "That's Hal."

"Thanks for clarifying, because there's no way in the world I would've seen that and thought *animal* of any description."

"I hope you're nicer to your students," Jess mumbled. Her tongue poked out as she went back to her task. A few moments later she stepped back and gestured to the completed scene. "Ta-dah!"

"Great. Let's not show Sofia this, or she may change her mind about coming with us. It's a struggle enough getting her to Wales, without suggesting she'll be heading there with a bunch of deformed aliens and their demented cloud-stick dog." Although she'd taken surprisingly little convincing on the idea. They'd moved their trip to the start of the summer holidays instead of the end because Sofia had flights already booked to go to Italy, and everyone had been happy to accommodate.

"Has Anya really put her off Wales that much?"

V took the pen, trying to correct some of Jess's terrible scribbles. "Yeah, unfortunately. We've had a few more chats about it and there's a lot of stuff mixed up in there, not just to do with Anya. I think Sofia struggled to express herself or be heard in that relationship, and as much as anything she's exasperated that she stayed for so long." Snapping the cap back on the marker, V shrugged. "I asked her how she feels about *our* relationship and she says it's completely different; she can be who she is. Long may that last, because who she is..." Nudging her eyebrows, V grasped the top of Jess's arm. "Well, let's just say I am very much into it."

"Yeah, no shit."

Quite prepared to gush a bit, V's hand dropped to her side and she shrugged again. "Sofia's incredibly sexy, clever, insightful, and there's something about her." She balled her fist and looked at the ceiling. "I can't really describe it, but we... fit."

Wandering towards the door and grabbing her mug on the way, she was about to unhook her bag from the peg when Sofia came through the door and held up a small square parcel. "Oh." Looking from one to the other, she laughed. "Well, this is embarrassing." She tore away her own paper and held up the same mug.

"Not at all. One for work, one for home. Then everyone will know that I am, in fact, the world's greatest teacher. Thank you." Snatching a quick kiss, V slipped both mugs into her bag and then chucked it over her shoulder. "We were just talking about you." She laced her fingers through Sofia's and gave them a squeeze.

"Should I worry, miele?"

"Absolutely. I hate to tell you, but I think you're stuck with me for a while."

Jess laughed as she followed them out, and the three wandered down the corridor. "What are you two up to this evening? Big celebration?"

"The biggest," V enthused. "We're chaperoning prom."

With a shot of laughter, Jess pushed open the door onto the car park. "Oh, now that brings back some memories. Hazy ones, but... have fun."

"We will. Grace is with her dad, I've spent far too much on a dress, and once the kids have had their little party, we're having one of our own."

Little party was a misnomer. Prom had gone big in the twelve years since Jess and V had snogged around the back of the rugby club. This event was in a fancy hotel on the edge of town, and there were limousines coming up the drive. Stood in a black dress with a slit as daring as she could get away with at a party which was technically for kids, V shook her head and wondered how many parents they had sent bankrupt for this.

There was no sign of Sofia yet. She'd gone home to change and was then on duty in the ballroom, setting up the awards for each department. It was Bob, almost inevitably, who V had was paired with on car park duty. To be fair to him, he looked quite natty in a black suit and a red bow tie. He'd even polished his bald spot.

Pointing kids through to the entrance, V gave him the once over. "Going out on the pull later?"

"Hilarious." He looked decidedly nervous, though, pulling on his collar and slicking back the greying hair along the side of his head.

"Definitely nothing going with this woman, then?"

"Come back to me on that."

"Ah, then there is gossip. Who is she?" Sidling up to him, V nudged his shoulder. "Is it Doris the lunch lady? Gillian from reception? Don't tell me you've got your eye on Sofia?"

"It'll surprise you to learn she isn't really my type, and I doubt I am hers."

"That doesn't surprise me at all, I know exactly who Sofia's type is. I also had the pleasure of meeting her soon to be ex-wife, and I can tell you she's upgraded."

He turned, his eyebrows surging up his forehead. "You've met the new woman as well? You're doing better than I am, she won't tell me a thing."

"Yep. She's stunning."

"I don't know, Anya is a good-looking woman." He shook his head and shrugged. "I can see how Sofia's head was turned, even if she was a—"

"Complete and utter confidence destroying manipulative bitch?" The smirk V had been wearing was completely wiped from her face and replaced with something scowl-like. Her disdain for that woman only increased.

"Yes. That. Head of finance, she was," Bob mused as he dug his hands into his pockets and rocked on his heels. "I remember saying to Sofia right from the start to watch out, after Anya fiddled me on the department budget. I don't care what this new one looks like, so long as she treats her right."

"That's awfully protective of you, Bob."

"Well, it's times like these you realise who your friends are." He sighed and nodded to a parent. "Everyone at work's been very supportive, through my... troubles."

"Things will get better."

"I bloody hope so. And on that note, wish me luck." He pointed towards the entrance and strode off.

"Not sure what I'm wishing you luck for," V called after him. "But you can have it."

Once all the cars had filtered back out, she made her way up the path through an ornamental garden and past reception. They'd propped open the double doors to the ballroom and there was music blaring from inside. Great glass chandeliers hung from the ceiling and reflected the disco lights from the dance floor in front of the stage. Thankfully the bar was open, but they were fastidiously taking ID from everyone.

Armed with two glasses of red, she went off in search of Sofia, but she was nowhere to be seen. Then, giving up and setting their drinks on the table and stopping to chat with some students, V felt a tap on her shoulder and spun around. "Fuck. Me." The thumping bass drowned out her request, which was probably for the best.

Sofia was in a black tux, perfectly tailored over her slim hips. She casually slid her hands into the pockets and acted as if it were absolutely nothing. "You look gorgeous. Stunning."

"Uhuh," V murmured, trying not to get too carried away in front of a hall full of kids, despite wanting to be backed up against a wall and fucked senseless. "You, er—" She expelled a quick breath. "Wow. You look quite nice too."

"Quite nice?"

"Well, you know." Fanning herself, she took a step forward and the waft of Sofia's perfume made the entire lower half of her body throb. "Yeah."

"Well, you know, yeah?"

Leaning closer to whispered in her ear, V was again resisting the urge to jump on her. "It would be inappropriate for me to express my thoughts about this outfit in present company but come back to me later." She picked up both glasses and handed one to Sofia, then raised hers in a toast. "To the tux."

They had a sit-down meal to get through first. It was another upgrade on her own prom experience, which had involved eating hot dogs from a barbecue and hoping not to chuck them back up at the end of the evening. All the teachers sat around the same table and she'd snagged a chair next to Sofia, trailing her fingers around her kneecap under the cover of a big white tablecloth. It was a dangerous game though, because she wasn't sure who was more aroused by the experience.

With that over they'd done the awards presentation, and Sofia had needed to get up anyway because she was giving the maths prize. All the kids looked bored rigid, desperate to get over the formal portion of the evening and stick their tongues down each other's throats while pretending to dance. To be fair, they weren't the only ones.

As she leapt down off the stage, V grabbed Sofia's hand and guided her towards the sea of teenage bodies. "Shall we show them how it's done?"

Sofia laughed but didn't put up much of a fight, her arm sliding around V's waist and pulling them tight. With one hand on Sofia's shoulder and the other loosely gripped, she was happy to let Sofia lead. "Have I told you how much I love this dress?"

"Not recently."

They were interrupted by some spotty oik in a white suit, who clearly thought he was the class clown. "Alright, miss? Can I cut in?"

"Absolutely not."

He looked Sofia up and down, doing some odd dance move that made it appear he'd shit himself. "Punching above your weight there, miss. Don't you reckon?"

Just as Sofia was about to reply, V clasped a hand tight over her mouth. "Yes, I am, but I'm hoping if I get her drunk enough, I may be in with a chance. Now bugger off back to your friends."

He skulked off, and Sofia laughed. "I'm not sure you should've said that."

"Probably not, but it's not like we'll ever see him again. Besides, it's his word against mine and did you hear anything?"

"Nope, not a sound besides you wishing him a pleasant evening."

As V peered up over Sofia's shoulder, she caught sight of Bob again. He was not alone. "Oh, hang on. Bob's going in for the kill. Look." She spun them around so Sofia could see. He was with the bubbly blonde from their department and she was talking his ear off, but he did not look entirely unhappy about that. Was it possible...? "Don't tell me we have two maths department romances?" Whatever it was, she gave him a big thumbs up and he went bright red, from his throat right over his head.

They danced for a while and then had to go back to chaperoning duties, which somewhat killed the mood, but thankfully being a teenage party, it didn't go on until late. At ten the lights came up and there was a mass groan, from everyone but the teachers. As the hotel staff helped push them all out, wanting to get tidied up and not caring about who was crying because their friend was going to a university in a different part of the country, the adults all picked up their leftover awards and presentation bits and enjoyed a last drink.

"Another year down," Bob declared, raising his glass. They all clinked and watched as the cleaners unwound streamers from every fitting. "And congratulations to Sofia, our new permanent head of maths."

V twisted sharply. "They gave you the job? Why didn't you say anything?"

"It was a formality. Didn't seem a big deal."

"Of course it's a big deal." Setting down her wine glass, V wrapped her arms around Sofia and whispered in her ear, "I'm so proud of you." When she pulled back, Sofia's grin was wide, and her eyebrows raised. "Oh, too far?"

"No, miele. Not far enough."

"Okay." She cupped Sofia's cheek, her other hand still tucked in the small of Sofia's back, and kissed her. "Now?"

"Much better."

"Hang on a minute," Bob interjected, pointing at them and frowning. "How much have you had to drink? I thought you had a girlfriend?"

Before Sofia could reply, V cut her off. "She does. I told you the new woman was gorgeous. Really, Bob, that should've been enough of a giveaway." She gestured in a long sweeping motion down her own dress, and then let out an exaggerated sigh.

As she laughed, Sofia's eyes glistened, and she leant in for another kiss. "I think it's time that we call it a night. Shall we go back to our room?"

"Room?"

"Yes, I booked us one. I packed a few of your things at the weekend. There is a bottle of Champagne waiting on ice, and a super king size bed. What do you reckon?"

Noting they were still being gawped at and he'd been reduced to complete silence, V raised her eyebrows suggestively. "I reckon sorry Bob, but we'll talk about this after the holidays." Taking the glass from Sofia's hand and discarding it on the table, she laced their fingers together and dragged Sofia towards the double doors. She still maintained that everyone else could be buggered.

31

They slowed when they reached the hallway, and V pointed to the cocktail bar at the end of the corridor. There was soft music coming from inside, and the room was lit with shimmering pinks. "Shall we get a drink first? I haven't had a proper evening out in ages." And never one like this. Besides which, it seemed a shame to get all dressed up and then waste it on a bunch of teenagers. "What do you reckon?"

"Well, we do have all night. Might as well make the most of it."

Leaning over to kiss Sofia's cheek, V whispered, "My thoughts exactly."

Scattered around the dance floor were a few middle-aged couples. V ordered another glass of red for Sofia and a martini for herself, perching on a chrome stool with a black leather seat, and watched them while she waited. She smiled and felt almost light-headed at the prospect of an impromptu night away. It was a rare treat.

Sofia, on the other hand, only had eyes for her girlfriend, but her smile was just as wide. "You look beautiful this evening. Have I already told you that?"

Rubbing a hand into her leg as she continued to watch the dancing, V shrugged. "Once or twice, but don't feel you have to stop."

When the drinks arrived, they each took a quick sip, then Sofia stood and held out her hand. They stepped onto the dance floor and she placed a palm in the small of V's back, drawing their bodies together. Neither of them really knew what they were doing, but it didn't matter. They wanted to hold each other a while, not win Strictly Come Dancing.

This time, V didn't need to be careful or worry who saw them. She rested her head against Sofia's shoulder and inhaled deeply of the scent, her stomach doing cartwheels. "Do you get butterflies, too? I never realised it was an actual thing, but I feel them with you."

Pressing her lips to V's forehead, Sofia laughed. "Yes, miele. From the first time you kissed me. Although come to think of it, that may have been shock. I invited you for food and you took off my shirt."

"Oh, please." V scoffed and peered up. "You did *not* only invite me to your house for food."

Smirking and shrugging, Sofia turned them to sway back in the other direction before they reached the edge of the floor and hit carpet. "No, okay. I didn't think anything would happen, though, not really. In my head I hoped it would, but... I thought it would remain a very nice fantasy."

"What happened in this fantasy?"

After a few moments pause, Sofia apologising as she almost trod on V's foot, she let out a long "ummmm". Then she bit her lip, her face filling with colour. "There is a sparkle in your eyes when you're about to say something clever or speak about Grace, and every time it melts me. The first time I saw it, I was completely immobilised. From that moment on I imagined what it would be like to kiss you afterwards. Or before you even got to the words."

Pausing for a beat, V was in a playful mood, even though her insides had dissolved. "Really? My fantasies weren't nearly as soft as that, I was just thinking about you fucking me senseless in the store cupboard." Letting out a sigh, she tousled the hair at the base of Sofia's neck. "Well, I suppose one of us has to be practical."

They danced a while longer, or at least managed some approximation of it. Then, as the barman announced last orders rather than yelling it and banging a loud gong, V knew she'd outstayed her welcome. She was holidaying in fancy-land, but at her heart would always be a dancing on tables kind of gal. After they'd downed the rest of their drinks, Sofia held out her arm and V took it, doing a little curtsey for good measure.

When they made it up to the first floor, Sofia swiped her key card and pushed open the door with a little flourish. She twisted the dimmer to illuminate the room with soft light, then wrapped her arms around V's waist and held her from behind. "What do you think?"

There was a bed in the middle of the room with crisp white sheets, then at the far end a chaise longue. In front of that was a low table with a silver bucket of Champagne next to a tray of expensive looking chocolates.

V inched forward, dragging Sofia along, and took a truffle. Biting it in half, she tipped her head back as it slowly melted over her tongue, and then shoved the rest in Sofia's mouth. "Are you secretly in with the mafia? I don't mind, it'd just be useful to know."

Laughing and licking the cocoa from V's fingers, Sofia didn't bother answering that. Instead, she walked them towards the bathroom, her arms still around V's waist, and flicked on the light to reveal a big whirlpool bath. "I know I've asked you this before, but is this enough pampering?"

"Mm." V considered, inclining her head. "I don't know. I suppose if we took the Champagne and the chocolates and ate them in the bath with the jets on, it might be quite relaxing." Unwinding herself, she set it running. "Only one way to find out."

When she turned back, Sofia had disappeared. Following her out, the Champagne cork was being firmly squeezed, and as it popped a trickle of liquid ran down Sofia's hand. She licked it off and poured, handing over a glass and then picking up the tray of chocolates.

Once they'd been set on the side of the bath, V strained for her own zip, but she couldn't reach it. Stepping behind, Sofia took a gentle grasp and slowly lowered it, laying kisses as she went and causing a tingle of goose bumps.

"I almost don't want to take this off," she whispered, her hands now smoothing over the straps. As the dress fell away, she wrapped her arms around instead and the silky material of her tux met V's bare skin.

"I feel the same way about that suit."

Turning and slipping her fingers under the jacket lapels, V closed her eyes as she luxuriated in Sofia's scent. Brushing their lips together, she unhooked her own bra and discarded it. Simultaneously Sofia had pulled down her underwear and V kicked that away too, pressing her hands into Sofia's arse to feel the slip of the material against her breasts and between her legs.

With the water still thundering into the bath and steam filling the room, Sofia turned V and backed her against the cold tiled wall next to the tub. Raising her foot and planting it on the edge, V pulled Sofia's hips against her own, her clit fluttering. They kissed again, Sofia's tongue slipping into her mouth as they rocked together, the chocolate both bitter and sweet to taste.

Her frustration building, V slid her hand down her own stomach and rubbed her clit, letting out a gentle moan of relief, but Sofia seized it. Lacing their fingers together she stepped away, V's body instinctively drawn forward.

"What is happening?" she just about got out, her core throbbing.

Switching off the taps and hitting the jets, Sofia let their hands drop and began unbuttoning her shirt. "You said we have all night." Seeming to think that constituted enough of an answer, she was out of the tux in lightning time and slipping under the water, leaning back against the edge of the tub. Coolly sipping from her glass, she pulled up her knees to make some space at the other end. "Aren't you getting in? It's very enjoyable."

Standing with her hands on her hips, V stared down at Sofia. "Is it?"

"Yes, it is." With a little shrug, Sofia splashed some water, and it sprayed across V's torso.

Still grumbling, she got in and sat opposite, her feet coming to rest somewhere around Sofia's arse. Thankfully, the taps were in the middle. Someone had really thought this through. "You're very cruel, do you know that?"

"Oh I know, the cruellest. I book an upmarket hotel room, order Champagne and chocolates, then expect you to sit in a bath with me." Shaking her head, Sofia mumbled, "Just horrible. It's a wonder you can find anything to love about me at all."

Flicking water in her face, V leant over to take a glass and a chocolate. This time it had a gooey caramel centre, and it dribbled down her chin as she bit in. "So true. That tux somewhat made up for it, though." She held out the other half and then placed it on Sofia's tongue. When it remained there, she laughed and sucked it off.

After a quarter of an hour spent feeding each other chocolates and sipping Champagne, jets of water hitting them from all angles, V was feeling light-headed again. She covered her mouth as she giggled; bubbles always sent her a bit silly. When Sofia hiccupped she did it again, her cheeks aching from smiling so much. It was another common theme.

The plastic squeaked as she nudged herself forward a bit, tilting down Sofia's chin to kiss her slowly. If she wanted to draw this out, they could. This time as their tongues met, V felt her chest contract and heat flooded up her neck. She gently trailed her fingertips over Sofia's breasts, her sides, and then her knees but didn't linger anywhere. It wasn't long, though, before Sofia was hooking a hand behind V's neck to deepen the kiss, little murmurs of pleasure and grunts of frustration echoing off the walls.

"Shall we get out?" she whispered, her eyes heavy as her lips parted slightly.

Stroking the damp hair from her face, V gently sucked on her bottom lip before pulling back again. Sofia's head fell forward, desperately seeking another kiss. "There's no rush. We have *all* night. And as you know, you can only have one orgasm so you should really build up to it." When Sofia became more alert, her lip hooking up as she narrowed her eyes and scowled, V laughed. "Oh, I'm sorry. Did I get that wrong? You see, I was under the impression we were rationing them now. That's why we had to stop so abruptly earlier; otherwise, we wouldn't have had anything to do for the rest of the night."

"You think you're *so* clever." With a superior smirk, Sofia hauled herself up and turned off the jets. She stepped out, grabbing a towel from the heated rail and dabbing herself dry as she exited the bathroom.

Leaning back with a little shrug, V took another sip of Champagne. Only when the glass was empty, did she get out, drying herself off as the sound of the television floated through from the bedroom. Clearing her throat to keep from laughing, she wandered out and stood in front of it to check her phone. Sofia sprawled on the bed, propped on some pillows, and began shuffling around.

"I'm sorry, am I blocking your view?"

Setting the phone back down, V stayed exactly where she was for a few moments, reaching for the Champagne and taking a swig from the bottle. Then she wandered back to the bathroom and picked up Sofia's shirt. Slipping her arms into the sleeves, she wrapped it around herself and pressed the collar to her nose.

"Fuck," she murmured. "Always with the butterflies." Buttoning it as she stepped back through, she then made herself comfortable next to Sofia. "What are you watching?"

As Sofia glanced over, she suppressed a smile. "A film. I thought I should kill some time. You know, since we have a lot of it." Her eyes settled back on the television. "You are wearing my shirt."

"Yep. Do you like it?"

She only shrugged, but seeing that her gaze kept flicking away from the television, her tongue running over her bottom lip, V ramped things up a notch. She parted her legs slightly and slid her hand up the inside of her own thigh, teasing her finger over her clit. Sofia's head shot around now, and she swallowed hard. Her legs slipped together as she pressed them tight and she pulled herself further up the pillows, grabbing the remote to switch off the TV.

Thinking she was going to join in, V took away her hand, but Sofia only whispered, "Keep going."

The desire in her eyes caused a growl in V's core and her nipples tingled against the shirt. She parted her legs further and rubbed over her swollen clit, closing her eyes and allowing herself to get into it this time. A few moments later when she opened them again, she could see the arousal flushed down Sofia's throat. She massaged a hand into her own breast now as she continued to circle and play, squeezing a taut nipple between her thumb and forefinger as she pressed harder along the side of her clit so that her hips bucked up slightly. Her breathing heavier, she could feel how wet she was becoming again.

When Sofia rolled off the bed, she carried on. Sofia was delving into the overnight bag she'd packed and returned with one of their joint purchases in hand—a slick high-end vibrator. V tried to suppress a smile, the mattress tilting slightly as Sofia knelt between her legs. She dabbed a little lube and chucked the tube to one side, their eyes locking. She made V wait, and her walls throbbed in anticipation. She wasn't willing to plead, still feeling entirely in control.

Parting her own lips, she ran two fingers around her opening and watched Sofia's tongue move over her bottom lip again as they slipped inside. Sofia switched on the vibrator and it let out a gentle buzz, but still she didn't move. She was breathing harder, though, her thumb rubbing over the controls as if she were imagining it somewhere else. V was right there with her, closing her eyes again and picturing Sofia's hand where her own was.

When the bed creaked, she looked up again to find Sofia now leant over her with a hand beside her head. Their lips brushed together as Sofia teased the vibrator around V's entrance and V's eyelids fluttered as she tipped back her head, the sight of Sofia over her the ultimate aphrodisiac. Wrapped in Sofia's spicy scent, she inhaled deeply and her core clenched, then again as the vibrator inched inside and slowly withdrew.

Her fingers still slipping over her own clit, she tried to relax, easing in all seven inches. Then Sofia changed the setting to massage her G-spot, and she groaned, squeezing her eyes shut. As the vibrator glided slowly in and out, Sofia arched her back and bent to press her lips to V's nipple through the material of the shirt, warm at first but the resultant moisture quickly cooled against V's skin.

With each wave she felt her orgasm build, rubbing faster while Sofia watched, her eyes darkening as she bit down on her bottom lip. "Are you going to come?" she whispered, a tremor in her voice.

"Uhuh," V panted, her cheeks flooding with the warmth that was radiating her entire body. Throwing back her head, the cotton moved over her sensitive breasts and she let out a low moan, every touch taking her closer. When Sofia increased the speed, first of the vibrator and then of her own movements with it, she was completely undone. Wet heat trickled onto the sheets and she gripped the duvet with her free hand, twisting it as she arched her back and felt the full force of her climax.

Only when she stilled did Sofia withdraw the vibrator, causing her to shiver. She laid it to one side and then Sofia lowered herself, a hand stroking over V's hip and under the shirt as she trailed her fingertips there and they lay pressed together. Stroking her hair, V tilted up Sofia's chin as it rested on her shoulder, kissing her lightly at first but quickly deepening it. She still tasted of chocolate and Champagne; her lips cool where she'd been breathing hard.

When the wet patch she was lying in became uncomfortable, V giggled and rolled them over, and Sofia fumbled behind herself as she grunted and writhed, pulling out the vibrator and lobbing it at the end of the bed. Cupping Sofia's cheek, V kissed her again, working down to cover her neck. "Thank god this is a super king size, or we might start running out of bed to sleep in."

"Sleep? I have no intention of sleeping." Sofia glanced at the clock on the bedside table. "There are eleven hours until we need to check out. You decided you wanted your orgasm ration now... but I am still considering. We'll see how the night progresses."

Bringing them face to face again, V raised her eyebrows. "We'll see? Also, surely at midnight that resets, so I'm entitled to another."

"I suppose."

Chewing on her bottom lip as she considered, V shrugged. "Okay. Well, you just let me know once you've decided how you'd like to spend the rest of our time. I'm going to have some more Champagne." She patted Sofia's side and got up, rolling her hips as she rounded the bed because she knew for damn sure that Sofia was watching.

After grabbing her glass from the bathroom, she filled it and took a sip, wandering over to the doors. Throwing them open, a cool gust of air dried the sweat in the base of her back. She stepped onto the balcony, leaning forward on the metal railing, and stared up at the stars. It was perfectly peaceful, the only sound of owls hooting in the distance.

Moments later, as expected, a pair of arms wrapped around her middle. "Come back to bed, miele."

Kisses peppered her neck and V reached behind to find Sofia was still completely naked, her skin soft but covered in goose bumps. Turning and leaning back against the railing, she set her glass on the small round table next to her.

Placing her mouth over Sofia's left breast, she sucked slowly and teased her tongue over the swollen nipple before pulling back. "I don't want to go to bed."

"No?"

She shook her head, repeating the action on the other side. Then V laced their fingers together and led Sofia into the bedroom and pushed her up against the wall by the door. As Sofia parted her legs slightly, her free hand landed on the wall beside V's head and she leant in to whisper against her ear, "Do you want to know what I love?" As V's finger circled her clit, Sofia grasped V's hand and slid it back, taking it around her opening and then in a zigzag through her folds. "Your tongue... just here."

As she repeated the action, V tensed slightly. She was usually quite careful in that area. "Do you?" she whispered back.

"Mhm."

"Do you prefer my tongue over my fingers?" Plying her tongue on Sofia's collarbone and trailing her fingertips over the curve of her arse, V waited for a response.

Withdrawing her own hand and leaving V to rub over her throbbing clit, Sofia murmured, "It is a very good tongue..."

"Is that so? I don't think my tongue has ever been complimented specifically before."

"Sometimes," Sofia continued, pausing for a lingering kiss. "When I'm on top." She dipped her head for another. "You pull me straight down onto your mouth..." Her eyelids fluttered now, and she allowed herself to be pulled towards the chaise longue.

Sitting and encouraging Sofia to put her foot on the seat, V wrapped both hands around the tops of her legs. Kissing down her stomach, she felt Sofia's hips tilt forward and fingers lace through her hair, but she wouldn't rush. As she breathed warm air, Sofia let out an anguished groan. She'd made it entirely clear where she wanted V's tongue, and her frustration was growing.

When it finally made contact, she whimpered, an achingly slow motion along the centre of her desire eking that out and causing her to shiver. Repeating the action, V still took her time, swirling delicate circles around Sofia's clit and then holding her firmer as she drew the swollen nub into her mouth. Sofia was close, and she'd been that way since they were in bed, but V wanted to tease out every sensation.

She stiffened her tongue and circled Sofia's entrance, taking care never to slip inside, and Sofia ground her hips ever faster. This time when V flicked over Sofia's clit, she let out a high-pitched cry, her legs trembling and her foot slipping over the fabric of the seat. Picking up the pace, V sucked and swirled, reaching a hand up to rub a firm line over Sofia's nipple until she couldn't hold on any longer and her hips bucked wildly. Her foot landed on the carpet as she bent over trembling with a hand on the chaise longue to steady herself.

Wiping her mouth on the sleeve of the shirt and breathing heavily, V peered up with a devilish grin. "Is that the sort of thing you quite like?"

Stuttering out a few incompressible words, Sofia used the arm of the chair to guide herself and pitched forward onto the bed. "Something a bit like that," she mumbled. After a few moments she raised her head and looked at the alarm clock. "I've got good news for you."

"Yeah?" Unbuttoning the shirt and chucking it over the back of the seat, V climbed on top of Sofia and kissed across her shoulders.

"Mm. It's just gone twelve and you know what that means."

"Witching hour?"

With a grunt of laughter that shook them both, Sofia dangled her arm over the side of the bed and strained for their overnight bag. "Funnily enough, no. But I have a wand..."

32

"Here we go," Sofia whispered excitedly as they hit the Severn Bridge. She wore a wide smile and stroked V's knee, her other hand on the steering wheel.

It was odd being in a separate car and staying somewhere different. Like a Welsh holiday but not a Welsh holiday. Similar to everything else in their lives these days, the old gang were together but not together, enjoying each other's company but coming apart afterwards. Even Grace was settling into this new way of being, probably because she'd just added a fourth adult to her collection of people who doted on her. Sofia was almost softer than Jess, and she used that fact to her advantage.

"Sofia, can we listen to my music now?" She leant forward and grabbed the back of V's seat, using the tone she'd perfected to get her way.

"What's *your* music? Isn't music for everybody?"

Trust her to have a clever answer. There was silence for a few moments and Grace sat back, considering her response. "The music I like. This is rubbish."

"Rubbish?" Sofia scoffed, turning briefly before fixing her eyes back on the road. "This is not rubbish."

"But I can't understand the words."

"That's because your Italian isn't good enough yet, give it time. You'll soon be able to understand every word, and just think how clever you'll feel when you can torment your mother in a whole other language."

Grace let out a little snigger. "Yeah. And Daddy."

"That's my girl. Now, do you still want me to turn it over?"

"No."

Sofia wore a satisfied smile and gripped tighter around V's leg, then they both laughed as Grace hummed along to the tune, trying to pick out words. She managed a few of them, her determination paying off.

As they reached the end of the bridge, Sofia let out a loud sigh and gestured to the sign. "That's it, I'm back in Wales. I hope you're both happy."

V rubbed a hand into Sofia's shoulder and mocked her with a pout. "My poor baby, did the country really hurt your feelings?"

"Yes, it did, but I intend to spend this week building sandcastles, eating ice cream and fish and chips, and reminding myself of all the reasons I love this place."

Grace had been staring out the window, but she turned back, her face quizzical. "Why don't you like Wales?"

"That is a very long story, cucciolo."

"I've got time."

As Sofia laughed, she bobbed her head. "Okay, well it all has to do with the Welsh girl you met. We were in love once, but it ended badly."

"Oh, I don't like *her*. That's not Wales's fault though, is it?"

"No. And now I have someone new to love, so I don't suppose I should hold a grudge. Thank you, Grace. Once again you have shown me the light."

It was another half an hour or so from there to wherever Sofia had booked for them to stay. Usually everyone crammed into Melissa's grandparents' house but that was unmanageable this year, so they were inflicting two screaming babies on a pair of pensioners alone.

Having had visions of a luxury hotel or a swanky Airbnb, V frowned when Sofia turned down a lane sign-posted to a campsite. "Are we camping?"

"Not exactly, we're staying in a static caravan."

The frown deepened. "You booked a static caravan? You, who will only eat your own fancy cooking and sleep in expensive silk sheets?"

"Yes, that me. I thought it would be fun, and there are lots of facilities on-site for Grace: a swimming pool, play-ground, adventure golf..." She slowed as they went over a speed bump. "Granted, I booked the nicest caravan they had."

"Thank god for that." V leant over to kiss the top of her arm and then turned, her elbow on the armrest. "What do you reckon, will this be fun?" When Grace was already busy rifling through her bag on the seat next to her, excitedly pulling out her swimming costume, armbands and goggles, V left her to it. "Never mind, I think I have my answer. Thank you, it was very sweet of you to pick somewhere for Grace."

Slowing again for the entry barrier, Sofia entwined their fingers and kissed the back of V's hand. "It wasn't just for Grace; it'll be fun for us all." She pulled up outside a little wooden reception hut and popped open the door, jumping out and grabbing their keys. A few moments later she was

back in the car, handing over a pack of welcome information and wrist bands for them to access all the facilities.
"Right then, lets dump our stuff and get to the beach."

"What?" Grace whined. "I want to swim!"

"What do you think the sea is for, cucciolo? Auntie Jess
will be waiting for you, and I bet Hal will want to do a little
doggy paddle." As Sofia demonstrated, Grace laughed.

After they'd thrown their bags into the caravan, quickly
changing Grace into her swimming costume, they set off in
search of the beach. When they arrived in the clifftop
carpark, Grace sprang out of the car, grabbing the bag
holding her towel and other gear for the day, and pulled
open the passenger side door before V even blinked. "Come
on, Mummy." Then she ran around the bonnet and almost
slammed into Sofia. "Come on, Sofia." She tugged at Sofia's
loose tank top and tried to drag her towards the steps, but as
they got there, she stopped and peered down. "It's a long
way."

"You need a lift?" Sofia crouched down and patted her
back.

V rubbed a hand into Sofia's shoulder. "You don't need to
do that. She's just being lazy." And seeing how far she could
push it.

"I don't mind. Jump on."

Without a second thought, Grace handed V her bag and
leapt onto Sofia's back, wrapping both arms tight around
her neck. Then there was a grunt as she was lifted from the
ground. This was definitely not going to fly long term, but V
relented for now, happy that they were still bonding.

When they reached the bottom Sofia ran across the sand
and Grace squealed, her hair flying in all directions as a
strong gust blew in off the sea. She was finally dropped
about a hundred metres away where Jess had already set up

camp and immediately started rolling around on the blanket with Izzy and Ruby.

"Come here, sweetheart. Sunscreen before you do anything else." She wasn't getting away with that under any circumstances because it only took five minutes before she burned to a crisp.

"No thank you."

"Yes, thank you. Up." V pulled a tube of factor one million from the bag and flicked off the cap. "Here. Now."

Sofia stepped behind and took the bottle, squeezing a blob onto her hand and rubbing it into V's shoulder. "For you too, miele," she whispered. Then she raised her voice again. "I bet Izzy and Ruby have on their sunscreen. Come here so we can do you." When Grace immediately pushed herself up and ran over, Sofia laughed. She squeezed cream into V's hand this time so they could work in tandem. Once she'd finished, she wrapped her arms around V's waist and leant into her ear. "You smell delicious."

Quickly twisting, V snatched a kiss. "Save that for later, I'll see if we can score a couple of babysitters so we can be alone for an hour. What do you reckon?"

The hushed tones had raised suspicions and Melissa peered up as she tried to reattach a sun hat to Izzy's head. "What are you two plotting?"

"Nothing." They'd both said it in unison and then burst out laughing, Sofia lifting V clear of the ground and walking towards the sea.

Grace had already surged into the water, squealing when the cold hit, and as they approached, V tried to wriggle free. "Put me down."

"Okay." When Sofia let go, she landed right on top of a lump of seaweed. It caused her to cringe, turn, and leap right back into Sofia's arms. Steadying herself, she wrapped V's legs around her middle. "Hello again."

"Slimy. Didn't like it." With a shudder, V hooked her arms behind Sofia's neck and kissed her.

"I'm not complaining, miele." She took a few strides forward until the waves were rolling into her knees.

"Don't you dare drop me in here. I mean it. You can forget returning to this position again tonight if I end up in the sea." She went in for another kiss to seal the deal but just as their lips met, Grace and Hal both barrelled into Sofia's legs and knocked her over, sending them toppling.

Even now, that dog was a pain in the arse.

* * *

They spent their evening at a restaurant on the seafront, then walked back along the beach and fit in a quickie before Grace returned. It was probably the only chance they'd get with a six-year-old the other side of a flimsy caravan wall, and it was the one aspect Sofia hadn't thought through very well.

They were still rapidly re-buttoning and tucking in clothes as Jess's car pulled up onsite and stopped in the space next to the Mini. She popped open the back door and then leant against the chassis. "She's been fed and bathed. I'll email my invoice."

As she peered through the window to see Grace's eyes nodding and her head lolling, V laughed. She stepped around Jess and reached out her arms, finding Grace clung to her front, nuzzling into her neck. With a grunt she adjusted the weight. "Thank you for taking her."

"No bother."

Sofia had hung back but ran a hand over Grace's head,

affectionately stroking the hair from her eyes. "Would you like me to take her?"

"What do you reckon, sweetheart? Will you let Sofia carry you in? She's got bigger muscles than me."

Grace nodded and suckered herself to Sofia instead, closing her eyes completely as a kiss pressed to her forehead. They wandered up the path together and Jess nudged Vs shoulder. "So, how was your evening?"

"Oh, you know, just the standard amount of amazing. I really love her."

"Looks like you're not the only one."

"Yeah, that is all pretty cute. We still have some hurdles to overcome, like the fact Sofia lets Grace get away with murder, but I think I know how to handle that. After all, you were the same and now look at you. Proper mum and everything."

Jess let out a long, wistful sigh and folded her arms. "Still let her get away with murder, she decapitated a gingerbread man this evening, and I said nothing."

"Mm." V laughed, but then glanced back at the figures moving behind a hideous net curtain. "You know what we almost feel like?"

"A family?"

"Yep." She stressed the P and turned back to face Jess with a shrug. "Everything I thought I never wanted. It's pretty good, though. I can see the appeal." Pausing for a beat, she raised her index finger "However, the minute I catch her in a pair of comfy slippers this is over."

"Speaking of comfy slippers, I need to get back to my wife. She promised to keep them warm for me."

"Still feels to hear you say *wife*."

"Does it?" Jess pushed off the chassis and opened the driver side door, resting her arm on top and her chin in the crook of her elbow. "She's always been that to me," she murmured, going all doe eyed. "Even if she'd never wanted me like that, I know I'd still have loved her and wanted her in my life. Same with all of you, really. I'd choose you as my best friend, even if you are a sarky bitch sometime. Grace, despite my biscuit bill. Hal... well, I guess he's hairy. The girls, no matter how many times they puke up on me." She scrunched her nose. "Is that soft?"

"Completely. It's perfectly you and I love you for it."

Her entire face scrunching now, Jess laughed. "Wow, you really are dropping those bombs all over the place tonight. Catch you at the arcades tomorrow?"

"We'll be there."

They hugged good night and then parted. V waved her off and then wandered back up to the caravan. Inside, Sofia sprawled on the sofa with Grace draped over her, quietly reading the end of a book. Taking Sofia's wrist to lift her arm and then positioning herself underneath it, V cuddled in and listened, but it was Jess's words still replaying in her head. For once she felt completely in control of her own path; her own life; her own choices.

She'd choose this a million times over.

Printed in Great Britain
by Amazon

81946034R00181